DOG SPELLED BACKWARD

By
Fernando Camacho

This book is a work of fiction. Names, characters, places and incidents are products of the author's imagination or are used fictitiously. Any resemblance to actual events or locales or persons, living or dead, is entirely coincidental.

The environmental statistics within this novel are entirely factual.

*To Michele for believing in me
and Hayley for inspiring me.*

AUTHOR'S NOTE

Since I was a little kid, I've always had a love of reading and was always excited when I discovered a new story to get lost in. My favorites were adventure and fantasy books, where I was transported into another world with interesting characters who explored strange lands and had amazing adventures. I would disappear into the story and happily lose myself in each new world. It was a fun distraction from everyday life and a place where I could use my restless imagination constructively to paint pictures from the words I read.

As I got older, my love of reading continued and I soon felt the creative tingle to write my own story. In my early twenties I started two or three different novels but never could get past the second or third chapter. I seemed to lack the inspiration and motivation to go any further, so I abandoned them, unfinished, and moved on with my life. However, the creative tingle remained and the idea of writing my own novel someday was always lurking in the back of my mind.

Then, in 2001, at one of the lowest points in my life, I adopted a white and brown Pit Bull named Hayley. Since that day my entire life changed. Looking back now, fifteen years later, I realize that Hayley has shaped my entire life since my decision to adopt her. A few months after adopting Hayley I met my now wife, Michele. Together, those two girls have fueled everything I've accomplished since (now my two daughters have added their octane to the mix and I'm constantly propelled by endless girl power).

The book you hold in your hands right now was their first influence on me. I found my dormant creative juices flowing again and one day while in the shower (yes, it really happens that way sometimes) the title popped into my head. Then, as I was drying off, the character of the dog took shape as did the message I wanted the story to deliver. Soon my mind was churning with ideas and storylines that I wanted to include. It seems I only needed the right inspiration to kick my mind into gear, and who would have thought it would be an unsuspecting Pit Bull that would be the catalyst.

Inspiration alone, however, does not get a book written. To actually find time in my busy days to prioritize this little passion project, I would need motivation as well. Luckily for me, I had another girl in my corner to give me exactly what I needed, exactly when I needed it most. My super supportive girlfriend Michele was there to help me set aside the time (often sacrificing our time together), encourage me when I got stuck, and really push me to finally finish my dream novel. Without Hayley to inspire me and Michele to motivate me, my dream of being a writer would never have come true.

Writing this book was initially just a personal thing for me – something to cross off my bucket list – and I was initially planning to just get a few copies printed and give it to my family for Christmas. But as I finished the story I immediately wanted to share it with the world, to entertain and even inspire people the way so many books have done for me. So, I decided to make it available to everyone. The only problem was I didn't have a lot of money or resources to do it the way I really wanted. Now, however, with this second edition, I'm ready to revisit the story and improve it.

I hope you like my epic tale of adventure and that you will be entertained by the events, touched by the characters and inspired by the underlying message. Read on and feel free to lose yourself in the story, forget about the real world for a bit, and enjoy the ride.

Fern (aka Fernando Camacho)

PROLOGUE

Thunder boomed above Manny's head as he stepped out of the truck. The sky was thick with black clouds that had been looming overhead all morning. The air was dry and hot, and he felt filthy inside and out. This job was no good for him. This job was no good for anyone. It was two years ago when he first set foot into this glorified dirt pit. Utah had never been his first choice, but he had to go where he could find work.

That was something that Manny's father had told him as a kid, each time they moved to yet another new city: "You got to go where the work is, son," was the only explanation Manny ever got. It was the only answer Manny had as to why he had to change schools again, make new friends again, and try to fit into a new place once again. It wouldn't be until Manny was much older that he realized the brutal truth of that statement.

Now it seemed that he would be stuck at this damned copper mine forever. Another ear-shattering crack of thunder sent Manny ducking to the ground. He quickened his pace toward the office as he glanced up at the sky, cursing the heavens.

Then his ears picked up a garbled sound in the distance. As it got louder, Manny looked up to the sky as it filled with squawking birds. Hundreds of them streamed overhead, their voices echoing throughout the copper plant.

Manny had never seen so many birds flying together at one time. There were all different kinds of birds, jumbled together in a totally unorganized frenzy. Didn't they always travel in some sort of a "V" formation? It struck him as very unnatural that they would be hightailing like that.

Damn birds must have lost their minds, Manny thought as he ducked inside the office doorway.

The inside of the office wasn't much cleaner than Manny's clothing. Dirt seemed to get into everything here no matter how hard you tried to keep it clean, and there was definitely no one here trying.

"Hey man, what's the word?" Manny said to the foreman, who was sitting with his feet up on a cluttered desk smoking a cigarette.

Although the name plate on his desk said Bill Chambers, around the mine he was known simply as "The Overlord." He was a round, pudding of a man who seemed to always be covered in a shiny coat of sweat.

"The word, my friend, is trouble," the Overlord replied, sitting up and jamming the remains of his cigarette into the ashtray on the desk. "It seems we're under fire again."

As if on cue, another burst of thunder rattled the windows and made both men jump. The Overlord grabbed a newspaper out of the pile of papers on his desk, and forced his bulk out of his seat. "It seems that Utah has been rated second in the whole friggin' U.S. of

A. for its toxic waste release, and they say that we're the main reason this state's in the shitter."

The Overlord thrust the paper into Manny's hands. Manny quickly skimmed the article while the Overlord stood, panting. The article went on to say that the state of Utah was responsible for 954 million pounds of toxic releases. The copper mine they were standing in was credited for 814 million pounds of that release.

"What's the big deal? So the lizards around here have a few more heads than they should," Manny said as he threw the paper back on the desk.

"The big deal is that now there's going to be people coming here and asking questions, making my life more of a living hell than it already is. And you know who's going to get the blame? . . . Me! Well, not this time. I don't care who —"

The Overlord's mouth was silenced by a series of loud cracks that shook the building down to the foundation. Manny quickly turned his attention to the large window over his shoulder and gasped. Outside, the sky was raining lightning.

Big thick bolts charged down from the black clouds overhead, crashing into the mine and the surrounding buildings. Fire shot up as the combustible materials inside the buildings exploded. Wood burned, glass broke, and cement crumbled. The sky was lit up with as many as fifty lightning bolts at one time; all concentrated on the copper mine.

Manny thought he screamed, but didn't hear any sound come out of his mouth. The terror overcoming him was mirrored in the bloated face of the Overlord, who stood frozen at his desk. Manny got his feet moving and was almost to the door of the building when it crashed down on top of him. Within minutes nothing was left of the copper mine but large plumes of smoke.

About a mile away, on a rust colored mountaintop, a small lizard with one head looked toward the smoke of the crumbling copper mine. It pivoted its head slightly, then quickly turned and scampered away.

CHAPTER 1

Another Day in Paradise

There was something about a hot cup of coffee that just makes the morning feel all right, Ryan thought as he filled his cup. A little milk added and there it was – perfection in a mug. He enjoyed a quick sip as he headed into the dining room to gather his things for work.

Looking out the window of his first floor garden apartment, he could see that it was going to be another cloudy day. The sun had been in short supply these last couple of weeks and Ryan was starting to miss it. Although it hadn't rained for a month and the entire area was bordering on a serious drought, the gray clouds always remained.

Sun or no sun, Ryan tried to keep in good spirits, and if it turned out to be a nice weekend maybe he would go for a hike or hit the batting cages. Having a whole weekend free was kind of cool. Not long ago, he felt like a loser if he didn't have his Friday, Saturday and Sunday filled with activities. There was always so much pressure to have a spectacular weekend so you could go into the office on Monday and tell everyone how much fun you had, thereby validating your life. Not to mention all of the wasted energy spent trying to meet that special girl every weekend.

Not anymore. He was done with that. It never panned out the way he planned it, and always left him wondering where the weekend went. Now he just took each day as it came, and didn't try to force something to happen. Good things seemed to happen when he least expected it anyway.

He walked to the bathroom to give himself a quick once over before heading out. His apartment was a simple one bedroom unit, but that was all he really needed. The front door opened into a dining area that held a small table with four chairs around it. Beyond that, a clean white counter separated the small kitchen from the dining area. Off to the left was the living room, framed by a brown couch and loveseat. Everything was well-used, leftover from his parent's house from when they moved to Arizona two years ago. The living room contained the only new item in the house, an entertainment center complete with a big flat screen TV and the latest Xbox video game system.

A small hallway led to the bedroom and bathroom. Looking into the bathroom mirror, Ryan saw that although the years had been kind to him, age was beginning to make itself known. Last month he blew out thirty-six candles, and now he was starting to notice some changes. His five-foot-ten body was thin with a hint of muscular definition, but some things had started to ache and creak a bit. He couldn't complain too much though; he was still holding up pretty well compared to other people his age. He'd led a fairly clean life, free of all the popular vices. He liked to have a few beers once in a while, but all night benders where you woke up in a strange bed wondering where your pants were, had never been his style.

He ran his hand through his hair, pleased he could only find one or two grays hiding among his short brown hair. It didn't seem like there was a receding hairline or any hint of thinning in the back. The threat of baldness weighs on every man's mind once he passes the big three-o, but it seemed that Ryan would be spared the trauma of deciding if he should do the comb-over, the shave, or go for the throw rug.

He had to get moving if he was going to make it to work on time. The office was only ten miles away, but New Jersey traffic was always unpredictable. He finished his coffee, put the mug in the sink, grabbed his suit jacket and cell phone, and was out the door.

He walked into the courtyard and was hit by a breeze that seemed a little too cool for this time of year. Spring had sprung, but it seemed winter was not ready to let go just yet. As much as he hated wearing a suit, he was glad to have his jacket's added protection.

The two courtyards outside his apartment were quiet and well kept, with neatly trimmed bushes and cut grass. Each was framed by four identical two-story brick buildings. Ryan lived in a first floor unit on the north side. The buildings were built back in the Sixties, but were holding up well. The worn red bricks gave it a very charming feel that made him feel good about coming home at the end of each day. He was renting his apartment from a young couple who lived a few towns over, and although he had moved into the complex three years ago with the intention of eventually buying a unit, now he wasn't so sure. He liked living here, but Ryan had dreams of getting a bigger and better place sometime in the future. The apartment was only three miles from the house where he grew up, and even though it had been a number of years since his parents moved to Arizona, Clifton still felt like home.

When he heard approaching footsteps, Ryan glanced up to see one of his neighbors walking toward him. It was Vivian, an attractive redhead, who lived in the upstairs unit across from him. He and Vivian had become friends as soon as he had moved in. She was petite, no more than five-foot-two, with a slim body and fair skin. Ryan had found her attractive, and initially thought of pursuing a romantic relationship, but the timing never seemed right. Now they had slipped into what felt like some kind of sibling relationship.

It was kind of nice, though. Through Vivian, Ryan was always able to get a girl's view on everything. It often felt like he was doomed to never understand women, but she was able to give Ryan a window into their world. It was nice to have someone on the inside helping him.

Unfortunately, their relationship changed with the arrival of Brad, Vivian's boyfriend of six months. The house where Brad had been living was being sold and he was forced to find a new place quickly. It was Brad's idea that he should move into her place, and although it seemed like it might be too soon in their relationship to live together, she said she had a good feeling about it.

Right from the start, Brad seemed a little threatened by Ryan's relationship with Vivian. It probably wasn't intentional, but little by little, Vivian became less available to him. Although he was sad to lose his time with her, he hoped that everything worked out for Vivian.

The day Brad came home and said that she no longer "did it" for him Ryan had been cleaning up around his place. He could hear

Vivian across the courtyard pleading for him to stay, as she struggled to understand why this was happening to her. Brad walked out of her life with little more than a wave goodbye, and left her sobbing on her living room floor.

That was last week.

Ryan had made a few attempts to talk to her since the breakup, but she had been unwilling to open up to him. He figured she just needed some time to grieve and deal with this unexpected turn in her life. After a week's time, however, she only seemed more rooted in depression and despair.

This morning she was walking slowly, with her head downcast, wearing faded blue jeans and an oversized sweatshirt. Her long red hair was pulled back into a pony tail and in her hands she gripped a small paper bag. As she neared him, Ryan said cheerfully, "Good morning, Viv. It's nice to see you up and about today."

Lost in her own thoughts, she hadn't even noticed him coming. Timidly, she lifted her head up. Her green eyes looked like they had cried many tears in the last few days and were streaked with redness. It hurt Ryan to see anyone like this, let alone a friend. The dark bands under her eyes showed that she hadn't been sleeping much and the pained expression on her face made him want to cry himself.

"Hi, Ryan," she said softly without stopping.

Ryan turned as she passed him, "Viv, I know this is tough, but it's going to get better. How about we get together this weekend and rent a movie? I'll make us some dinner, we'll both agree I still can't cook and then order a pizza. It'll be just like old times."

"Maybe some other time," she whispered, as she reached her door.

"Just think about it. I'll check in on you when I get back from work." Ryan called, as Vivian shut her door.

That poor girl has got to snap out of it, he thought as he walked around the building to the parking lot. Crying over some nobody like Brad just wasn't worth it. She was too good a person to be so unhappy.

He got into his black Jeep Wrangler, started it up and pulled out of the lot. Soon, he was on the highway, the soft top gently flapping overhead. He wished that the temperature would climb just a little bit more so he could take the top down. Riding around on a warm sunny day with the top down and the wind in your hair just put you in a good mood no matter where you were going.

The traffic was uncharacteristically light and Ryan reached his office in record time. *I guess everyone is starting the weekend early,* he thought as he closed the door to the Jeep and walked toward his building.

The twenty-six story office building was one of three fairly new office buildings that stood over a scattered assortment of restaurants and shops. JNR Technologies, the computer sales company Ryan worked for, took up the entire fourteenth floor of the second building. He had a small cubicle in a room filled with small cubicles.

He wasn't quite sure how he had ended up here. It's funny how you go to college with all of these aspirations about doing good work, making good money, and making a difference in the world. Then you get out of college and don't get the job you want, don't make the money you want and end up wondering what the hell happened to all your dreams.

As a young, ambitious college student, he would never have guessed that in fourteen years he would be stuck selling office computers to unfamiliar companies. Maybe he should have made some different career choices. Maybe he should've gone back to school. Or maybe it was just bad luck that stuck him in a job that left him feeling empty and yearning for something more. Ryan knew that this job, like all the others, was only a temporary stop for him, but until he figured out what he really wanted to do, he would have to face yet another day of peddling computers.

In the last ten years Ryan had worked at two financial institutions, an advertising agency, a printing company and now at JNR selling computers. He knew the job-hopping didn't look good on his résumé, but he had just never been happy at any of his past positions. He was searching for something more. The perfect job was out there waiting for him somewhere - the hard part was finding it.

He was fifty feet from the main doors when his mood darkened. Standing in front of the building sucking down a cigarette was Gabriel Reese, by far Ryan's least favorite person at JNR, and maybe even on the whole planet. Since Ryan had started working here, five and a half months ago, he'd never heard anyone call him by his first name – everyone called him Reese. Reese was a wiry, chain-smoking scoundrel who always wore the most expensive suits money could buy. He was about five-foot-seven with black hair slicked back on a bony head that contained beady eyes. In the event of a fire, Reese was the sort of man likely to run over small children trying to save himself. He was also the best salesman at JNR. He had shattered every sales record in the company – and he was only thirty-two years old.

Ryan had to give him some credit. Reese was definitely a great salesman, mostly due to the fact that he could pile on the lies without hesitation, and cared for no one but himself. It never seemed to bother him if he screwed people out of thousands of dollars, as long as he kept getting his fat commission checks. That's probably why Ryan could never excel at JNR; he actually cared about other people more than making money.

Hovering next to Reese was Scott Batling, a spineless leach that everyone called "Scott Buttlicking" behind his back. Overweight, middle-aged, and balding, he was definitely not turning any female heads. It was fairly obvious to everyone that he hung on Reese's every word in the hope that he would slip him some leads. Ryan was sure that Reese knew Scott was just a parasite, but liked the attention too much to care – anything to hear the sound of his own voice.

As Ryan walked toward the door, Reese took a long last drag from his cigarette and tossed it to the ground, among the dozens he had discarded earlier in the week.

"Hey there, Ryan, how ya' doing, buddy?" he asked insincerely.

"I'll be better in about eight hours," Ryan replied, as he continued toward the door.

"I'm not sure all the time in the world could help your numbers."

With that both Reese and Scott started to chuckle.

Ryan turned away from Reese, shaking his head in disgust.

"Hey, seems like I hit a soft spot. Well, I think I happen to have the monthly numbers right here." Reese reached into his pocket, unfolded a piece of paper and cleared his throat. "Seems the Reese-Man is on top again. And, oh, who's this way down toward the bottom? Well, shit, that's your name."

"Screw you, Reese. I really don't care about the numbers, and I care even less about you."

Reese's smile was so wide it threatened to engulf his entire face. In the background, Scott continued to chuckle.

"Aw, I never meant to make you mad, buddy. We'd better just get rid of this." He crumbled the paper up into a ball and threw it at the garbage can next to the door, missing it by about a foot and a half. Then he turned and started to go inside, with Scott stuck to his heels.

He made it about halfway through the doorway before Ryan called, "You missed the garbage."

Reese turned back, pushing Scott's plump body aside and faced Ryan. "Looks like I did. So what?"

"Just because your very existence pollutes this planet doesn't give you the right to cover it with garbage too." Ryan said staring squarely into Reese's beady eyes.

"Well, well, what have we here? Seems like we got us a tree-hugger," Reese said with a sneer. "Let me tell you something, tree-hugger-mother-fucker. I'll make more money before lunch than you'll make all year, so maybe I should hire you to follow me around and collect my garbage for me. Why don't you pick that up and we'll consider this your audition."

As Ryan stared down Reese he could feel his anger rising up. His face reddened and his hands slowly formed into fists.

Reese could see that he was getting to Ryan. "Maybe you'd like to take a swing at me. Go ahead, take your shot." Reese paused and took a half step closer, so that they were almost touching. "I would love to sue your ass and take the loose change you call a life savings."

Although Ryan was certain he could send Reese to the emergency room with one punch, he resisted the urge. It would never be worth it. Slowly, he let go of his anger and began to relax his hands.

Seeing that the moment had passed, Reese stepped back. "That's what I thought, my little tree-hugger-mother-fucker." He turned again, bumping into Scott, and went inside. Scott gave Ryan a quick dirty look and scampered after Reese.

Ryan let out a deep breath, picked up the paper, threw it in the garbage can, and went inside.

Ryan lost himself in his work for the first three hours of the day. It was a morning filled with cold calls and mindless paperwork, which were about the crappiest tasks anyone could be forced to do, as far as Ryan was concerned. The repetitive dialing of numbers, hoping to make it through your first sentence without getting hung up on was not the most fun thing to do, but somehow Ryan made it to lunch.

He ordered in and had a pretty good turkey sandwich at his desk, while pondering his weekend possibilities. Just as he swallowed the last bite, he felt a hand on his back. Turning, he saw his coworker and friend, Diane, wearing a troubled expression.

"Did you hear about the volcanoes?" she asked, brushing her shoulder length blond hair out of her face.

Diane occupied the cubicle directly behind Ryan and they worked back to back every day. When they weren't out on sales calls they would talk periodically throughout the day, often without even turning to face one another. She was a nice person and probably his best friend at JNR.

"No, what volcanoes?" Ryan replied.

"There have been a number of eruptions around the world. It's all over the news. Come on, everyone's watching it in the conference room."

He followed Diane through the maze of cubicles until they reached one of two conference rooms in the back of the office. A long, rectangular table filled the center of the room with a white board on the back wall and a large flat screen TV on the opposite wall. About two-thirds of the people in the office were gathered around the table staring up at the television.

As images of lava flowing and mountains exploding rolled on the screen, Ryan could hear the voice over, "...tragedy I can imagine. These eruptions at Mt. Vesuvius and Mt. Merapi in Indonesia bring the total to nine volcanoes currently erupting worldwide. It's impossible to say how many people have lost their lives so far, but it's estimated to be in the hundreds, maybe even the thousands."

"Oh my God, that's horrible. How long has this been going on?" Ryan asked Diane, while everyone else in the room began their own private conversations with one another.

"Only about an hour. It's crazy, first the storms in Utah and Nevada, and now this."

Ryan's heart sped up. "Wait, what happened in Utah and Nevada?"

"Wow, Ryan, you really ought to pay attention to the news. For the last two days there were severe lightning storms throughout Utah and Nevada. They seemed to be concentrated around industrial areas and factories, but both states are pretty much on fire."

Ryan felt shell-shocked. He never really watched the news. Every time he gave it a chance there was nothing but murder, terrorism, and destruction. He had decided a long time ago not to depress himself with it. The only information Ryan took in was from random posts on Facebook.

He made it back to his desk trying to digest everything that was going on. Lost in his thoughts, Ryan stared blankly at his computer screen.

A smack on the cubicle's wall startled him, snapping his head up and sending him rolling back on his wheeled chair.

"Wake up, my little tree-hugger-mother-fucker." It was Reese.

"Jesus, Reese. What the hell do you want?" Ryan scowled and rolled back to his desk.

"Easy now. Don't get your panties in a bunch," Reese said smiling. "I just wanted to check in and see how you were doing. With all of this craziness in the world, I wanted to make sure you were all right. I know how sensitive and fragile you can be."

"Shouldn't you be busy conniving your way to another commission?" Ryan replied, trying to contain his hatred.

Reese smiled. "Oh, I'm so sorry. You can't play the part of the poor jealous coworker in the epic story of my life. You've already landed the role of the pathetic loser, and I think that's really all you can handle."

Ryan was far from being a violent person, but for the second time today, his hands were balled into fists. Using all of his self-control, he slowly opened his hands and leaned back in his chair. "I have enough to deal with without listening to your bullshit."

"I know all of these disasters have you wondering what the future holds, but I wouldn't worry too much. Even if the world gets tossed upside down, you can bet the Reese-Man will land on his feet at the top. And I'll always have a nice place saved at the bottom for you, tree-hugger-mother-fucker."

With another slap against the wall, Reese sauntered away, leaving Ryan with a pounding headache.

It was obvious that no one was going to get back to work today, so he decided to cut out early. Watching the news was not how he wanted to spend his weekend, but it seemed that's how it was going to start.

CHAPTER 2

A Quiet Dinner for Two

Ryan pulled the Jeep into his assigned parking spot in his apartment complex at ten minutes after four. On his way home, he had stopped off at the supermarket and the bank. The start of every good weekend began with food and money.

He walked through the courtyard carrying two bags full of groceries and thinking about electrical storms and volcanoes. Glancing ahead toward his building, he noticed something in front of his door. Calmly sitting on his doormat watching him approach was a white and brown dog.

Dogs never really scared Ryan, not even the big Great Danes that seemed like they could swallow your head like a piece of kibble. Still, he wasn't sure what to make of this dog. It seemed to be a mixture of a number of breeds. Ryan could identify the square jaw and muscular build of a Pit Bull, but it lacked the bulk and size of a full Pit. It was lean and athletic looking, probably weighing about fifty pounds or so, with a disarming sweetness in its eyes.

Ryan put his groceries down and walked up to the dog, crouching with his hand outstretched.

"Hey there, are you waiting for me?"

As soon as Ryan approached the dog, it started wagging it's tail. Kneeling beside it, he noticed that it was a female, maybe three to five years old. She had short white hair with a number of light brown patches throughout her body, including a large spot that covered her left eye and ear.

"Well, you're certainly friendly," Ryan said, as he rubbed the dog along her flank.

Now the dog's entire body was wagging.

"Where do you live, girl?"

Ryan stood up, searching the courtyard for the dog's owner. A few doors down, a middle-aged man emerged and started walking toward the parking lot. Ryan recognized him from his building, although he had never met him formally.

"Do you know whose dog this is?" Ryan called as he stood up.

Looking over, the man yelled, "No, I don't. Sorry," and then continued on his way.

There were no tags or even a collar on the dog. She seemed to be in great shape, so Ryan thought it unlikely that she was a stray. She was very clean, her coat flawless, and her belly full. *She must have slipped out of somebody's door without being noticed,* Ryan thought. But if she lived in one of the apartments, why had he never seen her before?

Ryan scanned the courtyard one more time and then opened his door. The dog casually walked in and sat down on the carpet.

"Yes, please make yourself at home," Ryan said from the

doorway.

After retrieving the groceries from the walkway, Ryan set them down on the kitchen table and took off his suit jacket.

"So, what am I going to do with you?" Ryan asked, as the dog walked into the living room and curled up into a ball as if it had lived there for years.

"Don't get too comfortable, now. You won't be staying here long."

Looking up, he glanced out his window into the courtyard and got an idea. "We're going to find your home girl, but first, you just may be able to help me out."

Ryan quickly changed out of his suit and into a pair of jeans and a long sleeve t-shirt. Then moved into the kitchen, where he got out some pots and pans and began cooking.

Thirty minutes later, Ryan had the table set and chicken and vegetables simmering. Peering out his window, he picked up the phone and dialed. The phone rang four or five times before Vivian's answering machine picked up. Ryan hung up the phone without leaving a message. Up at her apartment there was a dim light shining through the window.

"Stay here, and don't even think about touching my dinner," he said to the stretched out dog on the living room floor as he walked outside.

Even though it was only five o'clock, the dark clouds overhead made it seem like late evening. As he reached Vivian's door across the courtyard, thunder cracked overhead. He pressed the doorbell three times in long bursts. After no one came, he rang it a few more times and then knocked loudly yelling, "Vivian, it's Ryan! I need you – it's very important!"

A few seconds later he heard footsteps coming down the stairs. The door opened a crack and Vivian's red, puffy eyes peered out. "It's really not a good time Ryan," she said softly, her face a vision of melancholy.

"I'm sorry Viv, but I've got a major emergency," Ryan said dramatically. "When I got home, there was this thing and . . . and I don't know what to do. Please, you've got to come over and help me."

As Vivian opened the door a little more, Ryan noticed that she was wearing a white bathrobe and that her bare feet were dripping water onto the floor.

A look of concern flashed in her eyes, "Slow down. What the hell are you talking about?"

"I don't know what to do. You just have to come over and help me. I can't explain it. It's something you need to see for yourself."

Ryan thought he might have laid it on a bit too thick, but she seemed to bite.

"All right. Stay here and I'll be right down." She closed the door and ran upstairs.

Moments later, she emerged wearing the same outfit he saw her in that morning. "Okay, let's go," she said as thunder rolled through the clouds.

They ran across the courtyard together, and she followed him as he burst into his apartment. Before she had time to register what was going on, she was greeted by a happy, affectionate, tail wagging dog that seemed to be very excited she was there. Vivian knelt down to say hi to the dog, and got a pretty good face licking in return.

Good dog, Ryan thought, *that's exactly what I was hoping you'd do.*

"I think she likes you," he said.

"She's beautiful," Vivian said, as a reluctant smile began to appear on her face. "Where did you get her?"

"I found her outside my door, and I need help finding out who she belongs to."

"Hold on a second," she said, standing up. "This is your big emergency?"

"Yes, it is. It was *very* important that I see you smile."

The dog was at Vivian's feet prancing around demanding attention. She knelt back down and continued rubbing her.

"This is about the lowest thing you've ever done," she said, as the licks to her face continued. "She is damn cute, though,"

"I need you to help me figure out what to do with this little girl. Let's sit down and see if we can come up with something." Ryan said and led her toward the table.

Vivian began to move, but slowed as she noticed the table settings.

"Ryan, you son of a bitch," she said softly, as she reluctantly sat down.

During dinner, their conversation started with the dog, who had curled up under the table between them, but soon moved on to various other topics. Ryan was careful to keep the mood light and stayed away from anything to do with her recent breakup. Vivian was a little quiet and guarded, but seemed to loosen up a little with time.

Even after their forks hit the plates, they continued to talk for a while. After spending the last week withdrawn and quiet, Ryan was hoping that all Vivian really needed was a simple night of friendly distractions to get her back on track. Finally, he sat up and said "I'm going to clean up a little. Do you think you could take the dog out for a walk? We don't want any accidents, do we?"

"I guess I could. Do you even have a leash?" Vivian asked, standing up.

"A leash . . . . No, I guess not, but maybe I have something we can use." Ryan went into the closet and returned with the belt from his bathrobe. Bending down, he tied it around the dog's neck and gave the end to Vivian. "Now, don't disappear on me. I need you back here for dessert."

He opened the door for them and watched as the two girls walked down the path. The sky was thick with black clouds and the wind was really picking up.

We're in for quite a storm, Ryan thought as he closed the door and started bringing the dishes over to the sink.

Not more than five minutes had passed when the front door opened in a rush of wind. Vivian came in with the dog and quickly closed the door behind her.

"Yikes, it's getting pretty nasty out there," she said as she untied the terry cloth belt from the dog's neck.

"Everything go all right?" Ryan asked from the kitchen.

"Yeah, it's weird though. She kept looking up at me as we walked, and before I knew it, she'd led me right back here. It was almost as if she was walking me."

A shot of thunder sounded so loudly that Ryan thought the

clouds must be sitting directly on the roof. That's when the dog started barking and jumping at the door.

"It's okay girl, just a little noise, nothing to be afraid of," Ryan said softly.

Then they heard a large crack, followed by a dull boom coming from somewhere outside. The dog went crazy, barking at the door and then staring up at Ryan.

"What the hell was that?" Vivian asked as Ryan reached for the door.

As soon as he opened it, the dog ran outside, stopping about ten feet away, looking back at them in the doorway. One of the big trees that dotted the courtyard had fallen over and was lying on its side across the path with its roots exposed.

The dog barked at them a few more times and then darted past the tree and toward the parking lot.

"Hey, where're you going, girl?" Ryan called, as he and Vivian chased after her.

They ran past the tree and around the corner to the parking lot. Squinting in the wind, Ryan scanned the area for his new friend.

They heard some barking over to the left and ran over to find the dog barking in front of Ryan's Jeep.

"What's she doing?" Vivian shouted, as the wind whipped against them.

"I don't know, but this weather is a little too dangerous. We should get back inside." Ryan shouted back.

Ryan and Vivian began jogging back to Ryan's apartment. At the corner of the courtyard, Ryan stopped and turned back to see the dog still standing in front of the Jeep watching him.

"Here, girl!" he called, patting his leg.

The dog gazed at the Jeep for a second and then reluctantly trotted over to Ryan. Once together, they both ran after Vivian and followed her back into Ryan's apartment.

Inside, Vivian caught her breath as she regarded the dog. "That was weird," she said. "It looked like she wanted to go for a ride."

"Yeah, but she was waiting on my doorstep when I got home from work. She's never seen my Jeep before."

"Then why would she run over to it like that? Could she have known it was yours?"

"I don't see how. I know dogs do have a great sense of smell. Maybe she could smell my scent on the Jeep."

"I don't think her sniffer is *that* good, do you?" Vivian asked skeptically.

"No, probably not."

Thunder cracked overhead, and a bolt of lightning flashed nearby. The wind whipped against the windows and another loud burst of thunder shook the building. *Maybe it was time to turn on the TV and see what was happening,* Ryan thought.

Ryan went into the living room, followed by the dog and Vivian, and turned on the TV. One of the local channels broadcasting out of New York City had a newswoman reporting.

". . . out of nowhere. The entire tri-state area is covered by thick clouds, and wind speeds are almost at hurricane force. There really is no explanation for this quick change in the weather. There was no indication or warning that a storm of this magnitude was headed our way."

Ryan, Vivian, and the dog stood in silence and stared at the TV as the reporter continued.

"We can only assume that this is in some way connected to the recent volcanic eruptions worldwide and the tragic storms in Utah and Nevada. The weather seems to be turning violent all around the globe. Reports are coming in from every continent describing everything from high winds and tornados, to volcanoes and electrical storms.

"There is also evidence of increased seismic activity throughout the United States and Canada. Even locations that have never had a recorded incidence of an earthquake are experiencing tremors. On the coast, seas have risen dramatically in the last five hours, with swells reaching twenty to thirty feet. Scientists are baffled, while some people are saying this is the end–"

Glass shattered, as the living room window exploded, causing Ryan and Vivian to cover their faces. Wind rushed into the room, and the dog barked frantically at Ryan's feet.

"I've got a really bad feeling about this," Ryan said.

"What should we do?" Fear had replaced the sorrow in Vivian's eyes.

It was hard to think clearly with the noise of the storm and the wind rushing into the apartment. Loose papers swirled around the room in chaotic circles and another window shattered somewhere back in the bedroom.

Ryan panned down and locked eyes with the dog. Then, they were plunged into darkness as the power went out. It took a moment for Ryan's eyes to adjust to the dim surroundings. Luckily the sun, wherever it was hiding, had not yet set and left them with a dim grayness instead of total pitch black.

The dog let out a soft, but stern growl, bringing Ryan out of his indecisive daze.

"We've got to get out of here," he said.

"Leave the apartment? Why? Don't you think it's safer to stay inside?" Even in the darkness, Ryan could see the worry on her face.

"I just have this really bad feeling. I think we need to get out of here. It's not safe." Ryan felt a bump on his knee, and peered down to see the dog watching him, with what seemed like concern.

"You've got to trust me on this one, Viv. Go to your apartment and throw a few things in a bag and meet me at the Jeep."

"Where are we going?"

"We'll go to my parent's lake house in Pennsylvania. Think of it as a weekend getaway, but we need to get away right now. If everything calms down, we'll come back tomorrow, or maybe Sunday."

The dog was barking again. They both went into motion without another word. Vivian opened the door and ran through the wind across the courtyard as Ryan went to his bedroom and started throwing clothes into a duffle bag.

He wasn't sure what he should be packing, so he just grabbed whatever was closest. In the end, about a week's worth of clothes, a flashlight, his hiking boots and a few towels made it into the bag. Then, he went to the kitchen and filled another bag with food and some bottles of water.

Ryan picked up his cell phone, but it showed that there was no service. He always got good reception in his apartment, but now his phone showed that he wasn't getting any signal.

He wanted to check up on his parents in Arizona, and see what was happening out west. The dog barked from the living room, and Ryan put the phone in his pocket and headed for the door.

He didn't know what he was going to do with the dog. Looking around he couldn't seem to locate the bathrobe belt they had used as a leash, and he didn't have the time to find something else. He would have to just go without it and hoped the dog would stay with them.

He opened the door and the wind almost knocked him off his feet. The dog shot out in front of him, ran around the fallen tree and was out of sight. *Oh well, so much for staying with me,* Ryan thought.

More thunder boomed above Ryan's head and somewhere in the distance, and lightning lit up the sky. As he ran past the tree and rounded the corner to the parking lot, the sky lit up again. This time there were a series of flashes followed by a distant rumble that seemed to shake the ground beneath his feet.

Ryan reached the Jeep and was, again, met by the dog. He opened the door, threw the bags in the back seat, and held the door open.

"Come on, girl," he called, but the dog stood in front of the jeep stoically.

"Come on," he said again louder. When the dog made no move he said, "Suit yourself, but I'm leaving."

Closing the door, he started the engine and switched on the lights. The dog was still standing there, now in the glow of the headlights. She looked back toward the apartments and Ryan followed her gaze to see Vivian running toward them. As Vivian opened the door she was pushed aside by the dog, who jumped inside the Jeep and into the back seat. Vivian threw the two bags she had packed in the back with the dog and climbed in.

The sky lit up again, as more lightning shot down somewhere just out of sight. Ryan got the Jeep moving and pulled out into the street. There were a number of other cars slowly navigating the street, making the journey much slower than Ryan was comfortable with.

Driving through the darkened roads demanded all of his attention. Apparently, the entire area had lost power, and with the exception of car headlights and the occasional lightning bolt, there was only darkness – and it seemed to be getting darker by the second. Ryan didn't know what time it was, but it seemed like night had finally fallen upon them, and fallen hard.

He pulled onto the onramp for the highway. The dog let out a few yelps as Ryan suddenly jammed on the brakes. The highway was a mass of traffic. Brake lights lit up the road as cars and trucks sat motionless, bumper to bumper.

Quickly, Ryan turned the wheel, hopped the curb and drove over the grass embankment and back onto the street. They would have to try their luck on the local roads. The wind was blowing papers and loose garbage across their path as Ryan navigated around other cars that were moving too slowly. He wanted to head west, but it seemed there was traffic everywhere. With the feeling of dread still firmly rooted in his stomach, Ryan decided their best bet would be to get on a major highway and try to eventually make their way onto Route 78. Last year, a friend of his had shown Ryan some seldom used local roads to the New Jersey Turnpike. It wasn't exactly where he wanted to be, but he would have to give it a try.

The twenty minutes it took them to reach the Turnpike seemed like an eternity. He was forced to drive on more than a few lawns and jump a number of curbs in order to keep moving. Once on the Turnpike, he let out the breath he was holding. The traffic was moderate, and Ryan hit the gas as he weaved around cars and trucks. On the left side of the Jeep, off in the distance, there was a large orange glow.

"What is that?" Vivian asked Ryan.

Keeping his eyes on the road ahead of him, Ryan quietly replied, "It appears New York City is burning."

CHAPTER 3

Good Karma

The journey south on the New Jersey Turnpike was slow. For the most part, Ryan and Vivian sat in silence, their eyes scanning the road ahead. Various obstacles dotted the highway causing Ryan to swerve the Jeep right and left quickly. In the back seat, the dog sat quietly, gazing out the window.

Even in the darkness of night, Ryan could feel the thick clouds weighing down on him from above. Lightning streaked down sporadically, illuminating the horizon with a flash. The wind was still blowing hard, but not a single drop of rain had fallen. As they drove past Newark airport, they could see the planes parked motionless, most of them in darkness. Although the electricity was out, the airport must have had emergency power, because some lights were visible in the towers.

They passed a number of fires as they drove. Most were off in the distance, but when they passed through the town of Elizabeth, flames seemed to be everywhere. Ryan remembered driving this way many times in the summer, when he would take weekend trips to the beach further south. Even on a sunny day, the sky would always seem gray here. On either side of the Turnpike, huge factories pumped plumes of smoke into the air from tall chimneys. The landscape was the color of steel and concrete, without a tree or blade of grass anywhere in sight. He had always quickened his speed here, feeling that the polluted air was poisoning his lungs.

Tonight the smoke was again pouring out of the Elizabeth factories, but for the last time. The fires were so intense and consuming that he could feel the heat of the flames, even though the buildings burned hundreds of yards away. Ryan was greatly relieved when he finally left the fires behind, and returned to the darkness of the highway. From the lessening tension he could visibly see in Vivian's posture, he knew she felt the same.

Ryan was able to traverse a few smaller roadways, finally reaching Route 78 heading west. He crossed the border into Pennsylvania with a sigh of relief, even though the wind was still blowing fiercely. Leaving the highway, they went north on a rural road flanked by thick trees. The road was winding and dark, and he was having trouble keeping the Jeep on the road.

Exhaustion was creeping up on them, and he knew he would have to stop driving soon or he might fall asleep at the wheel. Next to him, Vivian was also starting to doze. The darkness around them was all encompassing. They hadn't seen a single car since leaving the highway, and the few houses they passed were dark and appeared abandoned.

Startled, Ryan hit the brakes. The Jeep headlights illuminated the remains of a car accident in the center of the intersection ahead.

Several cars and a pick-up truck were locked together blocking the road. Another car lay on its side off in the trees. By the severity of the damage, Ryan could tell that some of the vehicles must have been traveling at a pretty high speed.

"Stay here," Ryan said to Vivian, as he opened his door.

He walked around the scene, gazing inside the cars and pickup truck. The Jeep's headlights lit up the first two cars, but the rest were nestled in shadows. As he approached a beat-up Cadillac, he saw that the broken windshield was streaked with blood. Through the window, he saw an old man's slumped body. Ryan figured that the man must have died on impact. The other vehicles were empty, their engines cold. Ryan assumed the accident must have taken place a few hours ago.

He returned to the Jeep and filled Vivian in on what he'd seen. "There's nothing we can do here," he said, eyeballing the intersection. "We can't get around this mess, so I think we should turn around and see if someone will be kind enough to let us stay the night."

"I don't know, Ryan," Vivian said softly. "Do you think it's a good idea to just knock on someone's door? This might not be a friendly neighborhood."

Ryan glanced around, noticing some lights shining through holes in the foliage, confirming that the area still had some electricity. He took his cell phone out of his pocket and noticed that he still had no service.

"It's not my first choice," Ryan said, "but we're exhausted and I don't know these roads too well. Maybe we can find a way to the house in the morning."

Vivian nodded, and Ryan reached toward the back seat and patted the dog on the head. "Sound good to you girl?"

The dog leaned forward and gave Ryan a few licks on the chin.

"I'll take that as a yes," Ryan said as he pulled the Jeep in reverse and turned it around.

About a half mile down the road, they came to a mailbox on the left. There was a gravel driveway alongside it, and somewhere hidden in the darkness was presumably a house. Ryan turned the Jeep into the driveway and headed into the woods. The driveway went straight back for about one hundred yards and led to an old log cabin style house with a beat up pickup truck parked in front. The house was dark and quiet.

Ryan and Vivian got out of the Jeep. Before Ryan had a chance to close the door, the dog jumped out.

"I guess you're not waiting in the car," Ryan said, as the dog ran to the cabin door.

Once at the door, the dog began cautiously sniffing up and down. She seemed a bit uneasy and this made Ryan nervous. Although they never had a chance to talk about it, both Ryan and Vivian were unsure what to make of this dog, but right now they didn't have time to think about it. It was late and they needed shelter for the night.

Ryan got to the door and knocked loudly.

The only sound they heard was the wind blowing against the trees.

He knocked again and said, "Hello, anyone home?"

Again, no answer.

"Stay here. I'm going to take a look around," he said to Vivian, who stayed at the door watching the dog continue her sniffing.

Ryan went to the Jeep and got the flashlight out of his duffle bag and turned it on. Walking around the side of the house, Ryan saw a pile of firewood stacked in a neat pyramid against the house.

Continuing to the back, he came to a big deck attached to the back of the house. A small picnic table and a propane barbeque grill sat in the middle against the wooden railing. Ryan climbed up on the deck and to the sliding glass doors that led into the house. Squinting through the darkness, he made out a dining room with a kitchen off to the left. There was no sign of anyone. He shined the light on his watch, which read 1:16.

Maybe everyone is sleeping, he thought.

He continued walking around the house, pausing to peek in every window. There were three bedrooms and a bathroom, all of which were empty. Outside, the wind continued to blow leaves and branches around, startling him whenever one landed close by. He heard more thunder and lightning, but it seemed to be some distance away.

He finally completed his circle around the house and ended up back at the front door, where Vivian was kneeling down petting the dog.

"There doesn't seem to be anyone here," he told her.

"Well, what do we do now? Try another house?"

"I don't really want to go door to door all night," Ryan said as he walked up to the door. "This has been one crazy night. So let's continue the craziness."

He turned the door knob, silently praying for it to be unlocked. It turned easily and Ryan let out a gentle sigh of relief as he opened the door. There was nothing but darkness inside. Slowly, Ryan inched his way inside with Vivian and the dog following closely behind.

"Let me find a light switch," Ryan said walking to the far wall. Just before he flicked the switch, the dog made a subtle whining noise.

The switch turned on a lamp resting on an old wooden end table. In the light, they saw that they were standing in a small living room with a stone fireplace at one end. There was a couch against the front windows and a love seat cutting across the room, opposite the fireplace. End tables filled the corners of the room, which led to a dining room, with a kitchen off to the left. The walls were merely the wooden logs that made up the exterior of the cabin, and the ceiling went all the way up to the peak of the roof. Just before the hallway that led to the bedrooms, stood a six foot high cabinet filled with guns. Five rifles were mounted vertically, with three handguns neatly positioned underneath. But what disturbed Ryan the most was that he was surrounded by animals.

A huge deer head was mounted above the fireplace, two stuffed pheasants adorned the opposite wall, ducks sat on the mantle, rabbits and raccoons stared blankly from the dining room and a huge brown bear stood in the far corner, its face forever locked in a ferocious snarl. In the center of the living room floor was a big bearskin rug and various animal pelts were draped over just about every piece of furniture they could see.

Ryan had never killed an animal in his life and couldn't comprehend how someone could get enjoyment out of gunning down an innocent creature. Every year, when hunting season began, there were always stories about hunters shooting each other by mistake. Although he never said it out loud, Ryan always felt some kind of justice hearing how some big, bad hunter finally got to feel what it was like to be unsuspectingly shot.

Vivian appeared equally disgusted as she looked around the house. Even the dog seemed to be bothered by the sight. She padded around the cabin quietly, giving the occasional sniff here and there.

"This is a bit creepy," Vivian said, walking toward the gun cabinet. "Maybe we should have broken into a place with a little less firepower."

Ryan picked up a picture sitting on one of the end tables. It showed a bearded man of about fifty years holding a rifle, and standing over a dead bear – presumably the one standing in the corner. This was probably the hunter's cabin, and Ryan started to get concerned with what this man, so fond of guns and killing, would do once he discovered them in his house.

"I'm going to take one more quick look around outside. I have a feeling that this is not the type of guy who likes surprises. Keep checking out the rest of the rooms in here. I'll be right back." Ryan grabbed the flashlight and went outside.

He walked around the house again searching for anything that might suggest the hunter's whereabouts. In the back of the house, he walked a few steps into the woods, panning the flashlight beam around. Something caught his attention off in the woods, directly behind the cabin. Holding the flashlight in front of him like a weapon, Ryan moved ahead. He came to a small well in the center of a clearing. He looked into the well, but couldn't really see anything.

The wind began blowing again, as the smell of burnt wood reached Ryan's nose. He turned into the woods to the right. Lying under a small tree was the crumpled form of a man. Both the man and tree were black with ash, as was a circle of grass and some of the surrounding shrubbery. Ryan recognized the blackened face as that of the hunter in the picture. Ryan felt for a pulse, but wasn't surprised when there was none.

Back in the house, he found Vivian and the dog checking out the bedrooms.

"We'll stay here for the night," he told them.

"What about the Great White Hunter?" Vivian asked.

"I don't think he's going to need the place anymore. I found him in the woods out back. I think he was struck by lightning."

"Yikes. Do you think I should take a look at him?" Vivian worked as a nurse and was always there whenever anyone needed so much as a band aid. Although she graduated at the top of her nursing class, it wasn't her knowledge that made her a good nurse, but the way she interacted with the patients. She had a talent for putting people at ease, even when they were in pain or had a grim diagnosis.

"No one can help him now," Ryan said. "He's gone."

Ryan brought their bags in, and they both got into a change of clothes.

"We should get some sleep," Ryan said, with a yawn. "Which bedroom do you want?"

"If you don't mind, I'd like it if we stayed together. After everything that's happened, it would be nice to have you close by."

"Sure," Ryan replied. "No problem."

They made their way to the back bedroom and climbed into the queen sized bed together. Before they had time to pull the covers up, the dog jumped onto the bed, and curled up between them.

Laying with the light on, they both stared up at the ceiling thinking about all that had happened in the last ten hours.

"I feel kind of weird sleeping here while that guy is lying dead outside," Vivian said, leaning toward Ryan.

"I know, but try to get some rest. I have a feeling we're going to need it."

Ryan shut off the light and they both closed their eyes and fell asleep to the sound of the wind whipping through the trees. Nestled in the covers between them, the dog was the last one to close her eyes.

The next morning the sun came up, but nobody saw it. A wall of clouds blanketed the sky making the morning seem gray and dismal. After a full night's sleep, Ryan awoke in silence to an equally quiet Vivian. He noticed that she seemed a bit somber, and he feared that she might be slipping back into her depressed state. With the excitement of the past day, she seemed to forget about being miserable. Now, awakening to a new day, he worried that she was feeling the weight of her sorrow once again.

Ryan walked to the back window. It was still pretty windy, but it didn't appear dangerous. The refrigerator supplied them with a breakfast of eggs, toast and some fruit, which they shared with their furry companion. Ryan made a mental note to find some dog food somewhere soon.

After quiet breakfast, Ryan said, "What do you say we take the dog for a little walk in the woods before we head out of here?"

"I'm not really in the mood. You go ahead." Vivian said, taking a seat on the living room floor.

"Come on, it will do you good to get some fresh air." He wasn't about to let her settle back into her depression. Besides genuinely caring for her, he also needed her alert and watchful. Something serious was going on in the world and they needed to be ready for anything.

The dog, who had been sitting close by, walked over to Vivian and looked up at her intently.

"Okay, okay, I'll go," she said, and Ryan caught a slight smile showing on Vivian's face as she stood up. The dog pranced around the living room excitedly. "What about a leash?"

"I have a feeling she'll stick with us. She likes you too much to take off."

They walked out into the breezy morning and into the woods off to the left of the house. Ryan made sure they stayed well away from the area where the hunter's body lay. The dog walked about ten feet ahead of Ryan and Vivian, stopping to sniff a tree every so often.

About twenty feet into the woods they picked up a path that led them up a small hill. Ryan studied Vivian's face and realized she was battling her inner demons again.

"How're ya doing there, kiddo?" he asked as they walked up the hill.

Vivian was silent for a moment or two and then replied, "I've had better times."

"I know you've been really hurting lately, and it's natural to feel bad about the situation, but don't for a second feel bad about yourself."

At the top of the hill, the trees gave way to a small clearing. Ryan and Vivian sat down in the grass while the dog nosed around a few feet away.

Once they sat down Vivian looked at Ryan. "It's just very hard for me. I thought I knew exactly how everything in my life was going to go. I had it all planned out in my head. Brad and I would live together, love each other and live happily ever after. Then one day, my whole world gets shattered, and I'm left sitting among the broken pieces of my dreams trying to figure what I did wrong."

Vivian paused and wiped the wetness gathering in her eyes. "I never thought I could feel so utterly alone and worthless." She lowered her head and closed her eyes.

Ryan was trying to find the right words when the dog walked over to Vivian. A tear ran down her face, fell from her chin and landed on her leg, quickly absorbing into her jeans. The dog sniffed the spot where the tear fell, then looked up and licked the trail the tear had left on Vivian's face.

Vivian opened her eyes and was nose to nose with the dog. There seemed to be a quiet understanding in the dog's eyes that was comforting. Vivian stroked the dog's head a few times and slowly began to smile.

Ryan finally gathered his thoughts, as the dog walked a few feet away and curled up in the grass. "Out of all of the people I've known in my life, you are one of the most genuinely good souls I've encountered. Unfortunately, bad things sometimes happen to good people. I mean, look at everything that has happened in the world the last day or two. The thing you have to remember is that it's not your fault. I believe that the harder things get, the bigger the rewards are at the end. And I firmly believe that you are destined for the happiest times of your life, so you can't give up now."

Some of the pain seemed to be drifting from Vivian's face. "Thank you."

"Besides," Ryan continued. "That dog seems to think you're the best thing since bacon."

"She's sweet," Vivian said, then glanced up at the sky.

Above them, big, thick clouds were moving quickly in every

direction. Clouds of every size and shape swirled and churned back and forth. Every so often a small patch of blue would show through and the sun would shine down, but only for a moment. Ryan had never seen anything like it. How could the wind be moving the clouds in every direction at once?

"Do you think this is the end of the world?" Vivian uttered so calmly that it caught Ryan off guard.

"I don't know what's going on. But I think that whatever is happening will change how we live forever."

"I think that dog sensed something back at your place. It ran right to your Jeep, without knowing it was yours. I think she was trying to tell us to get out of there."

"As much as I'd like to believe that, I think it was just a coincidence."

Vivian gazed back up at the clouds. "Don't you ever believe those stories about dogs waking up their owners in the middle of the night when their house is on fire?"

"I don't know. I've never known anyone that happened to, so to me, they're just stories." Ryan paused and glanced over at the dog curled up in the grass, being warmed by a sunbeam.

"Well, I think she's special no matter what you say," Vivian said defiantly.

He nodded and stood up, offering his hand to Vivian. "She's been pretty good luck to us so far. And anything that can bring that smile back to your face is good in my book."

Vivian accepted his hand and he helped her up. "Well, it would seem she plans on staying with us, so we should probably call her something other than *the dog*."

Ryan studied the little white and brown dog for a moment or

two before he realized something very strange. The clouds were still swirling at high speeds overhead and only parted once in a while to show the sun for a brief second at a time. But somehow, a flickering sunbeam always shone down on one spot. That spot was where the dog lay resting.

"You still think she's not special?" Vivian said, with wonder in her voice.

The dog got up and walked over to them, leaving the warmth of the sunbeam, which disappeared behind the clouds a moment later.

"I honestly don't know what to think," Ryan replied as his mind struggled to make sense of what he just saw.

They began walking back toward the house, with the dog jogging ahead.

"She doesn't seem like the Fido or Rover type," Ryan said.

"No way, she deserves something better than that." Vivian paused, watching the dog bounce down the path ahead of them. "As the whole world goes crazy, this dog found its way to you. You may say it's just a coincidence, but maybe it's more than that. Maybe she was meant to find you. Maybe she was meant to find us. I think she's our good luck charm, and that nothing bad will happen as long as she's with us."

Ryan glanced at Vivian. "So you want to call her Lucky?"

"No, it's more than luck," Vivian said. "I think you're a truly great guy. And if even half of those nice things you said about me are true, then it's much more than luck. It's karma. And I think that's what we should name her."

Up ahead, the dog had stopped and was waiting for them to catch up. Once they reached her, Vivian bent down and gently patted her head. "Good Karma," she said, and smiled at Ryan.

He returned her smile. "That sounds perfect."

They walked back down the path to the house, and turned the corner just in time to see a large man slicing open the Jeep's soft top with a knife.

CHAPTER 4

Things Get Heated

The guy with the knife was big – real big. He stood at about six-foot-five and looked to be around two hundred and fifty pounds. He was African American and had fairly dark brown skin, a long mane of dreadlocked hair and a wild beard that covered the lower portion of his face. Even though his body was covered by a pair of dark gray pants and a faded gray short sleeve shirt, you could see the outlines of a very muscular body. The knife he was using to cut through the Jeep's soft top appeared to be some sort of large pocket knife. He was standing by the driver's side door slicing just above the window frame.

Ryan surveyed the scene and tried to think fast. There was no doubt that a physical confrontation with this monster would be suicide, so it seemed he would have to talk his way through this.

"You know you don't have to cut it. It just zips open," Ryan said, walking ahead of Vivian.

Startled, the big guy whirled around, holding the knife before him.

"Jesus. You scared the hell out of me," he said, letting out a big breath. Even startled, the big guy seemed very sure of himself. "I take it this is your Jeep."

Ryan was standing about ten feet away, trying his best to figure out what kind of person he was dealing with. "That it is."

The big guy seemed to realize he was still holding the knife out in front of him, and closed the blade up and put it in his pocket. Karma, who had been standing beside Vivian, ran past Ryan and straight at the big guy, who took a cautious step backward. The dog reached him before he had time to consider any kind of action. With her tail wagging furiously, Karma stood up and placed her front paws on the big guy's legs and looked up at him.

Soon the apprehension on his face was replaced with a smile, as he bent down to pet the dog.

Turning back to Vivian, Ryan said, "Great watch dog."

After a moment or two, the big guy stood back up to his full height and faced Ryan and Vivian. "Sorry about your Jeep, I didn't think anyone was here. With the planet falling apart and all, I just figured it was abandoned."

Suddenly, the front door of the house swung open and out walked a man holding Vivian's duffle bag. He was about thirty years old with wild dirty blond hair that fell to his shoulders. His face was covered with light scruffy facial hair, and he also wore a gray shirt with gray pants.

Vivian walked up to him and grabbed her bag from his hands. "That would be mine!"

"Sorry, sweetheart," he paused, leering at her. "If I knew it belonged to a beauty like you, I would have spent more time checkin' out the delicates."

Vivian shot him a disgusted look and walked back to Ryan.

"You'll have to excuse my insensitive friend. As you can probably tell, he doesn't have much experience with women," the big guy told them.

"Screw you!" the man in front of the house yelled back at him.

Ignoring him, the big guy continued to Ryan and Vivian. "We were just passing through when our bike ran out of gas." He gestured to a beat up Harley Davidson motorcycle parked at the end of the driveway. "We needed to borrow another vehicle and get some food."

"Don't you mean steal another vehicle?" Vivian said accusingly.

"I guess you could call it that, but I figure we're working on a whole new set of rules since the world's turned upside down." He stepped toward Ryan and Vivian. "My name's Marcus, and that's Mikey over there. I'm sorry we snuck into your house and ripped up your Jeep. I just assumed the owner bolted, like everybody else."

"Actually, this isn't our house," Ryan said. "We traveled all night from New Jersey in the middle of the storms. We needed a place to crash for the night, so we let ourselves in. I'm Ryan and this is Vivian. Do you have any idea what's going on?"

"The fucking world is coming to an end, man." Mikey said.

Marcus glared at Mikey and took a deep breath. "Lightning storms rained down on the entire Northeast causing raging fires and massive devastation. New York City burned to the ground. There's nothing left of Manhattan now except blowing ash. The surrounding areas of New Jersey and Connecticut are piles of rubble. I'm not sure where you two came from, but I hope you don't plan on going back anytime soon."

The gravity of this information hit Ryan hard. Next to him, Vivian looked equally stunned. Everyone he knew was gone. Everything he owned was gone. The events of the past night had happened so fast that he never really had a chance to deal with it. In one night, life as he knew it had been tossed into the air, and was now tumbling around and around. The big guy was right; the world did have a new set of rules. Ryan just didn't know what they were.

Seeing the turmoil on their faces, Marcus said, "Why don't we go inside and get some food, and I'll tell you everything I know. And by the time we're done eating, we'll all be good friends"

The big man didn't leave much room for argument, so Ryan and Vivian followed Mikey into the house. Before going in the house, Marcus turned back and studied the Jeep. "Well what do you know? It does have zippers." Then he went inside, with Karma walking just ahead of him.

Marcus was a blur of motion in the kitchen, and within thirty minutes he laid two heaping stacks of pancakes on the dining room table. Mikey barely waited for Marcus to set the food down before he had a forkful in his mouth. Ryan and Vivian sat at the table watching the men eat, as they digested all the new information.

"Show a little manners, Mikey," Marcus said, watching Mikey stuffing his face. "You know, you don't always have to act like such a savage."

Mikey stopped chewing just long enough to say, "You keep shooting off your big mouth, and I'll show you what a kind of a savage I am."

Ryan didn't trust these two strangers and didn't want them around, but it seemed he was stuck with them whether he liked it or not. Karma was sleeping soundly at Ryan's feet, and since coming into the house, she had remained very close to him.

"Where are you guys from?" Ryan asked.

"Ossining, New York," Marcus said between bites. "Mikey and I are neighbors, and we took off together when we heard about New York City. We figured it might be safer to head away from the coast, but I'm not sure it makes a damn bit of difference. Our car broke down about forty miles away. We came across the motorcycle lying on the side of the road, so we got it going and made it here."

"And a wild ride it was," Mikey said with a mouthful of pancakes.

Ryan and Vivian told them about what they had seen in the past twenty-four hours, but didn't get many more details about their two new friends. Marcus did most of the talking and seemed a bit uneasy whenever Mikey would open his mouth to say something.

After the two men ate their fill, Vivian called Karma into the living room, where they rolled around playfully together.

"That's a beautiful dog you got there," Marcus said, watching from the dining room.

"Yeah, she's one of a kind," Ryan replied.

Mikey leaned over the table to get a look into the living room. "That's a Pit Bull isn't it?"

"I'm not really sure what kind of dog she is, but she does kind of look like one."

"If you bulk her up a little, I bet she'd make a damn good fighting dog. I know a guy who runs some fights in his basement. I could probably hook you up," Mikey said, leaning back.

"No, thanks," Ryan said coldly.

"I don't think she's the fighting type," Marcus said, as he stood up and walked into the living room, where Vivian was getting licked all over her face. "No sir. This dog's a lover."

As he lowered his huge body to the floor, Karma came over to him and started to lick his face, but pulled back after only a few licks.

"I don't think she likes your beard," Vivian said.

Marcus smiled, but seemed disappointed. Mikey came into the living room and bent down with his hand out to pet Karma.

Karma stepped back, staying out of Mikey's reach and let out a low growl. Mikey quickly stood back up, bringing his hand back to his side.

"Seems like female dogs like you as much as female people do," Marcus said smiling.

"Fuck you, Marcus. Dumb mutt. I'm going to the can." And he stormed down the hall, to the bathroom.

"Don't give Mikey there much thought. He's harmless," Marcus said to Vivian, seeing the distrust on her face. Then he turned to Ryan. "So where are you headed?"

Ryan thought for a minute trying to decide how much he should say. He didn't trust these two guys, but since he really didn't have much of a plan, he felt he could be honest. "I'm not really sure. We were headed out to my parent's lake house not far from here. We were going to stay there for the weekend and see if things calmed down, but now it doesn't seem like we'll be going back any time soon."

"From what I saw, I don't think you want to head back that way," Marcus was petting Karma again.

"We really haven't talked about it yet, but I was thinking about maybe driving to Arizona to check in on my parents. Have you heard about anything out west?"

"I only know about the storms in Utah and Nevada a couple days ago. Other than that, I haven't heard a thing. Does this place have a TV or radio?" Marcus asked glancing around.

Vivian shook her head. "No, I checked last night. I would imagine this guy spent all his time hunting."

"And I haven't been able to get any cell reception since the storms started," Ryan said, looking once again at his useless cell phone.

Ryan put his phone away and watched Marcus on the floor with Karma. This big guy, who had seemed so menacing when he was cutting open the Jeep, now seemed totally unthreatening. Although he knew nothing about him, Ryan got the feeling that Marcus was a man who could be trusted.

Suddenly, Karma stood up very rigid, with her ears raised as if she had heard something. She stayed like that for a few moments, and then started to bark.

Mikey walked out of the hallway and into the living room. "What got up her ass?"

Karma was moving back and forth in front of Ryan, barking. Vivian stood up nervously. "Ryan, maybe we should go."

Marcus also stood up, trying to read the expression on Vivian's face. "Go? She probably just heard something outside - an animal or something."

Ryan glanced at Karma and then back to Vivian. "Maybe we

should get going."

"Because the stupid dog is barking? Are you kidding me?" Mikey said. "The dumb mutt probably just heard a squirrel or something."

Mikey walked to the sliding glass door that led to the back deck. They all saw the movement outside, as Mikey stared in disbelief. "What the . . . ."

A large herd of deer were running from the woods at top speed. They were moving very quickly, as if being chased by a predator. It took a full twenty seconds for the stream of animals to disappear around the house, and Ryan estimated close to one hundred deer must have shot by. Everyone in the house continued staring out the back window watching the dust settle, even after the last deer was gone.

Karma's bark snapped everyone back to attention, and Ryan turned to see the dog run to the front door and look back at him.

"Get our stuff together, Viv," Ryan said, as he reached into his pocket for his keys. "You guys are welcome to stay here all you want, but we're out of here."

Mikey's voice stopped Vivian as she reached the hallway, "Wait! You can't leave us here. You know we've got no ride. Besides, it could be nothing but some spooked deer."

Ryan shuddered. "The last time Karma acted like this, the tri-state area went up in flames," he explained.

Marcus put a hand on Ryan's shoulder. "Hang on a second. Let me go check outside and see what's going on." Seeing the indecision on Ryan's face, he added, "Please, just give me two minutes."

Ryan stared into the big man's eyes and quietly replied, "You've got two minutes. One second more, and we're gone."

Marcus opened the glass door, jumped the stairs of the deck and ran into the woods where the deer came from.

Inside, Vivian had continued down the hall and was filling the duffle bags with their belongings. Ryan walked into the kitchen and started packing up food into a shopping bag. To Mikey, he said, "Why don't you go search the back bedrooms and see if there's anything we might need?"

"Listen, I don't take orders from no one. And I sure as hell don't give a shit if some dumb mutt is yappin' its head off," Mikey said, but slowly moved toward the hall, pausing briefly to show Karma his middle finger.

As soon as Marcus stepped out of the house he smelled it – the distinct odor of something burning. As he ran down the path through the woods, the smell got stronger. The day was blanketed in a solid wall of gray clouds. The only sign of the sun was a hazy bright gray spot within the monochrome sky.

Marcus was surprisingly quick for a man his size. He ran along a narrow path, leading to a small hill. He was charging up the incline, when he saw a huge black cloud rising up, just over the hill. He also heard a strange sound, sort of like rushing water.

At the top, he stopped and stared at the woods ahead. The sight took his breath away. The sound wasn't rushing water, but raging fire. Flames as high as thirty feet had engulfed the trees and nearby houses, blowing ash through the air like pollen. The wall of fire seemed to go on for miles and was rapidly approaching the hill he was standing on.

Marcus quickly turned and fled down the hill, picking up speed as he barreled back toward the house.

Vivian had joined Ryan in the kitchen, and they were filling their third bag with food when Marcus burst through the sliding door.

"We've got to get out of here now," he said, panting.

Ryan grabbed the bag they were filling and turned for the front door as Mikey came into the living room.

"What's the deal, Big Man?" Mikey asked, but Marcus ignored him, continuing his big strides forward, catching Ryan as he turned the door knob.

"Please, don't leave us here." Although Marcus towered over Ryan, there was no threat in his eyes.

"If you can fit yourself in the Jeep, we'll get you out of here," Ryan told him.

"Thanks, we'll fit." Marcus nodded at Ryan.

Ryan and Vivian went out the front door with Karma, and headed for the Jeep.

"What did you see out there?" Mikey asked, watching the serious look on Marcus's face.

"A wall of fire," Marcus replied. "Now grab the rest of those groceries and get your ass outside." He turned and went outside where he helped Ryan put down the Jeep's soft top, while Vivian loaded the bags in the small cargo area. Karma waited by the Jeep door.

A Jeep Wrangler is not a big vehicle. Ryan didn't see how Marcus was going to squeeze his body in, but maybe with the top down he could somehow shoehorn himself in.

Ryan quickly got the soft top down and looked at Marcus, "You're never going to fit." They could hear the fire now, crackling on the other side of the house, and black ash started to flutter down.

Marcus hopped into the back seat and stood holding onto the roll bar. "I'm ready."

Not the safest option, but it would have to do. The front door of the house swung open and out came Mikey carrying a green army bag.

"What the hell is that? I told you to get the food, jackass!" Marcus yelled, as Mikey jumped in the back next to Marcus.

"I got me some new clothes," he replied, clutching the bag on his lap.

"I'll get it," Vivian said, moving Karma who was sitting on her lap and running back into the house.

"Hurry, Viv," Ryan shouted, as he and Karma got into the Jeep.

Inside the house, Vivian ran into the kitchen and grabbed the remaining bag of food. As she scooped it up, she glanced up at the back window and saw a sheet of orange flames about five feet from the house. It wasn't until she saw the fire that she noticed the house was filling with smoke.

Coughing, she spun around with the bag and headed out of the kitchen. She ran toward the front door, but paused as she passed the gun cabinet. The door was ajar and one of the pistols was missing.

Smoke filled her lungs, causing her to cough harder, and she ran out the front door. Outside, she stuffed the bag into the small cargo area and climbed in the front seat, moving Karma onto her lap again. As soon as her door closed, Ryan hit the gas, and gravel shot backward as the tires spun.

Everybody held on tightly, as Ryan turned out of the driveway and headed back the way he'd driven the night before. Marcus, standing in the back, tried his best to anticipate Ryan's turns so he could properly prepare himself and not get thrown out. They made it about a quarter mile south before they saw the first flames chewing through the trees on the left side.

The fire seemed to be moving at an unnatural speed and the back country Pennsylvania roads didn't provide many cross streets as escape options. Peering ahead, Ryan could see an intersection about two hundred feet away. Ryan felt a surge of heat as the flames neared the street. Smoke and burning ash clouded his vision as he hit the accelerator and prayed that the fire would take some time to jump the street.

The Jeep made it to the intersection just as the wall of fire engulfed the tree line next to the road. Ryan put his foot down on the brake as he cut the wheel and made a sharp right turn. Marcus' scream, as he was tossed out of the Jeep, was almost drowned out by the crackling of the flames and the squeal of the tires.

Ryan would have kept driving unaware of the big guy's ejection, if it weren't for Mikey's shout and Karma's barking. He jammed on the brakes and everyone was pushed forward as the Jeep skidded to a stop.

Turning, they saw that Marcus was already up and running toward them. Behind him, they watched in horror as the fire closed in from every direction. Flames crackled in the woods on either side of the road as the inferno advanced toward them. They screamed for Marcus to run faster, and the big man seemed to quicken his sprint a bit, but soon the flames were all around him. The road became a narrow corridor with flames leaning over on both sides. Marcus finally made it back to the Jeep, and barely had enough time get back in before Ryan hit the gas.

The Jeep raced through the fire. The heat was unbearable and the smoke made Ryan's eyes sting. Slowly, he sped the Jeep past the flames and got them clear of the inferno. Ryan had no idea where he was going – he was just trying to put as much distance between the Jeep and the fire that appeared to be chasing them.

Ryan didn't slow down until the last line of fires was about five miles behind them. They passed a few other cars along the way that were packed with supplies and seemed to be fleeing the area. They talked briefly about where they were going to go and decided it was best keep driving until they found a gas station where they could get a map and fill the tank.

It took about an hour of westward travel to find the first gas station. It was a small Gulf station with a little garage connected to an office.

Ryan pulled the Jeep up to the pumps and cut the engine. For a moment, everyone sat there in silence. Finally, Ryan got out and turned to Marcus, who was sitting on the back rest of the rear seat with his hands still clutching the roll bar.

"You all right?" Ryan asked.

Marcus had a coating of dust and ash all over his clothes, and bits of sticks and gravel stuck in his dreadlocks and beard. His shirt had come out of his pants and was torn along one end, and his left forearm had a bloody scrape down the entire length of it.

Dazed, he tilted his head toward Ryan. "I'll live. Nice driving."

"Sorry I lost you back there. I'm not used to taking corners like that with people standing in the back," Ryan said sincerely.

"I'm just happy to be alive."

Vivian and Mikey had also gotten out of the Jeep and were both trying to steady themselves. Karma sat in the front seat watching everyone. In the distance, over the trees, the big cloud of smoke slowly grew.

Once the tank was full, Ryan went in the office to pay the attendant who was sitting lazily behind a beat up desk. Ryan stepped in and was overwhelmed with the smell of marijuana. He put a twenty dollar bill on the desk and looked into a pair of bloodshot eyes.

"There's a huge forest fire headed this way. I think you may want to get out of here," Ryan told the kid, who couldn't have been more than eighteen years old.

"Don't you worry about me. I've seen a fire or two before, and I can handle just about anything ol' Mother Nature can throw at me," the kid said slowly.

Ryan didn't have the time or the patience to argue with him. "Do you have any maps?"

The kid slowly reached into the desk and pulled out a folded Pennsylvania map.

"Three bucks," he said softly.

Ryan threw an additional three dollars on the desk, grabbed the map and left the office. As he walked back to the Jeep, he noticed that the smoke cloud in the distance seemed to be closing in on them. It was time to go.

Everyone was back in their places in the Jeep. Marcus was still sitting on the back rest leaning forward on the roll bar, his ripped shirt hanging out behind him. Ryan hadn't noticed it before, but now he realized that Marcus and Mikey had the exact same shirt on. And as he walked around the back of the Jeep, he could see there was black writing along the very bottom of Marcus's shirt.

It read: Sing Sing Correctional Facility.

CHAPTER 5

Dark Revelations

Although the fires were fading in the distance behind them, Ryan drove the Jeep at a brisk pace. A million thoughts swirled inside his head, making him feel dizzy and confused. Everything was happening so quickly.

If you asked him, Ryan would tell you he had led a pretty average life. He had a nice childhood, with plenty of friends and loving parents who took good care of him. He grew up in a typical suburban New Jersey town, in a small white Cape Cod style house on a dead end street. His dad worked as a teacher at the local high school, and his mom was a secretary at a printing company. As a young man, Ryan tended to be a little quiet and sometimes shy.

In high school, he played baseball and basketball, and kept a solid B grade-point average. He was accepted into three colleges out of the seven he applied to, and eventually decided to stay in New Jersey and attended Seton Hall University. During Ryan's four years there, he enrolled in a wide variety of classes hoping to find something interesting enough to concentrate in. Business was what everyone was being pushed toward and seemed to have the most financial possibilities, so that became his major.

After graduation he began the first in a series of disappointing jobs in the business field. He was a hard worker, but never found a position or company that he really cared about. Consequently, he never lasted more than a year at any of them. It seemed he was always searching without knowing what he was looking for.

Now here he was, driving west in the middle of Pennsylvania trying to outrun a number of natural disasters. And once again, he had no idea of where he was going or what he should be looking for. It made him feel lost and alone.

Since leaving the gas station several hours ago, they had traveled over a hundred miles. The roads were busy with cars zipping in every direction. Apparently, the fires had caused a lot of people to flee their homes, and they passed quite a few cars loaded with everything from clothing to furniture.

They had found their way north to Route 80 and decided to drive as far west as they could before it got dark. Smoke dotted the landscape in almost all directions, so it seemed that the fires were fairly widespread. The clouds covering the sky started to change from light gray to dark which, Ryan assumed, meant the sun was starting to drop. How he longed to see the sun again. It seemed like forever since he felt its warmth on his face.

There was almost no conversation between the Jeep's passengers during the ride, mostly due to the noise of the wind caused by having the top down. Marcus would occasionally stand up from his perch on the backrest to stretch his legs, always making sure to hold onto the roll bar tightly, so he wouldn't be tossed out again. Mikey dozed off shortly after they left the gas station, and muttered to himself whenever a bump jolted him from his sleep. Vivian seemed to be troubled by something, glancing over at Ryan periodically with concern in her eyes. He wasn't sure if it was just the effects of recent events or something more.

Ryan was a bit troubled as well. He was fairly certain that Sing Sing Correctional Facility was a maximum security prison in New York somewhere, and he could only assume that the shirts his two rear passengers were wearing were standard prison issue and not novelty items. He couldn't help but be a little afraid for their safety.

Ryan glanced over at Karma, lying on Vivian's lap. He still had so many questions about this strange dog. She seemed to know when the disasters were coming. Ryan did believe that animals were in tune with the environment and had superior senses, but there seemed to be more to Karma.

It was all too much for Ryan to handle. He didn't know what questions to try to answer first. Everything seemed to demand immediate attention.

As darkness began to fall, it became clear that the entire area they were in had lost power. The only light to be seen was the orange glow of distant fires.

Shortly after they passed over into Ohio, Ryan started searching for someplace where they could stay for the night. He noticed a small strip mall off to the right side and decided to pull into the parking lot. The strip mall consisted of five separate businesses connected in the same building. On the far left was a fairly large drug store, then a clothing store called *Now Fashions*, a discount shoe store, a small luncheonette named *Grammy's Place*, and an electronics store at the end.

There were two other cars parked in the lot, but Ryan didn't see any people. All of the storefront windows were broken and the glass door of the drug store was shattered. The stores were dark inside, but they could hear some noises coming from inside the electronics store.

When the Jeep came to a stop, everyone got out and stretched. Karma hopped out and began sniffing the sidewalk in front of the storefronts.

"Why the hell did you stop here?" Mikey whined.

"Do you know of a better place? It's getting dark, and my eyes were starting to close," Ryan replied.

Mikey glared at Ryan and was about to say something when Marcus put a hand on his shoulder. "This is perfect. We can sleep in one of these stores and get supplies if we need any."

Mikey smiled, "All right. It's about time I treated myself to some presents." He started to walk toward the electronics store, when Marcus's voice stopped him.

"Only what we need. We're not here to loot the place."

"Man, you are absolutely no fun," Mikey said shaking his head as he stepped through the broken window and into the store.

Ryan walked over to Vivian, who was leaning against the side of the Jeep staring at the smoke of distant fires.

"How ya' doing?" he asked.

"I'm okay, I guess. Just a little dazed by everything," she said straightening up and then whispered, "Ryan, we've got to talk about these guys. I think –"

"Hey, Ryan," Marcus cut in loudly from the sidewalk. "You said you think Karma's a Pit Bull Terrier, right?"

Ryan looked over at him a bit confused, "I think so, why?"

"I thought terriers chased everything that moved."

"Usually, yeah. It's in their blood," Ryan said, puzzled. "Where is she? Did she take off?"

Marcus lifted his arm and pointed. Ryan and Vivian followed his finger and were speechless at what they saw. Karma was standing at the end of the sidewalk, nose to nose with a squirrel.

Ryan could remember hanging out in the park by his apartment and smiling whenever he saw someone get yanked by the wrist as their dog lunged after a squirrel that was running for the safety of a tree. Never in his life had he ever seen a dog and a squirrel having an exchange like the one that was taking place in front of him now.

Karma was standing, leaning her head down as the squirrel sat on its hind legs with its tail curled up behind it. Their noses were so close they almost touched. The way they were focused on each other made it seem like they were sharing a thought together.

Ryan looked on in disbelief as the dog and squirrel continued what appeared to be their conversation. Then Karma leaned down a little further and licked the squirrel on the side of its head. The squirrel leaned up and touched noses with Karma and hopped off into the trees on the side of the parking lot.

Karma watched the squirrel depart and then walked over to Ryan and sat down, leaning on his leg.

Marcus found his voice first. "I wouldn't have believed it if I didn't just see it with my own eyes."

Vivian knelt down and cradled Karma's head. "You're just always full of surprises, aren't you, girl?"

"I'm starting to agree that is one special dog," Marcus said, watching Karma.

Ryan just nodded, still unable to speak.

After they made a quick inspection of each of the stores they decided the best place to spend the night was in the clothing store. Mikey had met two guys in the electronics store that were taking everything they could fit into their car. They must have either run out of merchandise or space in the car, because within an hour they pulled away.

The only other people they found were an elderly couple sitting in one of the isles of drug store stuffing their faces with candy bars. Ryan had discovered them, and they barely lifted their heads to acknowledge him as he paused while walking through. It seemed a very sad sight to Ryan, and he wondered what events had led them to this spot, wolfing down chocolate.

The clothing store seemed like the best place because it was carpeted and had plenty of clothing to use as blankets if the night got cool. As they cleared away some of the clothing racks to make a space to sleep, the gray sky finally finished changing over to the black of night.

Ryan grabbed the flashlight from his duffle bag and switched it on. The beam cut through the air, illuminating dust particles that they disturbed moving the clothing racks. They got settled in and made peanut butter sandwiches with the supplies they had taken from the old hunter's kitchen. Ryan set down his flashlight with the beam facing the side wall to give them some reflective light. A six pack of soda acquired from the drug store helped them wash down their sandwiches.

Ryan continued to try to figure out what to do with the two strangers outfitted with prison shirts. He didn't think it was wise to confront them just yet, so he would have to sit tight for now, making sure to keep a close eye on them. Vivian sat on the floor next to him, quietly chewing. She seemed very nervous and uncomfortable.

Karma was lying on the floor in front of Ryan, separating them from Marcus and Mikey, who were sitting opposite them. Mikey was reclining on a pile of shirts, while Marcus sat Indian style neatly eating his sandwich.

"You think we're safe from the fires here?" Marcus asked.

Ryan thought for a second and replied, "I think so. All of the fires seem to be a good distance away. We'll just have to keep an eye out during the night, just to be sure."

"Those fires were out of control today," Marcus said, appearing a bit menacing in the shadowy light. "I've never seen fire move so quickly."

"It's like they were chasing us, man" Mikey said.

"I'm starting to get the feeling that all of the elements of the world have taken it up a notch," Ryan said. "It's like they're moving with a purpose." He paused and then added, "And with a vengeance."

"It sure is some crazy-ass shit," Mikey said, wiping peanut butter on his shirt.

Marcus finished his sandwich and slid over to Karma, where he leaned down and got nose to nose with her. "Do you know something we don't?"

The dog licked his hairy face and then suddenly pulled back. Marcus sat back up, studying her. Then he stood up and told them, "I'm going over to the drug store to see if I can find another light and anything else that would make our stay here more comfortable. I'll need to borrow the flashlight for a minute or two."

Ryan didn't like the idea of giving up his light, but he didn't want to rock the boat with these two guys just yet. Somewhat reluctantly, he gave Marcus the flashlight, which left the rest of them in total darkness.

Once the light was gone, Vivian scooted up next to Ryan, found his hand and squeezed it firmly.

"Now this is some serious dark," Mikey stated. "With no power anywhere and the moon blocked out by the clouds, you really can't see squat."

Ryan and Vivian sat holding hands, squinting in the darkness trying to see Mikey. It made Ryan very uncomfortable not knowing exactly where he was.

"Are you two married or something?" Mikey's voice seemed a little closer.

"No. We're just friends," Ryan replied.

"Very good friends," Vivian added quickly.

"I almost got hitched once. But I caught the dumb bitch stealing from me, so I kicked that stupid whore to the curb nice and fast." Judging by the sound of his voice, Mikey sounded like he was inching his way toward them. "Yeah, she got what she deserved in the end."

Ryan and Vivian sat in silence for another twenty minutes, while Mikey rambled on about the "skank" who tried to ruin his life. Eventually, they saw the flickering light of the flashlight returning. Marcus walked in and emptied two plastic shopping bags of items on the floor. As he put the flashlight back in its original spot shining on the wall, Mikey noticed his face.

"Oh, shit!" Mikey exclaimed, leaning in to get a closer look. "You shaved your beard. Why the hell did you do that?"

Marcus sat back down in front of Karma. "Felt like I needed a change." Not a trace of the wild, untamed beard remained on his face.

"Since I've known you, you've been growing that ratty beard. You never so much as trimmed it and now you shave the whole thing off. I don't believe it."

Marcus laid down on his stomach with his face right in front of Karma's nose and started rubbing her floppy ears. Karma leaned in and started giving his face a good washing with her tongue, while her tail wagged in wide arcs. Marcus wore a big smile on his face and was obviously loving every minute of it.

Vivian couldn't help but smile herself, as Mikey called out, "No fuckin' way! You shaved for the dog!"

Marcus laughed and squirmed as Karma continued with the licks.

Mikey fell back laughing, "I don't believe it! Big, bad Marcus shaves for a dumb mutt!"

Marcus finally sat up, the smile slowly leaving his face. "I'd almost forgotten what it was like to smile."

Mikey continued to cackle, leaning back on the pile of clothes. Finally, he regained his composure and sat back up. "Now I know the world is coming to an end. Even the Big Man is falling apart and going soft."

Ignoring Mikey, Marcus gave Karma a final pat on the head and then leaned back and reclined on his own pile of clothing.

Ryan still didn't know what to make of these two guys, but he decided it was time to find out more about them. "How long were you guys in prison?" he asked bluntly.

Marcus and Mikey exchanged a look of concern, as Vivian squeezed Ryan's hand again. Then Marcus sat up, taking a deep breath.

"What makes you think we were in prison?" he asked.

"I saw the Sing Sing written on your shirts. That's a maximum security prison, isn't it?" Ryan said calmly.

"Oh, yeah," Mikey said, still lounging back on a pile of clothing. "They don't send you there unless you've been real bad."

Marcus shot Mikey a stern look, then turned back to Ryan and Vivian. "Yes, we were both inmates at Sing Sing when the lightning storms started. All hell broke loose and the guards started to run for it. A bunch of us were in the main yard when the first bolts came down on the buildings. Some started burning, while others just crumbled apart. The guards were just taking off, while all the inmates were still locked up. I had become friendly with one of them and convinced him to free a bunch of us. I'd say about twelve of us got out before the whole place went up in flames, and crashed down to rubble, killing everyone. Once we got clear of the prison, we all went our separate ways. Mikey and I just seemed to be going in the same direction. We found the bike and kept on riding as fast as we could until we ran out of gas. That's pretty much our whole story."

The pain of all he had seen and been through was written on Marcus's face. Ryan was trying to decide what he could believe, and more importantly, what he should do about it.

"What were you in for?" Vivian asked quietly.

Marcus made eye contact with her and replied, "Manslaughter."

Even though Vivian knew that was probably going to be the answer, she still wasn't prepared for it. A chill went up her spine as her heartbeat doubled, and the urge to flee overcame her. She squeezed Ryan's hand tightly, and tried to steady her breathing.

Marcus saw the fear in her face and continued, "About two and a half years ago, I was coming out of a bar late one night. There wasn't anyone around except one other guy who had left just before I did. He was walking off toward his car when three guys ran around the side of the bar and jumped him. Within twenty seconds they had him on the ground and were beating the hell out of him. I don't know why they jumped him or if he deserved it. All I know is that I couldn't stand there and let them beat him to death. So I decided to stop it. I pushed two of them off him and had the third up against the car. One of the thugs hit me in the back, so I turned and punched him in the face. He fell backward and slammed his head on the pavement. I'm not sure if he died from the impact or from the loss of blood, but either way, he died.

"The guy they jumped was beat up real bad and was in a coma for a while before he eventually died. The two thugs claimed that I attacked them and killed their buddy. They had a good lawyer, I had a bad one."

Marcus was staring off into space by the time he finished. He blinked a few times, shaking away the past, and turned back toward Vivian, "I never meant to kill anyone."

They were all quiet for a minute and then Ryan looked over at Mikey. "What about you?"

Mikey was lying back with his legs straight out in front of him. He slowly crossed his feet and smiled. "Well I'd love to tell you that I didn't mean to hurt anyone either, but that would be a lie. But don't worry, the bitch I killed deserved it." He paused and panned over to Vivian. "You know, she looked a lot like you."

"Knock it off, Mikey," Marcus warned.

Ignoring Marcus, Mikey sat up and continued, "Yeah, you have the same eyes. It's a pity what I had to do to her, but she made me angry. You would never make me angry, would you, baby?"

Vivian started to tremble in his gaze.

"I said that's enough!" Marcus shouted, and gave Mikey a firm push.

Mikey stood up, glaring down at Marcus. "Okay, that's it! I've had enough of you bossing me around. I'm not your bitch and I'm not afraid of you, so you can just fuck off."

"Sit down and shut your face," Marcus said sternly, without an ounce of worry on his face.

"I don't think so. I'm done listening to you!" Mikey threw his half-filled can of soda at Marcus, hitting him in the face and spilling soda on his lap.

Ryan noticed that Marcus had leaned up, resembling a coiled spring about to explode. Meanwhile, Vivian had taken hold of his arm tightly and was trying to scoot them back. Things were getting out of hand.

"Let's all just calm down for a moment," Ryan said in the most soothing voice he could summon, as he stood up.

Mikey's tilted toward him. "Now you're going to give me orders?"

During all this, Karma had remained lying in front of Ryan. But now she stood up, faced Mikey and let out a low growl.

Mikey lowered his gaze for second to consider Karma and then looked back up and addressed the group. "I'm not taking any more shit from any of you assholes. Not from you," he pointed at Marcus. "Not from this jackass," his finger moved to Ryan. "This bitch," he stabbed his finger at Vivian. "And especially not from this yapping, pain in the ass mutt!"

Mikey brought his foot back and swung his leg forward to kick Karma. Ryan moved forward but knew he would never get there before the booted foot connected with Karma's head. As Vivian cried out, Marcus shot up and took a firm hold on Mikey's neck with one of his huge hands, causing him to jerk as his forward momentum was suddenly stopped. Mikey grabbed feebly at the hand that trapped him, but Marcus held tight.

Ryan wasn't sure what he should do. Karma was barking at his feet and Vivian had stood up, moving just behind him, clutching his arm.

Marcus was staring into Mikey's eyes. "You always want to do things the hard way, Mikey."

In the dim light, no one noticed Mikey's hand reach back into his pocket. In a quick motion, he brought his hand up toward the arm that held him captive. Ryan saw the glint of the blade a second before the hunting knife bit into Marcus's forearm.

Marcus pulled his arm back, releasing Mikey who shuffled back a step holding the knife in front of him. If Marcus was hurt, he didn't show it. He stood tall, his eyes locked on Mikey. Karma was still in front of Ryan, barking.

"You want to do things the hard way, do you?" Mikey was in a half crouch, slowly moving the knife back and forth in front of him.

Ryan brought his hands up unthreateningly, as Vivian pressed against Ryan's body and said "Be careful, he's got a gun."

Marcus glanced over at Ryan and Vivian with concern.

"No, he doesn't," Ryan said reaching his hand under his shirt. "I do." And he pulled the gun that Vivian had seen missing from the hunter's gun case from his waistband.

All eyes were now on Ryan. Except for Karma, who was still staring at Mikey.

"I had a feeling we might be in for some trouble," Ryan said.

Before anyone could consider their next move, Mikey charged forward and kicked the flashlight, sending it spinning across the floor and under a clothing rack. The room plunged into darkness.

There was shuffle of feet and a series of muffled thuds, followed by a groan that sounded like Marcus. Ryan's heart was pounding so hard he thought it might burst through his chest. Somewhere in the blackness Karma barked again.

Vivian crawled frantically across the floor trying to retrieve the flashlight. A small line of light could be seen where the rack of hanging clothes met the floor. She reached her hand into the wall of fabric, found the flashlight, and swung it out.

The ten or fifteen seconds that it took Vivian to find the flashlight seemed like an eternity. She waved the beam of light around the room and finally found the form of Marcus kneeling stiffly with Mikey behind him, the knife pressed to his throat.

"Get that light out of my face, bitch," Mikey said and Vivian tilted the beam down a little. "If you don't like the sight of blood, you better drop the gun and back away," Mikey said, pressing the blade down and causing a trickle of blood to drip down Marcus's neck.

Ryan was trying to think fast. "I don't care if you cut him."

"Oh, I think you do. I'm going to count to three and then we're going to see how far his blood will shoot out." Mikey was smiling.

Ryan considered his options.

"One."

Karma let out two quick barks and then went silent.

"Two." Mikey's eyes seemed wild.

Ryan leaned down and let the gun drop to the floor and stepped back, as Marcus let out a pained "No."

Mikey punched Marcus in the kidney causing him to topple forward, threw the knife across the room and grabbed the gun.

"Ha, ha!" he said triumphantly smiling. "I'm afraid you just made a HUGE mistake. You see, now I get to kill all of you."

Marcus got his wind back and stood up, blood slowly leaking from the cut on his neck.

"The only question is who gets it first?" Mikey asked. "I should cap the Big Man for being such a dick to me. But since dumb Ryan was stupid enough to give me the gun, I guess he deserves the first bullet." He paused and looked at Vivian. "You know I'm saving you for last, baby." He then turned the gun to Karma, who was standing a few feet away watching him calmly. "No, I think it's time that the yappy mutt finally shut up for good."

Vivian held her breath and felt tears come to her eyes, as Mikey pointed the gun at Karma and pulled the trigger.

Click.

Nothing happened.

A look of bewilderment spread across Mikey's face. He pulled the trigger again.

Click.

Still nothing happened.

Click, Click, Click.

"It's a miracle," Vivian breathed.

"Not quite," Ryan said taking a step forward. "I just didn't feel comfortable with a loaded gun."

Marcus turned to Ryan, confused.

"So I decided to leave the bullets behind."

Slowly Marcus began to smile, as Mikey's face quickly changed to an expression of panic.

Before Mikey could make a run for it, Marcus stepped forward and jabbed his left fist into Mikey's nose, which shattered on impact. Marcus' right hand grabbed Mikey's shirt at the shoulder and pulled his body down to connect with his right knee. When Marcus let go of Mikey, his body crumbled to the floor in a heap, where he curled up, gasping for breath.

Marcus looked over to see Ryan and Vivian watching him apprehensively.

"Don't worry about me, I'm not like him," Marcus interjected quickly, seeing the concern on their faces. "You can trust me."

Ryan stared into the big man's eyes and tried to read them. Ever since they'd met him, Ryan felt that deep down, he was a good person. He had just about nothing to base the feeling on, but he decided to trust it.

"I know I can. What should we do with him?" Ryan pointed at Mikey, who was curled up in a fetal position.

"Let's tie him up and worry about it tomorrow," Marcus said looking around. "There must be some rope around here somewhere."

They searched the clothing store, but couldn't find anything suitable for the job, so Ryan walked over to the drug store while Marcus watched over Mikey.

Ryan returned with some rope that was sold as a laundry line and some first aid supplies. Marcus made sure he tied Mikey up tightly. He tied his hands behind his back, tied his feet together and then tied a line from his hands to his feet. Finally, he attached a separate line from the ropes holding Mikey to a clothing rack fastened to the wall. Stepping back, Marcus was confident that he wasn't going anywhere.

Vivian then used the first aid supplies to work on the cut on Marcus's forearm. She used a few butterfly bandages to close the wound, covered it in gauze and wrapped it in an ace bandage. The arm wound appeared worse than it really was, and would heal quickly, while the cut on his neck was only a superficial one and didn't need anything more than a few dabs with a tissue to stop the blood flow.

Once Marcus was all patched up, they made up beds on the floor out of piles of clothing. Ryan and Vivian set theirs up close to each other, with Marcus lying a few feet away where he could keep a watchful eye on Mikey. Karma curled up between Vivian and Ryan in a way that she was touching both of them.

Ryan looked over at Karma. He ran a hand down her back and smiled. He felt safe in her presence, and was struck by a feeling that everything would somehow work out. *Maybe I should have gotten a dog a long time ago,* Ryan thought.

Soon, they were all fast asleep.

CHAPTER 6

It's a Zoo Out There

A moist sensation on his face caused Ryan to open his eyes. Karma was sitting next to him, gently licking his cheek. He leaned up on one elbow and wiped the sleep from his eyes. For a moment, he forgot where he was. As he scanned the room and saw the sprawled out form of Marcus lying in a mess of clothing, everything came rushing back.

He had been in a really deep sleep. Usually when things were on his mind he had trouble sleeping. *I guess I was just exhausted*, he thought as he sat up, feeling rested.

Karma had moved on, and was now giving Vivian her wake up licks. She was curled up next to Ryan entwined in a number of long sleeve shirts.

"Good morning to you, Missy," she said, as she stroked Karma's head. Then she looked over at Ryan. "And good morning to you."

"Good morning. Did you sleep okay?" he asked.

"Like a rock," she replied, sitting up.

"Me, too," Marcus said as he stood up and stretched. "I don't know if my body was spent or it was just nice not to be in a cold prison cell."

"Well, I slept like shit," Mikey said from the corner. "You busted my fuckin' nose. Damn thing's been throbbing all night."

"You're lucky I let you wake up at all," Marcus shot back.

Ryan stood up and wiped sweat from his brow. "It sure is hot in here."

"Tell me about it," Marcus said raising his arms, showing the sweat stains on his prison shirt. "I can't believe I'm still wearing this. I do believe it's time for a wardrobe change."

He bent over and rummaged through the pile of shirts he was sleeping on. After a little probing, he found one that seemed like it would fit him and changed shirts. His new shirt was light blue, with long sleeves, a few buttons down the front with a thin red stripe going vertically down the left side, two inches from the buttons. Surprisingly, it was a little baggy on him.

"A nice change," Vivian told him.

Marcus balled up his prison shirt and threw it in the corner next to Mikey.

Ryan stretched and walked through the racks of clothing until he came to the remains of the glass store front. He stepped out onto the sidewalk and looked around. He would have called out to the others but he couldn't find the words.

Everything, in all directions, was burnt to a crisp. Trees were black and disfigured, houses were nothing but charred frames and cars were melted heaps. Small fires still burned in few places, and smoke rose from the blackened earth in wisps.

In a state of shock, Ryan didn't notice Vivian stepping out behind him.

"Oh, my God," Vivian whispered.

Marcus walked out. "What the hell happened out here?" he said in awe.

Ryan took a few steps forward and turned to face the strip mall. There wasn't so much as a smudge of ash on the entire building. Marcus slowly walked around the corner, as Ryan turned his concern to his Jeep. Luckily, the parking lot also remained untouched.

The gas station across the street was a pile of burning embers, the vegetable stand down the road had been reduced to black dust and the various houses they had passed on their drive were all gone.

Marcus came around the other side of the building, having finished his lap around, and stood next to Ryan and Vivian. "The fires came right up to the side of the building, but never touched it. This is the only thing, as far as I can see, that didn't burn."

"How is that possible?" Ryan asked stunned.

Karma came trotting out of the clothing store window and stopped in front of them stretching her back legs casually.

"You don't think . . ." Vivian began, as they stared at Karma.

"No," Ryan said, sounding uncertain. "It must be something in the building that makes it fire-proof."

"This is crazy," Marcus added.

Ryan looked around again, taking in the scope of the damage. He followed a trail of smoke as it floated upward. A ceiling of clouds still blocked out the sky, but they were much darker today. Although it was morning, it felt more like late evening.

A flash of light off in the distance caught Ryan's eye. The others saw it was well, and they all peered into the burnt landscape trying to find its source.

Another small flash blinked, and he was able to pinpoint it. Squinting through the haze and floating ash, he was able to make out the silhouette of a lone figure about a quarter of a mile away.

Suddenly, Karma barked and started jogging toward it. She got about twenty feet away, when she stopped and turned back at them. When they made no move, she barked again.

"Seems like she wants to go check it out," Vivian said.

"So it would seem," Ryan said. Then, he looked at Marcus, "What do you think?"

"If you asked me yesterday, I would have told you that there was no way I was going traipsing through that smoldering terrain." Marcus told them. "But today, I say I'm sticking with the pooch."

Ryan nodded and they all walked toward Karma. Once she saw they were coming, she turned and bounded off.

They had to watch their step because there were many small fires still burning and charred debris was everywhere. They were all struck by how massive the destruction was. There was nothing but ash and singed objects as far as the eye could see.

Karma would stop and wait for them whenever she got too far ahead. The heat coming off the ground made the air steamy, causing their vision to be hazy.

The only thing they could see that wasn't burned was a yellow pick-up truck that was parked on the road, not far from the mystery figure ahead.

As they got closer, they saw that the light they had noticed was the flash of a camera, carried by a woman who was studying the ground beneath her. Karma reached her first, and she seemed startled when the dog ran up to her, tail wagging.

The woman began vigorously petting Karma. "Hey there, how did you make it through all this?" Then she caught site of the approaching people and straightened up to face them.

"Well, what do you know, I'm not alone in the world," she said with a slight smirk.

She was tall, about five-foot-nine, with a lean build and friendly smile. By the sound of her slight accent, she seemed to be of Hispanic origin. Her face was plain, but pretty, with an olive complexion. She was dressed in faded blue jeans, a green t-shirt, and worn hiking boots that had seen better days. Her black hair was pulled in a ponytail and she was covered from head to toe in soot and dirt.

"Hi," Ryan said. "What's a girl like you doing in a place like this?"

She said, "Oh, you know, taking in the sights and sounds of the countryside."

"In this mess? That's my kind of girl," Marcus said, smiling back.

"Get any nice shots?" Vivian asked motioning to the camera.

"I don't know if you would call them nice, but I have been using up film," she said. "I'm actually trying to document everything that's happening to this planet. I've been following the fires, making notes and taking pictures. When this is all over, we may need this information to figure out what happened and why."

"What makes you think there will be anything left when all this is over?" Marcus had to ask.

"Well, I like to try to stay optimistic," the woman replied. "Even when things get a little hot."

A few raindrops began to drizzle down from the dark clouds overhead. As they hit the heated ground, they made a hissing sound as small trails of smoke drifted into the air. It was the first rain the entire planet had seen in months.

"What are you guys doing out here?" she asked. "Not exactly the best day for a walk with the dog."

"We've sort of been on the run for the last day or so. We stopped here and spent the night in one of those stores," Ryan said, pointing over his shoulder without turning.

The woman stood on her toes to look behind them and seemed confused. "In there?" she said, pointing behind them.

They all turned around toward the strip mall, which was now engulfed in flames.

"Oh no," Ryan gasped and started running back.

Marcus and Vivian were right behind him, followed by Karma. When they reached the parking lot they were stopped short by the intense heat. The fire had completely taken the building. Something exploded inside the luncheonette causing them to duck instinctively. It shattered the remainder of the front window and shot flaming debris into the air. Some of the flaming material hit the Jeep, and it, too, started to catch fire.

"No!" Ryan screamed and ran to the vehicle.

Ryan shuffled around frantically trying to figure out some way to stop the fire. He had to put a hand in front of his face to shield himself from the intense heat of the burning building. The flames rose high out of the Jeep, and his eyes stung from the smoke. It had all happened so quickly.

Just as he was starting to cough and hunch over, Marcus charged in and scooped him up by the waist and carried him back to Vivian and Karma, who were watching from the edge of the parking lot.

Marcus put Ryan safely down and they all stared at the fire in silence.

The Jeep was now a big fireball adding to the inferno of the burnt strip mall. The rain started to fall harder, sizzling as it hit the ground.

"Oh, my God, what about Mikey?" Vivian gasped.

Knowing there was nothing they could do, they just continued to stare at the burning building.

"I always knew that boy was going to burn in hell," Marcus finally said. "I just didn't think I would be around to see it."

They were beginning to get soaked from the rain which was now a full on downpour, but couldn't take their eyes off the sight in front of them. What little they had was now gone. Although they were all thinking it, no one voiced the fears about what was going to happen now.

Over the sound of the rain and the crumbling building, no one but Karma heard the pick-up truck pull up behind them.

A familiar female voice said, "You guys look like you need a lift."

The rain drummed down on the truck as they drove away from the burning strip mall. Luckily the pick-up truck was a Ford F-150, with four doors and a full back seat, so there was enough room for everyone. Marcus was in the front, seated next to the mystery woman, while Ryan and Vivian sat in the back seat with Karma. From the outside, no one would ever guess that the truck was only five months old. A covering of dirt and ash blanketed the yellow pick-up. However, the interior was fairly clean, with only a few signs of black ash on the floor mats. It also still had a trace of that new car smell.

"So where did you guys say you were headed?" the woman asked.

They all pondered the question for a moment, but no one could come up with an answer.

Finally, Ryan said, "We have no idea. The last couple of days we've been moving on adrenaline with no real destination in mind. And now that my Jeep's been torched we have no way of getting anywhere."

"Well then, I guess it's a good thing you met me," the woman said smiling.

She appeared to be about forty years old with the spunk of someone much younger. She worked the stick shift of the truck effortlessly as she talked.

"Well, it seems like we're stuck with each other, so we might as well get friendly," she said, as she tried to find the road through the rain. "My name's Melina."

"I'm Marcus," the big guy told her. "That's Ryan and Vivian back there, with Karma."

Melina looked up into the rearview mirror at them. "Pretty dog."

"Yeah, she's sort of an enigma," Ryan explained, as he put his hand on Karma's head. "A very good dog though."

"Well, I've got to head back to the office to reload my film and record some information," Melina said. "You guys might as well come along for the ride."

Marcus shifted in his seat. "Did you find anything that explains what the hell is going on?"

"Not really. But I have noticed something strange," she paused as she made a right turn. "I've searched through burnt rubble and blackened woods in two states so far. And I've come across more charred human bodies then I care to count. But I haven't found any animal remains. Not a cat, or a squirrel, or a bird or even a mouse. Nothing."

"That does seem a bit strange," Ryan said. "But there's not much that surprises me anymore."

They drove on, heading south, as the rain continued to beat down on the truck. Melina told them that her office was in Louisville, Kentucky, over two hundred miles away. Ryan knew none of them had anywhere else to go, and figured that Louisville was as good a place as any. Melina directed the conversation most of the way. She had a good sense of humor and quick wit that was a good distraction from the world around them.

Melina explained to them that she's been studying environmental changes and effects for the last two years. Although her work had taken her across the world, she'd concentrated on North America for the last eight months or so. She detailed her findings concerning the fires and the electrical storms as well as the other events happening worldwide.

Ryan, Vivian, and Marcus listened in disbelief as Melina told them what she knew. Oceans around the globe had begun to rise at an alarming rate. Japan and the Philippines were almost completely underwater. Many of the islands in the Caribbean had disappeared and coastal areas in North and South America had become severely flooded.

The reality of the conversation seemed to depress everyone. Even Melina, who had started out so lighthearted, began to feel the weight of her words. They drove for hours in the pouring rain, stopping only a few times to stretch their legs under a highway overpass. They only passed a handful of cars, and for the most part the roads were dreary and deserted.

They crossed the border into Kentucky just southeast of Cincinnati and continued on toward Louisville. The fires had taken almost all of the land they drove through, but just before they reached Kentucky they began to see green trees and intact buildings. Along the way, they snacked on some granola bars that Melina kept in the back of the truck along with some bottled water.

"We're almost there folks," Melina told them. "Hang tight just a little longer."

The rain hadn't let up since they left the burning strip mall, and now they were noticing quite a bit of local flooding. Melina navigated through the Louisville streets, trying to stay on the water soaked road.

Suddenly, she hit the brakes as the headlights landed on a seven foot bird standing in the middle of the street.

Melina managed to avoid hitting the strange creature and still keep control of the truck. Marcus was amazed at how well Melina was able to handle the big vehicle.

"Ahhh, what was that?" Vivian asked.

"An ostrich," Melina said calmly, while steering the truck through an archway with a sign above it that read, *Welcome to the Louisville Zoo.*

"Your office is the zoo?" Ryan asked.

"You got it, my friend," she replied. "The ostrich wandering outside is probably a sign that things are falling apart here as well."

She drove into the large, empty public parking lot and down a small road with a "do not enter" sign in front of it. It led to a flooded parking lot surrounded by a few small buildings.

Melina stopped the truck. "Follow me," she said, and got out and ran for the closest building. Everyone stepped into the rain and ran after Melina, who was putting a key into a side door.

Once inside, they shook the rain off as best they could and followed Melina through a series of cubicles. Without electricity the room was a bit dark, with only gray light coming in from the windows. Melina led them toward the front of the building and into one of the offices. On the walls were framed photographs of animals and a large map of the world with a number of pins stuck in various locations. There was a shelf against one wall, piled high with all kinds of books about nature and wildlife. A big wooden desk scattered with papers filled the middle of the room.

Melina sat down at the desk and started taking out equipment from a backpack she had carried from the truck. Ryan, Vivian and Marcus wandered around the room, while Karma sniffed around the outside of Melina's office.

Marcus picked up a thick booklet from the desk and flipped through it.

Melina glanced up at him, "That's just some of the information I've been compiling about the state of the environment. Most people don't realize just how much the human race has been abusing this planet. I think that if we can educate people about what's going on, maybe we can motivate them to stop it."

"I'm not sure it's going to matter much now," Marcus said, handing the booklet to Vivian.

"This seems to paint a pretty bleak picture for the future," Vivian said, reading one of the pages. "If nothing is done now, our children won't have much of a world to grow up in." Melina shuffled through a few papers on the desk until she pulled out a specific page, and began reading. "If the current rate of deforestation continues, the world's rain forests will vanish within one hundred years, causing unknown effects on global climate and eliminating the majority of plant and animal species on the planet." She paused to let that sink in and continued reading down the page. "Tropical deforestation may exceed 130,000 square kilometers per year."

Ryan thought about that statistic. Most people took their conveniences for granted and didn't want to know about the cost that might have to be paid to get them. Just as long as we could get to work faster, feel important wearing fancy fur coats, and eat animals that bordered on extinction. Ryan felt guilty. Even though he knew he wasn't directly responsible, he couldn't help feeling ashamed for being human.

"And that's just one small example," Melina added. "Half of the world's wetlands were lost last century; logging has shrunk the world's forests by as much as half; nine percent of the world's tree species are at risk of extinction; fishing fleets are forty percent larger than the ocean can sustain; nearly seventy percent of the world's major marine fish stocks are over-fished; twenty percent of the world's freshwater fish are extinct, threatened or endangered; and since 1980, the global economy has tripled in size and the human population has grown by thirty percent to six billion people."

As Melina was quoting the statistics, she got more and more animated. You could tell she felt strongly about the topic.

"That sucks," Marcus said, while everyone looked on, still

speechless.

"Very eloquently put," Melina replied, as she dropped the paper on her desk. "Now, what do you say we see how our friendly zoo animals are holding up in this storm?"

Melina got up, walked past everyone and into the main room. Karma was sniffing at a puddle forming on the floor from a leak in the ceiling that was steadily dripping water.

Melina considered the drip for a moment and gave Karma a pat on the head.

"I think it's time for a new roof," Ryan said, pointing ahead to a few other spots that were leaking.

"Unfortunately, most of the money coming into the zoo goes to the exhibits. Not many people who donate money want to see their name on a plaque in front of an office building," Melina said.

She grabbed a garbage pail from a nearby cubical and put it under the leak, then went around the office and did the same for a number of other leaky spots.

Looking around at all the pails collecting water, she said, "If this rain keeps up, the whole office will be soaking wet." She turned and walked into one of the side offices, leaving the others in the main room watching the water drip from above. A moment later she came out and threw everyone a green Louisville Zoo rain poncho, with a line drawing of a giraffe on the breast.

"With these jackets I hereby deputize you as official emergency caretakers of the Louisville Zoo," Melina declared. "We'll skip the speeches for now and get right to work."

After struggling into his jacket, Marcus asked, "Don't you have any adult sizes?" The sleeves of his poncho only made it down to the middle of his forearm and the length barely reached his waist.

Melina smiled at him. "Sorry Big Daddy, one size fits most."

They followed Melina outside, as she ran around the building and down a path that led them into the zoo. The rain was still coming down hard, and it wasn't long before they were all soaking wet from the waist down. Karma was the only one who didn't seem to mind at all as she ran up ahead with Melina.

Their first stop was a wetland exhibit that consisted of a big pond with about twenty flamingos huddled together in one corner. The water level was very high and was threatening to spill onto the path.

After surveying the exhibit, Melina said, "They don't look too happy, but they're safe for now. We usually have a ton of local birds swimming around in here, but I guess they all flew away."

"Why don't the flamingos fly away?" Vivian asked through the rain.

"Their wings have been clipped to keep them grounded," Melina replied.

They made it to the Reptile House, and were filing inside when a man in a long rain jacket came running over to them.

Once everyone was inside and out of the rain he said, "I'm sorry but the zoo is closed. You shouldn't be in here."

Lowering his hood, he revealed a wet, tired face. His eyes were sunken and dark showing that he obviously hadn't slept in days.

"Hi, Daryl. I was starting to wonder if anyone was here," Melina said, putting down her hood.

"Oh, Melina, I didn't know you had gotten back," the guy said, and he looked the others over to see if there was anyone else he recognized. Finding only strange new faces, he wiped rain off his gray-streaked beard, and turned back to Melina. "I'm glad to see you're okay."

"It's been a harrowing few days, but I made it back," she told him. "What's the situation here?"

"Just about everyone went home to be with their families. I think I'm the only one left. The zoo's got a lot of water damage. I brought most of the exterior animals inside their housings, but some of them are flooding. The emergency power seems to be holding for the tropical exhibits, but I don't know how much longer the generators will last. In a few hours this place could all be underwater. I was also forced to let a few animals loose, with the hope that they can survive this on their own. We just don't have enough safe places for them all."

"That would explain the ostrich we saw coming in," Melina said, her expression shifting to concern. "How come you aren't home with your family?"

"These animals are my family. I'm not leaving them."

Melina put a hand on his shoulder. "Let me get my new friends here to a safe, and hopefully dry, place. Then I'll help you make sure that everyone is tucked in safely."

The guy shook his head, "You're not going to find any dry places today, but your best bet would be The Cage."

Melina thought for a second. "You might be right. I'll take them there and then work my way over to you. I'll meet up with you at the African Outpost in about an hour and a half."

"I always knew you were one of the good ones," he said, raising his hood. "Be careful out there." Then he turned and went back into the rain.

Melina turned to the group, "Well, you guys ready to head back out?"

"That all depends on what 'The Cage' is," Vivian said softly.

Melina smiled, "It's one of the old steel cages they used to keep the animals in about thirty-five years ago when the zoo first opened. We still have one left to show the public how far we've come."

Pulling up their poncho hoods again, they followed Melina as she moved quickly around the exhibits. They went up a slight hill, and there to the Northeast corner of the zoo was The Cage.

It was basically a big box with bars – about twenty feet wide and twenty feet deep. There was an informative sign in front with a picture of the cage being used in its prime. It showed a male lion peering out between the bars at two small children. Now, the back wall of The Cage had a large square cut out so that zoo visitors could climb in and see how confined the animals had felt.

Inside, there was a big shelf built into the right wall where, Ryan imagined, the big cats would lounge. The floor was simple concrete and everything was a drab, dark gray color.

It seemed that Daryl was right, though. Because of the hill that it sat on, the area around The Cage was the least flooded place they had seen in the zoo so far.

Melina led them inside, and said, "All right, you guys make yourself at home here, and I'll swing by in about two hours. I'm going to open up the snack bar across the path on my way. Feel free to eat to your heart's content." She paused and looked at Marcus. "Except for you that is, big boy." And off she went.

Marcus slowly walked up and grabbed the bars. "This is a little too familiar."

Vivian walked up next to him. "It must have been awful. Sitting in that cell, knowing you didn't deserve to be there."

Marcus was staring blankly out into the rain. "You can't

imagine."

Karma walked up and sat next to Marcus, leaning her weight on him. The touch on his leg brought Marcus out of the past, and he bent down and gave Karma a pat on the head.

After pacing around The Cage for a few minutes, they ran over to the snack bar and filled up on junk food. The rain never faltered, not even for a second.

With their bellies full, they went back to The Cage and tried to relax. Ryan felt very sorry for any animal that had to call this home. It was small and bleak. Once again, he felt very ashamed that he was part of the race that had placed animals in such cramped quarters.

It wasn't long before the light gray of daytime began to change to the dark gray of night. Melina made it back to them just as the darkness finished swallowing the day. She drove her truck up the path and parked it on the side of The Cage.

Melina walked through the opening in the back wall with an armload of blankets.

"Well, the zoo is definitely taking on water," she said. "My office is just about floating and I think this may be the only place without an inch of water on the floor."

"How are the animals?" Ryan asked.

"All of the outdoor enclosures are pretty waterlogged and most of the indoor one's have some kind of damage. Unless this rain stops soon, Daryl is going to let all of the animals out and hope for the best. I told him we'd stick around in case he needs help."

"Let me get this straight," Marcus said. "There are going to be all kinds of wild animals roaming around here?"

Melina flashed one of her smiles, "Is Goliath scared?"

Marcus just gave her a dirty look.

"Well, don't worry, the animals will most likely jet out of here fast," she said. Then seeing the apprehension on their faces she added, "Don't worry, we're safe in here."

They spent the rest of the night hearing about the current state of the zoo from Melina. Soon they were all getting tired and decided they should try to get some sleep. Apparently, Melina had grabbed all of the blankets from a rhino or elephant exhibit, because they all had a strong animal smell.

One by one they drifted off, listening to the sound of the rain beating on the roof. Everyone was in a deep sleep when a huge grizzly bear stuck its head through the opening in the back of The Cage.

CHAPTER 7

Swimming with Tigers

Ryan looked down at himself walking across an open green field. Karma was running around him happily, circling a few times before coming in close for a playful nip. Up ahead, he saw that the field led to the edge of a cliff, which provided a view of the landscape beyond. Ryan walked up to the edge and gazed out. Piles of rubble and charred earth covered the ground for miles. Small fires were alight throughout the mess of concrete, steel, and blowing garbage. Smoke drifted up, making the air thick and polluted. Ryan felt sick with disgust.

Out in the distance he could see a beautiful green forest, with the sun shining down on lush trees. He wanted to go there, but it seemed so far away and he didn't see how he would ever be able to cross the ravaged land in between. He felt sad and discouraged.

Then, someone took his hand. Ryan turned to see Vivian's smiling face. Karma barked off to the right, and they turned to see her standing at the beginning of a path leading down the cliff into the charred valley below. The dog's eyes were so peaceful and calm. Ryan looked back at Vivian, and found comfort in the warmth of her smile and the touch of her hand. Slowly, they walked down the path holding hands, with Karma setting the pace just in front of them. Ryan tried not to concentrate on the horrible terrain they were about to walk through. Instead, he kept his eyes on the green forest off on the horizon.

Then, someone was shaking him. Slowly the heavy veil of sleep began to lift and he opened his eyes.

"Don't move," Vivian whispered in his ear.

The first thing Ryan's sleepy brain registered was that the rain was still beating down outside. Vivian was pressed against him closely, her face inches from his.

"We have a situation here," she said softly.

Ryan lifted his head slightly and saw that everyone else was already awake. Actually, they were very awake. Marcus was backed against the wall, his eyes wide and wearing an expression somewhere between bewilderment and shock.

Melina was to his right, and although she was alert, she didn't have the same tense look that Marcus carried. She was sitting up among a sea of blankets gazing at the far wall.

Ryan followed her gaze and lost his breath. A huge grizzly bear was lying on its side, sleeping against the opposite wall of The Cage. He was immense. The bear was probably over seven hundred pounds, with thick brown fur and sharp claws. Curled up in between those claws, sleeping peacefully, was Karma.

How could none of them notice a bear of that size coming into The Cage? Ryan had never been a heavy sleeper, and rarely slept through the night. However, this was the third night in a row that he slept soundly until morning.

Ryan looked over at Melina, "Weren't you the one who said we would be safe here?"

Without taking her eyes off the bear, she replied, "And you are. This here is Boomer, one of our resident grizzlies. He just stopped in to take a little snooze with us."

"So he's nice and friendly, right?" Marcus asked.

"He's been in zoos his entire life, but he's still a wild animal and I'm not sure how grumpy he is in the morning," Melina said.

"Great," Marcus added.

Suddenly the grizzly lifted his head and leaned up. He considered them very carefully for a moment or two, and then panned down to the dog between its huge paws.

Ryan's heart was pounding as he fought back a strong urge to run over and rescue Karma. He forced himself to stay put and waited to see what would happen next.

Just then Karma gently opened her eyes, slowly stood, stretched and turned to face the grizzly. They stared into each other's eyes for a moment and then the grizzly got to its feet. The size and sheer bulk of the animal made Ryan gasp.

The bear shook its head, turned toward Karma one last time and slowly padded out of the cage. Karma followed it to the opening at the back of The Cage, watched it walk away, and then turned toward the astonished group.

"That was the most amazing thing I've ever seen," Melina said, standing up.

"Keep hanging out with us and you'll get used to it," Marcus said, stepping away from the wall. "Karma has long lost friends everywhere."

Vivian went over to Karma and knelt down and hugged her. "I hope you don't have any larger acquaintances."

Melina walked over, knelt down and got nose to nose with Karma. "Simply amazing," she repeated.

Karma replied with a lick.

"Old Boomer coming to sleep with us can only mean one thing. Daryl must have been forced to let a lot of the animals go. And that means the zoo is in big trouble," Melina told them. "Let's take a look around and see how bad it is."

Everyone donned their ponchos and piled into the truck. If anything, it seemed like the rain had intensified. Going down the hill they could see that a good portion of the zoo was filled with large lakes of water.

Melina slowly negotiated the truck through the water filled paths. All of the outdoor exhibits they passed were filled with water. It was impossible to even figure out what animals used to live in each one. In some parts of the zoo, the water flooding onto the path came up to the bottom of the truck's doors.

Up ahead, they caught a glimpse of someone running into one of the exhibit buildings. Melina pulled the truck up to the door, and everyone stepped out into the river of water flowing down the path. Quickly, they ran into the building.

Inside, they were bathed in the dim glow of the emergency lighting. The building was a simple long rectangle with a number of glass enclosures running down the sides. There was about two inches of water covering the floor.

"Welcome to the Monkey House. This is where we have most of our small primates," Melina said, as she put her hand to her forehead and peered into one of the enclosures.

A door opened from the far corner and Daryl walked quickly down the hall to them. He was soaking wet and splashed with mud. In his arms, a chimpanzee huddled close to his body.

"I was just going to find you guys," Daryl said, slightly out of breath.

"How's the zoo holding up, Daryl?" Melina asked.

"Not good, I'm afraid." His face looked grave. "I figure the zoo will be completely flooded in another few hours. During the night, I let a number of the larger animals out to fend for themselves, and now I'm working on getting the smaller ones to safety."

"Will they be able to survive out there?" Vivian had to ask.

"The odds will be stacked heavily against them, but they will surely die if we leave them here," Daryl explained.

"Okay, how can we help?" Melina asked.

"I had a tough time making it out to the west side of the zoo. It was pretty flooded and I was rushing quite a bit. Maybe you could head that way in the truck and see if there are any animals I couldn't get to."

"You got it. We'll do a quick lap, but then I'm afraid we need to get ourselves out of here. We should all be able to squeeze into the truck."

Daryl was shaking his head. "No thanks, I'm staying here. I didn't let some of the tropical animals loose because I know they'd never survive. I'm going to stick around and see what I can do for them. We still have emergency power left for about twelve hours or so, and if the rain lets up I think I can keep them alive."

"Wake up and smell the apocalypse, Daryl," Melina said raising her arm out. "This place is going to be underwater. There's nothing more you can do here. You've got to come with us."

"I can't leave them," he stated.

The determination behind Daryl's tired eyes told Melina that he had made his decision. She gave him, and the chimp, a long hug. As she slowly released him, she left a hand on the back of his neck. "Be careful and take care of *yourself* too."

"I will," he said.

As they stepped away and walked toward the door, Karma stood motionless staring up at Daryl. He looked down at the dog, then bent down with the chimp still clinging to his chest and gave Karma a pat on the head who leaned in a bit and pushed her head into his midsection.

Daryl straightened up as Karma turned and walked past the group to the door. He stood holding the chimp and watched them disappear back into the rain.

Once they were back in the truck, Ryan said, "He's a good man."

"He's the best. I just hope he can make it through this." Melina pulled the truck away from the building.

As the truck sloshed through the rain soaked paths, everyone kept watch out the windows for any signs of animals. They drove through the African exhibits and past the African Outpost, where the outdoor benches sat in six inches of water. As they reached the corner and turned north, Karma, who was standing on Ryan's lap looking out the window, started barking.

Melina kept driving slowly, while Karma continued to bark at something out in the rain. Ryan peered out, but couldn't see anything. Karma kept barking.

"What's up?" Melina asked.

Ryan thought for second and said, "Stop the truck." He squinted in the rain and tried to see if there was something there that had gotten Karma's attention. "What exhibit is that?"

"Siberian tigers," Melina told him.

It was hard for him to see much in the pouring rain, but the tiger exhibit appeared to be a large sunken wooded habitat. There was a three foot high stone wall that circled the exhibit, which sat about twenty-five feet below. Water was pouring down from the path filling the exhibit. Ryan could just make out two stone hills that stood in the back. Each hill actually contained a cave that led to the tiger's indoor enclosure, but now, due to the rising water level, all that could be seen of the caves was about a foot opening at the top.

Karma was barking like crazy.

As Ryan opened the door, Karma hopped out of the truck and jumped onto the small wall, where she barked into the rain.

Ryan got out and stood beside her. He finally made out one large, adult tiger sitting on top of one of the hills watching as another tiger swam toward the second hill.

The others climbed out of the truck and joined Ryan and Karma at the wall.

Marcus pointed, "Look, there's a little one."

About five feet behind the adult tiger in the water a small baby tiger was struggling to keep its head above water. It was franticly churning its paws trying to stay afloat and follow the adult, but they could see it was tiring. Then, its head slipped below the surface of the water.

Without thinking, Ryan stepped onto the wall and jumped into the enclosure. He plunged into the water and immediately starting swimming toward the thrashing baby. The adult tiger on top of the hill stood up and stared at Ryan as he swam past. The other tiger made it to the other hill and began climbing up.

Ryan reached the little cub, grabbed it and lifted its head clear of the water. It thrashed for a second, and then calmed down once it realized it could breathe.

The baby tiger was only about four or five months old, but was a lot bigger then it appeared from the stone wall above. Ryan looked over at the two adult tigers gazing at him from the top of the stone hills. They were eyeing him with some interest, but soon had to deal with their own survival, as the water level had reached the top of the hills and was rising swiftly.

The rain continued to pour down relentlessly. Soon both tigers were half submerged as the water rose above the hills. Ryan couldn't believe how fast it was rising. He looked up at the stone wall and saw the astonished faces of his friends watching him.

The tiger cub splashed around every so often as water reached its head, but for the most part was surprisingly calm. Ryan, however, was starting to wonder what the hell he was thinking when he jumped into the water without any plan for escape.

"Ryan!" he heard someone scream from above.

He saw the water level steadily advancing upward and decided to swim back toward the wall. The tigers seemed to be thinking the same thing, because they too were paddling over to the wall.

Marcus was reaching down, but his outstretched hand was still ten feet above the rising water. Ryan was starting to get tired, and the combined weight of the tiger and his waterlogged clothes was starting to drag him under.

To Ryan's right, the adult tigers were clawing at the wall. Melina's head appeared at the wall and she threw down a rope, which landed a few feet from Ryan. He swam over to it, trying to keep the little cub's head out of the water, and wrapped it around his free arm.

Marcus, watching from above, made sure Ryan was holding on tightly and then began pulling him up. His progress was slow, but finally Ryan reached the top, where he handed the cub to Melina and then hoisted himself over the wall.

Ryan collapsed in a heap at the base of the wall and tried to catch his breath. Karma was the first to greet him with a wagging tail and wet tongue.

"You are one crazy dude," Marcus said, shaking his head. "Are you okay?"

"I think so," he replied between coughs, as Marcus helped him to his feet. "How's the cub?"

Melina held up the dripping little tiger, which seemed scared but well.

"I can't believe you did that," Vivian said at his side.

"Neither can I," Ryan replied, turning back to the exhibit. "What about the other tigers?"

They saw the two tigers still trying to get themselves up the wall. The water level was still eight or ten feet below the wall.

Karma jumped up onto the wall and started barking down at them. They looked up briefly and then started swimming off to the side, while the rain continued to come down in sheets.

"What can we do for them?" Vivian asked.

"I think they're doing it themselves," Ryan said, and pointed.

The tigers swam over to a half-submerged tree that was about ten feet from the wall, and started climbing.

"I didn't know tigers could climb trees," Marcus said.

Melina replied, "The drive for survival breaks all rules."

The first tiger got his back legs firmly planted on the base of the tree, gathered itself and jumped. It landed with cat-like grace on the wall and quickly ran away, disappearing in the rain.

The second tiger then made its way to the same spot, planted itself and sprang toward the wall. But it didn't quite make it. The jump was about a foot too short. The tiger got his upper body on the wall, but its lower half was dangling off. The only thing keeping it from falling was its muscular upper body and sharp claws. With all of its weight hanging over the wall it didn't have the leverage to get itself up. Then the tiger started to lose its grip.

Ryan bolted forward and grabbed a handful of fur and tried to pull the tiger up. At about five hundred pounds, the tiger was much more then Ryan could handle. But then Marcus was beside him, grabbing onto the tiger and pulling with all his might. Together they were able to move the cat enough so that it could get its back legs on the wall and pull its body over.

The tiger hopped off the wall and looked up at Melina, who was still holding the cub.

Melina, smiled, "I guess you're waiting for this little guy." And she plopped the cub down to the ground. It landed in about three inches of water and slowly walked over to the adult. The cub had to pass Karma on the way and paused briefly to look at the dog before moving on. Once the two cats were together, they took off down the path without turning back.

The rescue accomplished, everyone got back into the truck. Although Ryan was the only one who had jumped into the water, they were all soaked. Melina punched the truck in gear and drove down the flooded path. Ryan kept a close look outside to see if there were any more animals in need of help. It wasn't easy to see through the driving rain, but he didn't think he saw anything. Karma stood on his lap, and also seemed to be scanning the zoo. She was quiet though, which Ryan felt was a good sign.

Melina stopped the truck in front of another building. "Here's our next stop," she announced.

Back in the rain, they waited as Melina fiddled with a set of keys until she finally found the right one and opened the door to the large gift shop.

"Feel free to walk around, and pick out some dry clothes. Take whatever you like," then looking at Marcus, "or whatever fits you."

It took about fifteen minutes for everyone to get into their new clothes. They each selected a nice, new, dry Louisville Zoo shirt. Even Marcus was able to find a t-shirt that he could squeeze into. The girls found brown cargo shorts embroidered with the zoo logo, while Ryan and Marcus remained soggy from the waist down.

Next, they went across to one of the snack bars and stocked up on food. Melina had a big waterproof bag in the back of the truck that would keep everything relatively dry. The last stop was to a back corner of the zoo where the maintenance equipment was stored. Melina knew there was a supply of gasoline there for the various zoo vehicles. After a brief search, they were able to find pumps and fill the tank.

Once they were all back in the truck, Melina turned in the driver's seat. "Where to?"

No one had an answer.

Finally, Ryan said, "We've never really had a set destination since all this started, and somehow we're still alive. Maybe we should just keep moving and see what happens."

Marcus shrugged, "It's all the same to me."

Ryan looked over at Vivian who said, "Wherever we go, it can't be worse than here."

"All right then, I'll just start driving and we'll see where the road leads us," Melina said, and got the truck moving again.

They drove out of the zoo and headed southwest. Ryan wondered what would become of Daryl. He hoped that he would be able to keep the animals and himself safe. It seemed like such an unselfish act. Daryl was putting his life in jeopardy for a miscellaneous group of animals which had a limited chance for survival. In a world thrown into total chaos, where everyone was fighting to save themselves, it was nice to know that there were a few good souls around thinking of others. He silently wished Daryl well.

They drove on.

Due to the rain, Melina was forced to travel slowly, which didn't really matter because they weren't in a rush to get anywhere. They had to turn around a number of times due to roads that were flooded or blocked by abandoned cars, but for the most part they were able to continue traveling in a southwest direction.

For hours they drove, with nothing but the rain and some scattered conversation to break the silence. Melina turned the radio on a few times, but only got static out of the speakers. On all the roads and highways they traveled, they saw no one. Not one other living creature. It seemed they were alone in the world, and that made Ryan feel very uneasy.

Your whole life was spent in the midst of other people. No matter where you went, it seemed you were always surrounded by people. They were everywhere, all the time. Inside, outside, on the ground, in the sky, and on the ocean. Everywhere you turned there were people. Even alone in your house you still had the ringing of the telephone and a constant flood of emails. People always there. The towns and cities seemed busting with development. Soon there would be no more room on the planet to build anything. Then, we would have to just build upwards. Our buildings reaching higher into the sky until even that was overcrowded.

Ryan thought about some of the things Melina had told them yesterday. Six billion people were living on Earth, she had said. He had to wonder if one day the world would just be full. No more space for even a single person. Just people piled next to each other, everyone moving but no one getting anywhere. Would it ever stop? We would have to move to other planets, but would probably clog them up with people as well.

Ryan had always longed for some open space, but more people were being born every day and because of the amazing breakthroughs in medical science, people were living longer lives. People were living longer, using more natural resources and causing more pollution. We're able to live on this planet for longer than ever before, but we're also slowly killing our home.

Every animal species on the planet has a give and take relationship with the Earth. A particular species takes only what it needs to survive, and in turn gives something back. Insects pollinate flowers, birds spread seeds, plants give off oxygen, and every animal is food for another animal, helping to keep populations in check. Give and take.

It seemed to Ryan that the human race did more than its share of taking, however, and gave little back. We take so much from the Earth without ever providing a benefit, while our population grows out of control, spilling over onto every part of the planet. People everywhere, taking.

And now there wasn't a sign of a single person on any of the rain soaked streets. Maybe that should have made him happy, but it didn't. It made him feel alone and isolated. He never liked the crowds of people that were common to everyday city life, but this sudden lack of human existence unnerved him. It seemed unnatural, and he found himself studying the passing landscape searching for someone, anyone.

They drove on.

They crossed into Missouri briefly before heading south into Arkansas. The rain never let up and the dark gray sky made it impossible to tell the time of day. And the roads were getting worse. Melina was having a hard time controlling the truck on the rain swelled streets.

They were driving in about six inches of water when Melina stopped the truck at an intersection, in a rural neighborhood with houses on either side of the road. To the right, the road continued up a slight hill and disappeared. To the left, they could see a few store fronts, and straight ahead more houses.

"We should think of stopping somewhere soon," Melina said, looking back. "What do you think?"

"That's cool with me," Marcus said quickly, wanting to stretch his legs.

Vivian and Ryan both nodded. "Sounds good," Vivian added.

Ryan had one hand on Karma, who was sitting in the back seat between him and Vivian. "You've been a good captain so far, Melina. I think we can trust you to pick a place to stop for the night."

Before Melina put the truck in gear, Karma let out a single bark.

"Uh oh," Vivian said, as Karma stood up.

"What?" Melina asked. "What's the matter?"

"Things always get a little intense whenever Karma starts barking," Marcus said.

Everyone looked out, searching for any signs of trouble. Karma let out a series of rapid fire barks and stood up on Ryan's lap.

Through the rain, Ryan saw a river of water rushing toward them.

"Oh, no," was all he could mutter.

Peering out of the truck, they gasped as the wall of water hit them. The force of the impact gave them all a good jolt as water engulfed the truck. The rushing water grabbed the truck and sent it sliding down the hill. Out of control and at the mercy of the surge, the truck turned sideways as it picked up speed.

The truck slid down the hill, passenger side first, which is where Marcus and Vivian were seated. They looked ahead and noticed a big obstruction in the road. It was hard to see in the gloomy light, but as they raced closer they saw it was an overturned garbage truck. The truck was on its side, at a slight angle, with the bottom rear of the vehicle facing them. A stream of garbage was being washed out of the back of the truck. The garbage floated quickly down the hill, getting caught along the way on trees and immobile cars.

They braced themselves as they struck the garbage truck hard. The passenger side of the pick-up hit the underside of the garbage truck with a crash, and everyone was thrown to the side forcefully.

When Ryan got himself up, he immediately saw that Vivian was slumped over. Leaning her back, he saw that she had banged the side of her head on the window, and was bleeding and unconscious.

Ryan inspected the damage. The cut on her head was flowing freely and her body was limp. He leaned her head back and tried to stop the stream of blood.

"Is she hurt?" Melina asked, shaking off the effects of the crash.

With the exception of Vivian, they had only a few minor bruises. Karma had been thrown to the floor, but seemed unharmed.

"I don't know," Ryan said with concern in his voice. "She's out cold and is bleeding, but seems to be breathing well enough."

The rushing water had them pinned against the garbage truck. Melina glanced out her window and saw that the water level was up to the middle of the door. Water was trickling through the doors, slowly filling the inside of the truck.

"We've got to get this thing moving," Melina declared.

"How?" Marcus asked. "We're stuck against the damn truck."

Ryan was too concerned with Vivian to even think.

Melina eyeballed the bottom of the garbage truck then rolled down her window.

"What the hell are you doing?" Marcus said.

"We've got to get clear of that truck," she explained. "A little leverage might do the trick. I'll be right back." And she started climbing out the window.

"Are you out of your mind?" Marcus yelled at her, but she was already climbing onto the top of the pickup.

Once on top, she made her way to the bed of the truck and retrieved the shovel she kept there. Melina slid across the top of the cab to the hood. She jammed the shovel between the pick-up and the bottom of the garbage truck and pulled down with all her might, trying to separate the trucks and get them moving again. The rain was coming down in buckets all around her, making the hood slippery and causing her to have trouble keeping her feet as she pulled down on the shovel.

Then, both trucks shifted and turned forward a little. Melina lost her balance and landed flat on her stomach on the hood. She saw Marcus screaming something through the windshield, but couldn't hear him. She got herself up on one knee, when the water shifted the trucks forward again. The trucks were slowly turning down the hill.

Ryan opened his window and stuck his head out, "Melina, get back in here!"

Melina scrambled up onto the roof as a surge of water hit the trucks. The weight of the garbage truck kept it in place, but the lighter pick-up slid forward and separated from the garbage truck, sending it down the hill amidst the floating garbage. The sudden movement caused Melina to slip on the rain covered roof. She toppled down the windshield, rolled onto the hood and then slid off the truck. As her body fell over the driver's side of the hood, she frantically grabbed for something to hold on to. Somehow, she managed to grab hold of a windshield wiper blade and held on for dear life.

"Melina!" Marcus screamed.

Melina grimaced in pain, as the rushing water began to pull her under the truck.

Ryan knew that if Melina lost her grip she would surely drown. So, once again, Ryan acted without thinking.

He quickly climbed out the window and made his way onto the

hood of the truck. With his left hand, Ryan held onto the lip of the truck's hood near the base of the windshield wiper and grabbed hold of Melina's armpit with his right hand.

The truck turned in the current and now they were moving down the hill sideways, driver's side first.

Melina was close to exhaustion, but she grit her teeth and held on. Ryan closed his eyes, trying to prepare himself for one big pull. When he opened his eyes he saw that they were rapidly approaching a jumble of cars. The flow of water had the cars stuck against some thick trees, much as the pick-up had been pinned to the garbage truck. They were heading right for them, and Melina would be the first thing to hit.

Karma stuck her head out the window and barked.

Ryan took a deep breath and pulled as hard as he could on Melina's arm, as they approached the locked up cars. Slowly, Melina's body came up onto the hood. Ryan peeked ahead, saw they were about to hit a blue station wagon, and quickly gave a final big heave, that yanked the rest of Melina's body onto the hood.

Then they hit.

The entire driver's side of the truck hit the station wagon's side. If Melina had remained hanging off the hood, she would have been crushed between the two vehicles.

Ryan, who was kneeling over Melina on the hood, was thrown forward off the truck and onto the top of the station wagon. Melina was luckily lying flat on the hood of the pick-up, and although she was also thrown forward, she managed to keep her body on the hood. The pick-up only connected with the station wagon for a second or two before the water began to pull it away.

Ryan's forward momentum was stopped by an SUV that was

jammed on the other side of the station wagon. Groaning, he slowly got his feet under him and stood up on the top of the wagon in time to see the pick-up starting to float away.

Ignoring the many bruises on his aching body, he took two big strides and jumped, making a less-than-graceful landing in back of the pick-up, just as it was pulled away by the rushing water.

Luckily, the road that was now a river was straight without any other obstacles ahead. Soon, the truck slowed down as the hill leveled out. The water level began to drop and bring the truck back to the ground.

Finally, the wheels caught the pavement and the pick-up shuddered to a stop.

They were on a suburban street with houses lining either side of the road. Although the torrential rain continued, the water must have been draining somewhere because it was only about a foot deep now.

Ryan and Melina locked eyes over the top of the truck.

"This is going to sound pathetically inadequate," Melina said, "but, thank you."

Ryan smiled and nodded, but then thought of Vivian and jumped to the road and into the truck. Melina followed.

Inside, Marcus was staring at him from the front seat, while Karma stood wagging her tail next to the unconscious Vivian.

"Like I said," Marcus told him. "You are one crazy dude."

He reached over Karma and checked her head. The blood seemed to have stopped, but her face was very pale.

"We've got to get her someplace where we can lay her down," Ryan said, without taking his eyes off Vivian.

"Yeah, but where?" Melina asked.

Ryan looked up and squinted out the front windshield. "There," he said.

In the darkening sky a short distance ahead was a glowing circle. It seemed to be a multicolored mosaic of soft light floating in the rain.

"Head that way."

Melina got the truck moving, and they went towards the light.

CHAPTER 8

Soggy Sermons

The streetlights were out and there were no lights coming from any of the houses, yet they all saw the glowing circle in the sky up ahead. The light was very dim, and at first Ryan thought he was imagining it. It wasn't moving and seemed to be sections of colors all mixed together.

Intrigued by this strange apparition, Melina got the truck moving and drove toward it. After being half submerged, the truck was sluggish as water continued to drain from it. Melina crossed her fingers, hoping it wouldn't stall on them.

As they approached the circle of light, they discovered that it wasn't floating in the air, but sitting on top of a hill.

They drove up, keeping their eyes on the light, as the road curved up the hill. At the top there was a small parking lot adjacent to a church. The circle of light was actually a big, round stained glass window at the top of the church's front wall. There were similar small rectangular windows glowing along the sides of the church as well.

Melina stopped the truck alongside the church and everyone got out into the rain. Marcus stretched his legs quickly then went to help Ryan, who was already picking Vivian up out of the back seat.

"I've got her," Ryan told Marcus, who came over to help.

Melina shouted over the bed of the truck, "How about grabbing our stuff, big guy?"

Marcus took hold of the big waterproof duffle bag that held their food and meager belongings. The bag was fairly large, but Marcus lifted it like it was pillow, and heaved it over his shoulder.

They made their way to the front door of the church. Karma was already standing there, waiting to be let in. Melina opened the big wooden door and they stepped inside out of the pouring rain.

The front door opened up to a large foyer with stairs on either side leading upwards. About fifteen feet ahead was an archway that led into the church.

Karma walked into the nave and looked around. Following her, Ryan realized why they saw the light through the stained glass window. There were candles lit everywhere. Along the walls, on the window sills and at least a hundred illuminated around the altar. The nave consisted of two rows of pews separated by a center aisle with a row of columns along the sides dividing the pews from the two side aisles.

People were scattered around the church in small groups. Some sitting in pews, some bunched together in the corners and some lying in the center aisle. In total, there were about twenty-five to thirty people in the church.

Everyone was watching them as they walked in. Ryan put Vivian gently down on the back pew and moved the hair out of her face.

An elderly woman walked up and looked them over. "You poor things, what you must have been through. Not to worry, you're safe now. Let me go get the Reverend." She turned and walked quickly to the sanctuary and knocked on a door off to the right.

Ryan stood up from Vivian in time to see Karma jog over to a man sitting alone on the floor in the back left corner. As she passed a woman who was sitting in the last pew, the woman got up with a frightened look in her eyes and fled down the center aisle.

Karma paid her no attention and continued toward the man in the corner, tail wagging. Ryan chased after her, not wanting to scare anyone else.

Ryan got there, in time to watch Karma deliver a series of licks to the guy's face.

"I'm so sorry," Ryan apologized. "She's annoyingly friendly."

The man rubbed Karma's head and smiled. "Don't you worry about it," he said, leaning up off the balled up jacket he was reclining on. "I'm dog friendly."

Ryan extended his hand and was about to introduce himself, when a voice from behind him stopped him short.

"Greetings, newcomers."

Ryan turned to see a short middle-aged man wearing a long white clergy robe with ornate trim, walking down the center aisle with his arms outstretched.

"Welcome," the man said, smiling. "I am Reverend Holmes and you have found safe shelter now, I assure you." He had a smooth, calming voice, which Ryan found immediately comforting. His face was round, with the scattered lines of age around his eyes and mouth. A badly receding hairline drew attention to his large forehead, but the hair he had left was neat and well groomed.

"Hi, I'm Ryan. And this is Marcus and Melina," he said motioning to his soggy companions.

Reverend Holmes nodded at each of them in turn. "I hear that we have an injury?"

"Yes, Vivian," Ryan said, as he walked back toward her. "We got into an accident, and she hit her head pretty bad. She's been unconscious ever since."

The Reverend bent down and gently touched her forehead. "Don't worry, my child, we'll make sure you recover." Then he turned toward Ryan. "Let's make her as comfortable as we can. If you would bring her up to the front, I think we have a nice spot for her to rest."

Two men, who had been watching from the side aisle came forward and reached for the duffle bag Marcus carried.

When Marcus resisted, the Reverend said, "You've been through so much. Allow us to help you, while you get more comfortable."

Reluctantly, Marcus let the men take the bag and then followed the Reverend down the center aisle with Melina. Ryan carefully picked up Vivian and started down the aisle, then noticed that Karma was still pestering the man in the corner.

"Karma!" he called. "Let's go!"

Karma stared at Ryan for a moment, and then padded over to him.

The Reverend showed them to a spot in the front corner of the nave, just before the sanctuary, to the left of the altar. There was an open space between the first pew and a statue of the Virgin Mary.

"Let me see if I can find some blankets," the Reverend said, and disappeared through a door to the side of the altar.

He quickly returned with a couple of wool blankets and laid them on the floor. "It's not exactly a hospital bed, but I'm afraid it's all we have."

Ryan put Vivian down, resting her head on one of the blankets. "This is fine. Thanks."

"Please make yourself comfortable," the Reverend said. "I have a few things to attend to and I'm sure you want to catch your breath, after such a trying experience. Let's talk in an hour or so."

"That sounds good," Melina said.

The Reverend smiled, then turned and walked away, going through the door by the altar. As he walked away, Ryan noticed that his white priestly robe was a little too long. His hands disappeared in the sleeves and an inch or two dragged on the floor at the bottom.

Turning his attention to Vivian, Ryan sat down and checked her pulse. Karma sat down next to Vivian, opposite Ryan, watching.

"How's she doing?" Marcus asked.

"She's breathing and her pulse seems strong," he told them.

Melina put a hand on his shoulder. "I think she just needs some rest right now. She got quite a knock to the head. I bet she'll be up in no time."

Ryan wanted to believe that, but was very concerned. "I hope you're right."

The woman who met them when they first came into the church walked over. "The Reverend thought you might want to get out of those wet clothes and freshen up a bit. If you go through that door," she pointed to a door in the corner over Ryan's shoulder, "you'll find a bathroom and some spare clothes. Help yourself to whatever you want, but take only what you need."

Smiling, she walked back down the center aisle and sat down

in the back.

"You guys go," Ryan said. "I want to stay with her for a while."

"Let's go, giant," Melina said, taking Marcus's arm. And they walked through the door.

About twenty minutes later, Melina came out of the room with a big smile on her face. She was now wearing a faded green, long sleeve shirt and khaki shorts. Marcus followed, and Ryan realized why Melina was so giddy. He wore a pair of black shorts that were originally made for a guy Ryan's size, and an extra tight red t-shirt that said *Buster's BBQ Grill*.

They walked to the first pew and started laying out their wet clothes.

"Don't say a word," Marcus said, as he passed Ryan.

"I think–"

"Not one word."

Even though he was concerned about Vivian, Ryan had to laugh.

When Ryan looked back down to Vivian, he saw that she was beginning to stir. She let out a groan and lifted her hand to her head. Karma, who was lying next to her, lifted her head off her paws, her tail connecting with the wall as it moved back and forth.

Tentatively, Vivian opened her eyes.

"You're okay, Viv," Ryan assured her.

"I don't feel okay," she said groggily.

"You hit your head on the truck window. Do you remember?"

"I remember sitting in the truck watching a river of water coming at us, and that's it."

"Don't worry," Marcus said, standing over Ryan. "You didn't miss anything good."

"Where's Melina?" Vivian asked.

"I'm right here, kid," Melina said, as she walked around and knelt down by her head. "How're you doing?"

"I've got a mother of a headache," she replied and tried to lean up, but quickly fell back. "Ugh, and I'm very dizzy."

"Stay put, Viv," Ryan told her. "You need to rest."

Vivian noticed Karma next to her and put a weak hand on her head. "Hey, girl." Then she panned around the room and said, "You brought me to a church? Wow, you must have really thought I was in bad shape."

"The church sort of found us," Ryan said. "And we needed a place to rest. You just relax."

Vivian gave them a smile and a thumbs up.

Feeling relieved that Vivian was starting to function again, Ryan decided to get some dry clothes. He walked to the door Melina and Marcus had gone into earlier. Just before he closed the door he heard Vivian say, "Where's the ten-year-old you stole that outfit from Marcus?"

Smiling, Ryan found himself inside a small room with a stack of folding chairs along one wall. In the middle of the room, was a pile of clothes. After sifting through it, he found a pair of black pants and a pink shirt that seemed like the best fit for Vivian.

After assisting Vivian, by holding the blanket up while she squirmed out of her wet clothes and into the dry ones, Ryan headed back to outfit himself.

He decided on a pair of olive green cargo pants and a plain black t-shirt, then noticed the small pile of toiletries in the corner. Ryan checked for a toothbrush, but didn't see one. There were a few small bottles of mouth wash though, so he grabbed one and headed toward the one other door in the room, which led to a bathroom. He stared at himself in the mirror and thought, *you look like hell.*

His hair was a tangled, wet mess, he had a small bruise under his left eye and he had a dirty, thin coat of scruff covering his face.

He took a swig of mouthwash, swished it around and spit it in the sink. Then, he did is best to fix up his hair and returned to the church.

Marcus and Melina were sitting in the second pew talking to an elderly woman.

"We were so scared," the woman was saying with a slight southern accent. "There was water everywhere. The furniture was ruined, the carpets were soaked, and the basement was completely flooded." She stopped as Ryan walked over and looked down at the now sleeping Vivian. He laid out his wet clothes with the others and sat down.

"This is Rebecca," Marcus said. "She was just telling us how she made it here."

Ryan nodded, "Please continue."

"Well, Barry," she turned to Ryan, "that's my husband, thought we should come to the church so we could be close to God."

"Where is he?" Melina said, glancing around. Then added, "Your husband, not God."

"He's not here yet. I came alone, while he gathered some of our belongings. He should be here soon," the woman said unconvincingly.

Ryan got the feeling that Barry was never going to make it to church.

"Everyone here has a similar story," Marcus told Ryan.

"That's right," the old woman said. "We came here to be with

God in our hour of need. The Reverend has assured us that God will save us and lead us out of these times of trouble."

"The Reverend seems like a pretty nice guy," Ryan said.

"Oh, yes," she said, immediately, "He's such a kind and wise soul. His sermons inspire me so. I don't know what we would do without him."

"Well, it sounds like you're in good hands here," Marcus said to her.

"And now you are, too," she said, and then got up and walked to the back of the church.

Ryan studied the faces around him. Most looked tired and scared. Every person here had clearly felt some kind of loss over these last few days. The extreme situation that they were all thrust into had affected each and every one of them. Some of them appeared to be holding on to sanity by a thin thread.

They'd all found their way here, to this church, as a last hope. Their world was crashing in around them and they were desperate for some answers, so they turned to their faith. Ryan had never been a religious person. In fact, this was the first time he had stepped foot in a church since he was twelve-years-old. He was raised a Catholic, but lost interest in religion early on. His mother and father had only attended church for special holidays and never forced him to go. Although Ryan considered himself a spiritual person, he never found any connection in organized religion.

Still, he understood the allure. These people had made their way to this church while searching for hope. And if hope is what this church gave them, then maybe that was a good thing. Everyone needed hope, even in a hopeless situation.

Marcus's voice brought Ryan away from his thoughts. "Hey,

where's our bag?"

Ryan looked around. "I don't know."

"Two guys helped me with it when we came in here. Now I don't see it, or them," Marcus said with suspicion.

"Don't worry, Big Foot," Melina said. "I'm sure the good Reverend's keeping it safe and sound."

"I know," Marcus told her. "I'm just getting hungry and could go for some of that yummy food you packed."

"I think we could all use something to eat," Ryan said. "You guys stay put. I'll go ask Reverend Holmes about it." Ryan got up and started to walk toward the altar. "Keep an eye on Viv."

"Don't worry, Karma's keeping vigil," Melina said, motioning to the dog lying with her head on Vivian's arm.

Ryan walked up the three steps to the altar. Pillar candles of all shapes and sizes burned on tables, the floor and the altar itself – so many that he could actually feel a difference in temperature when he reached the top step. Ryan walked to the door that he had seen the Reverend enter earlier, and knocked.

There was some muffled movement from inside, then the door opened and the Reverend came out, shutting the door behind him.

"How can I be of assistance, my friend?" he said with a smile.

"We were wondering where our bag was," Ryan said. "A couple guys helped us with it when we got here. Now we're getting a little hungry and all of our food is in the bag."

"Ah, yes. Allow me to explain." The Reverend took a deep breath. "Here at this church we consider ourselves a community. You are not alone here. We are all in this together, and together we shall overcome this troubled time. God has brought you to us, and we will embrace you as our brother. What is ours, is now yours.

"You see, everything here is done for the good of the community," he continued. "Alone we would surely perish, but united we shall survive. So you, like all of these fine people before you, are asked to donate your food and belonging for the good of the group. We have combined all of our food together and have three communal feedings a day. Although I am certain that God will deliver us from these trials, it is necessary to ration our resources. The next rationing will commence shortly. So I ask you to put your faith in the community and together we shall come out of this united and strong."

Ryan took a second to absorb all that the Reverend had just told him. Then he said, "Well, of course, we would be happy to share. How much food do you have?"

The Reverend face turned grim. "Our supplies are small, while our numbers grow every day but God will provide. After all, he brought us you and your added supplies will help us continue on. Thank you."

"Uh, no problem," Ryan said.

"Please, go relax while I make ready this evening's meal," the Reverend said, guiding Ryan down the altar.

Ryan filled the others in on what the Reverend said, and then checked on Vivian. Her face, although still a little pale, was beginning to regain some of its natural color. He noticed her eyes were moving under her eyelids.

"She's dreaming," Melina said.

"I hope it's a dream of better days," Ryan said as he watched Vivian.

"Don't worry, she's going to be fine," Melina said, reading Ryan's mind. "How long have you two been together?"

Ryan gently put a hand on Vivian's forehead. He held it there for a moment, then walked over and sat down in the pew in front of Melina and Marcus. "We're not together, we're just friends."

"Come on now, I've seen that look in her eye," Melina told him. "She's definitely sweet on you."

Ryan shook his head. "No, she's just been through some tough times lately. Her boyfriend dumped her just before this all started, and she's not dealing with it too well. Then, when she thinks things can't get any worse, Mother Nature has a hissy fit, and she's forced to run for her life."

"And what's your story?" she asked.

"Me?" Ryan said. "I don't really have a story. "I'm just a guy trying to find his way out of this mess." He paused. "Actually, I've been trying to find my way for years. I've been through a series of equally meaningless jobs, as well as a number of meaningless relationships. I don't know what I want. And even if I did, I wouldn't know how to get there. I feel like I've been treading water, and although there's land all around me, I don't know which way I want to go. So, I keep treading water. I just wish someone would tell me where to swim."

"No way," Marcus said. "You need to find your own path. No matter how hard it is or how long it takes. No one can tell you what's right for you. Just keep your head above water and you'll figure it out on your own."

"He's right," Melina nodded, and then turned to Marcus. "You know, you're not so dumb for a giant."

"Hey, even I have my moments," Marcus replied.

"So it seems," she said. "How did you get mixed up with these two?"

Marcus was about to reply when they heard bells, and turned to find the Reverend standing at the altar in his white robe. The people scattered around the church slowly got up and made their way toward the altar and sat down in the first few pews.

Ryan noticed that the man in the back corner that Karma had taken a liking to sat down last, and was a few rows behind everyone else.

Once everyone was seated the Reverend raised his arms out wide. His body positioning mirrored the big crucifix on the wall behind him. "Good evening. It seems that the rains continue despite our prayers. Do not despair though. It rains because God deems it necessary and we must take solace in that. If it is His will, then it is done for a reason and we must trust in Him. He has brought us together and although we suffer, we live. And live we shall.

"Newcomers have joined our group," he motioned toward Ryan, Melina, Marcus and the sleeping Vivian. "And we will embrace them.

"Together we shall overcome the many tragedies that befall us. Together we shall persevere." He was slowly raising his voice. "Together we ride out the dark. And together we shall again bask in the light!"

The Reverend paused and considered the faces staring at him. "You must trust in me, as I trust in God. This time will pass, and only the pure of heart and loyal of body will reap the benefits of our new world. I have seen visions of it. He has shown me, and I want you by my side when the sun shines upon us and the new day has come."

He bowed his head as he finished. After a few seconds, he raised it and said, "Now let us commence the evening meal. Keep a strong heart. For as our rations are meager, our faith is grand."

The Reverend then nodded off to the side, and the two men who helped Marcus with the bag earlier came forward with two huge bowls. They walked up to the altar and stood next to the Reverend. One at a time, people stood up, got in line, and were given some food from the bowls. It was very organized, and resembled a normal communion service on any Sunday morning.

Ryan thought the Reverend's sermon was a little hokey but the people gathered in the church seemed to respect him.

Ryan, Melina and Marcus went up to the altar in line with everyone else. Marcus was first to receive his meal. He held out his hands like the people before him had, and Reverend Holmes gave him a small cheese sandwich.

Speechless, he walked back to his seat. Ryan and Melina soon followed with their sandwiches.

"You've got to be kidding," Marcus said, turning the small sandwich around in his hands, as Ryan and Melina sat down next to him. "This can't be all."

"The Reverend told me they were rationing the food," Ryan said. "I guess he's doing the best he can, given the situation."

The Reverend and his two helpers next passed out paper cups filled with water. Ryan sampled his sandwich as Marcus finished his in four big bites. The bread seemed a little stale and the cheese was warm, but it was better than nothing.

A cup of water was held out to Ryan and he lifted his head up to see the Reverend smiling down at him. Ryan accepted it and washed down his mouthful of sandwich.

"I brought you an extra sandwich in case your friend was feeling up to it," the Reverend said, handing him two more sandwiches. "And one for your dog, also."

"Thanks," Ryan replied.

The Reverend smiled again and continued the water distribution.

After they finished eating, everyone went off to their own private conversations and thoughts.

Ryan sat next to Vivian, while Marcus and Melina put some blankets on the floor nearby and got comfortable. It wasn't long before Vivian stirred and was able to eat her sandwich. She talked with them for a short while, but was soon feeling light-headed again, and decided to lie back down, where she quickly drifted off to sleep.

The rain continued to rattle the stained glass windows, as one by one the community of people in the church fell asleep.

Ryan awoke a few moments later, or so it seemed. He lifted his sleepy head and looked around. It was hard to tell what time it was, but it did seem to be a bit lighter then when he had closed his eyes. Over at the altar, he noticed the candles were burning very low. Everyone else was still sleeping, even Karma.

Ryan slowly walked down the side aisle, past a few bodies still huddled in slumber. He went through the foyer and opened the big wooden door that led outside.

Gazing out, he realized that the black of night had been replaced with the gray of day. The rain was pouring down as usual. He peered at the road at the bottom of the hill and could see that the water level had risen quite a bit since yesterday.

Ryan closed the door and walked back into the church. A few people had begun to stir, but the only sound to be heard was the drumming rain. As he approached the sleeping forms of his friends he caught sight of Karma curled up at the base of the Virgin Mary statue.

He smiled. *Such a sweet dog,* he thought.

Within an hour, everyone was awake. Vivian was still fighting a bad headache and some dizziness, and opted to remain lying down. Marcus complained about how hungry he was, while Melina went through a series of stretches. The clothes they had laid out to dry were still damp but wearable. Marcus didn't waste any time changing, and the others soon followed, returning the borrowed clothing back to the pile in the other room.

They talked about the rain and what they should do next. None of them wanted to stay in the church another night, but decided that they would wait until Vivian felt fit enough to travel before heading out.

Sometime in the late morning the Reverend rang his bell again and delivered another semi-inspirational sermon about how they were stronger and would make it through this together. It was pretty much the same speech as the night before, using slightly different words. Ryan guessed that the Reverend was running out of motivational material.

Following his speech, the Reverend passed out the morning rations. A few chocolate chip cookies and a glass of cranberry juice was all that was on the menu. Marcus complained that his prison meals were better, and no amount of lighthearted jokes from Melina could improve his mood. Vivian sat up and had a few cookies, but the more she moved, the more her head hurt. She wanted to get up and stretch her legs, but her body wasn't ready yet, and soon she was back on the floor resting next to Karma.

Ryan sat in the first pew and looked down at Vivian. He wasn't really sure how he felt about her anymore. When he first met her, there had been an instant attraction, but then as their friendship grew, she seemed more like a sister to him. Now, she was just about all he had left in the world, and recent events had brought them closer than ever. They were in this together, counting on each other to get through each day. But maybe it was more than that. Maybe he was feeling something deeper. Ryan couldn't really tell and he wasn't sure what Vivian was feeling. The only feeling she had given off the past few weeks was sorrow.

With all the craziness that had taken place, Vivian seemed to have forgotten her sadness. All the disasters and excitement had forced Vivian to concentrate on something else. *At least there was something positive to come out of this,* Ryan thought.

A shadow fell onto Ryan and he looked up to see Reverend Holmes standing next to him.

"Good morning, Brother Ryan," the Reverend said.

"Good morning, Reverend," Ryan replied.

"I wanted to take this time to invite you to a private counsel with me," the Reverend said, sitting down next to Ryan. "Every morning I meet with each member of our community, one on one, to discuss how you're feeling during this traumatic time. I find that spending a brief period talking each day helps unburden the soul and ease the spirit."

"I'm not really a religious person, Reverend," Ryan explained. "And I've never gone to confession."

"It need not be a confession, unless that's what you want it to be," he told Ryan. "Think of it more as a friendly chat. We can talk about a specific topic or something as trivial as the weather. I think you'll find that you feel much better afterwards."

Ryan didn't think his soul really needed to be unburdened, but he didn't want to offend the Reverend.

He saw that Marcus and Melina were engrossed in a conversation with each other in the side aisle. Then he panned down to Vivian. Even in sleep, the pain of her injury showed on her face. Next to her, Karma was watching them. She put her head down on her front paws, but her eyes stayed on the Reverend.

"Come now," the Reverend said standing up. "Just a short talk."

"All right," Ryan said, and followed the Reverend to the altar and into a small room off to the left.

There was a desk covered with books against one wall. The only other things in the room were two chairs set up in the middle, facing each other. One chair was a big, cushy office chair, the other a simple folding chair. The Reverend sat down in the office chair and then motioned for Ryan to sit.

"Why don't I start the conversation and we'll see where it goes?" the Reverend said.

Ryan nodded.

"I have spoken with everyone sitting out in that church," the Reverend began. "Everyone found their way here a little differently, but it's not an accident that you're here. Our paths have intersected here for a reason, of this I am sure. You are hurting inside and out. I can see it on your face. You are worried for your friend and unsure of the future."

The Reverend paused and looked at Ryan.

"Uh, yes," Ryan said tentatively. "I'm very worried about her. I mean, I know she's going to be fine. I just wish there was more I could do for her."

"We all want to cradle our loved ones in our wings and keep them from harm, but there is only so much that can be done. Sometimes we cannot stop bad things from happening. I'm guessing she's more than just a friend to you."

"No," Ryan answered. Then added, "I don't think so."

"Don't be shy or deny your feelings. They can only be pushed back for so long. If you open up with honesty and sincerity, you may be surprised by the results. But first we must concentrate our efforts on getting her healthy again. I know you may not necessarily believe in God, but that's okay. I'm not asking you to believe in Him, I'm asking you to believe in *me*. My faith is strong, and if you believe in me, I promise you that your Vivian will be back to normal in no time. Can you put your trust in me?"

Ryan wasn't really sure what to say, but replied, "Yes."

The Reverend continued, "No matter what you believe in, one thing is always certain. You must have faith to make it in this world. Faith in yourself, faith in those around you, and faith that everything will work out for the best. Unfortunately, these troubled times have caused many to doubt their faith. It's easy to see why. So many people have lost their loved ones, as well as their homes and possessions. Rain has replaced sun, darkness has replaced light and fear has replaced hope. It's no wonder that faith has been forgotten.

"But I am here to tell you that there is hope. Here in this community, there is hope. I ask you to put your faith in me, and I will help to lead you through this time, and together we will make tomorrow a better time and place."

The Reverend stood up. "Now, go back to Vivian. Attend to

her, while I pray for her recovery. Trust in me, and all will again be well."

Ryan stood up, surprised that their talk was over already. The Reverend led him out of the room and back to the first pew. Marcus and Melina were still talking when the Reverend left Ryan and walked over to them.

"My friends," he said, smiling. "I've just gotten done with my morning counsel with Ryan and would like each of you to join me for a brief moment."

Marcus raised one of his big hands. "No thanks, Reverend."

"It is something we do here every morning. It won't take but a moment and I think you will enjoy it," the Reverend said not giving up.

"Maybe later," Marcus replied.

The Reverend was about to say something more, when Melina jumped in. "We're right in the middle of something Reverend. How about if you come back to us later?"

Bowing his head, the Reverend said, "Certainly."

The Reverend turned and walked to a lonely looking man a few pews back. He said a few words and then led the man into the room Ryan had just left.

"Ryan," Marcus called.

When Ryan made eye contact, Marcus waved him over.

Ryan walked over to his two new friends. "What's up?"

"Melina and I have been discussing our situation here," Marcus told him. "And we think we need to leave."

Ryan was worried, "I want to move on, too, but we can't go anywhere until Vivian feels better."

"I know, but it's more than just her," Marcus said. "There's no way these people can survive here much longer with no food."

Ryan frowned, "I know the meals are little light, but the Reverend seems to be doing a good job rationing food so that everyone can survive until the weather clears."

Melina put a hand on his shoulder. "Ryan, the rain may never stop. Soon the food will run out, and the roads will be completely flooded. Then it will be too late to go anywhere."

"I just don't think Vivian's well enough to travel yet," Ryan pleaded.

"We don't either," Marcus said. "That's why Melina and I are going to go find some more food, and bring it back here."

"What? You can't go," Ryan said, alarmed. Although he had only known Marcus and Melina for a short time, the thought of them leaving sent a wave of panic through his body. "If you take the truck and can't make it back here, we'll be stranded. And who knows if you'll even be able to make it back. The streets have already flooded into rivers."

"If we don't go now," Melina said, "we may miss our chance forever."

"We're not going to go too far," Marcus added. "Just to get food and then we'll be back."

Ryan looked unconvinced.

"We *will* come back for you no matter what happens out there," Melina added. "I promise."

Ryan didn't want them to go. Partially because he didn't want to be left in the church with no way of getting out, but also because he was worried about his new friends. With all they had been through in such a short time, he had come to trust them and now he felt like he needed them. But he also knew they were right. They couldn't last much longer this way.

"All right," Ryan finally said. "Just don't forget about us."

Marcus smiled, "After everything we've been through?"

"Not to worry," Melina added. "We'll be back in no time."

Ryan walked Marcus and Melina to the main doors with Karma following closely behind. The rain was falling with its usual vigor, and the entire area was waterlogged.

They exchanged smiles one last time before Marcus and Melina climbed into the truck and drove down the road, where the water level came up to the middle of the truck's doors. As their tail lights moved away, Karma ran forward barking. She stopped in the middle of the parking lot and watched the truck disappear down the hill.

"They'll be back, girl," Ryan yelled from the door. "I hope . . ."

Karma turned to face Ryan, then back to the departing truck, and then slowly walked back to the church. In the foyer, Karma shook the water from her body and looked up at Ryan.

Ryan found it strange how Karma seemed so unfazed by the rain. Most dogs he had come across in his life had shown some discomfort with being out in the pouring rain. But as he had come to know, this was no ordinary dog.

He pushed the big wooden door of the church closed, looking out one last time where the truck had disappeared. Ryan had the uneasy feeling that he might never see Marcus and Melina again.

CHAPTER 9

The Price of Sanctuary

Ryan felt so alone. Closing the church doors felt like he was sealing his own tomb. He just watched two of the three people he had left in this world drive away into the harsh weather, in the only vehicle they had. Now once Vivian was feeling better, they would have no way of leaving this church unless they felt like walking in the rain, which wasn't too appealing.

It was official: they were stranded.

Following Karma back into the church, Ryan considered the people scattered about the room. The strange faces were so consumed by their own inner turmoil that most of them hadn't even lifted their heads when two of their community members left into the rain. Ryan took no comfort in their company.

Even the Reverend, who seemed like a nice and caring person, did little to sooth Ryan's unrest. No, there was only one person he cared about here, and right now he was going to do everything he could to make sure she made a full recovery.

Ryan walked along the back wall of the church to the left corner, where he found Karma wagging her tail over the same man she had pestered when they first arrived at the church.

"Karma." Ryan whispered loudly.

The man was sitting up, smiling as he pet Karma.

"I'm so sorry," Ryan said. "As you can see, I have no control over her."

"You can't stop a dog from being a dog," the man said. "What's this guy's name?"

"Actually it's a girl," Ryan told him. "And her name is Karma."

"What a beautiful name, for a beautiful dog." The man gave Karma one last rub on the head and then stood to face Ryan. "And how about you? What's your name?"

"I'm Ryan," he said holding out his hand.

The man grasped his hand and shook it firmly. "Pleased to meet you Ryan." He paused and looked down. "And Karma. My name's Leonard, but I prefer Leo. Leonard always feels a bit too formal."

Leo was around fifty years old, an inch or two shorter than Ryan, with hair more gray then black. He carried about twenty extra pounds under a blue short-sleeve collared shirt and black pants, and his welcoming face made Ryan feel like he was good friends with him already.

They released each other's hands but Leo's smile remained. All of the loneliness and isolation Ryan was feeling before seemed to dissolve in Leo's pleasant demeanor.

"Are you here by yourself?" Ryan asked him.

Leo's smile faded. "Yes."

Ryan could see there was pain in his eyes, but didn't feel

comfortable asking for any details. The uncomfortable silence only lasted a moment though.

"How's your friend?" Leo asked.

"She took a hard shot to the head, but I think she'll be fine," Ryan said.

"That's good to hear. Did your other friends leave already?"

"They went in search of more food," Ryan explained. "We have a feeling there's not much left."

Leo shared Ryan's concern. "These people are starving."

Ryan turned and looked around the church. "I'm sure the Reverend is doing everything he can with what he has. Have you known him long?"

Leo shook his head. "No, he's new I guess. Perhaps that's why I don't completely trust him yet."

"Oh? I assumed that Reverend Holmes was the resident clergy here," Ryan said.

"I don't know. Yesterday was my first day back here in a little while and he's not the priest that I'm used to seeing here," Leo said.

"Have you been coming to this church for a long time?" Ryan asked.

"Ever since we moved here from New York. I used to come here every Sunday with my wife and two boys." Leo paused and Ryan saw that the memories hurt him. "Then, about six months ago, a drunk driver took my family away from me. In an instant I lost my entire family, my entire life."

Leo lowered his head. "I lost my faith for a while as I dealt with the loss. It was a hard time for me. Then I realized that life must go on and that the church could be a friend. When the rain came and flooded my home, I knew this was a place I could come. When I arrived, I found Reverend Holmes here. He seems like a nice enough guy, but his sermons are a little weak in substance."

Ryan considered everything Leo had just said. "I'm sorry to hear about your family. But I am glad to know there's a New Yorker close by. I'm from Jersey."

Leo's smile returned. "I already knew that. After living down here for a while, it's easy to pick out a Jersey accent."

"I'll bet it is," Ryan said. "Well, I think I'm going to check on Vivian. Let's talk some more later."

"Sounds good," Leo replied, smiling.

"Come on Karma," Ryan gave the dog a tap on the side and walked down the side aisle. He sat down Indian style next to Vivian and looked down at her sleeping face, while Karma sat beside him.

So many different feelings were swirling inside Ryan. He had become such good friends with Vivian and treasured their relationship over the past three years. Now the circumstances of the last few days had brought them closer than ever before. He wondered why he had never pursued something more when they first met.

It seemed ridiculous to be concentrating on such things when there were so many other problems that required his attention, but he couldn't help it. His mind wouldn't let him move on.

Vivian's eyes slowly opened. Ryan smiled as Vivian stretched and tried to clear the sleep from her head. "Hey there," he said.

Vivian leaned up and received her morning licks from Karma. "Hey, back at you," she said to both of them.

"How are you feeling?" Ryan asked.

"My head's a little spinny and I still feel tired."

"Well, you still need rest," he told her.

"I think I've rested more than I can take." Vivian looked around and yawned. "Where are Melina and Marcus?"

Ryan scratched his head, not knowing how to tell her. "They went out to make a food run."

"What?" she asked. "Did it stop raining?"

"No, but they were concerned about the amount of food left here and decided to take the truck out while they still could."

Concern replaced the sleepiness in Vivian's eyes. "Is that safe?"

"The roads are flooded, but still drivable," Ryan said. "They promised to hurry."

"I hope they'll be all right out there," she said lying back down.

"Not to worry," Ryan told her. "Those two can take care of themselves."

For the next hour Ryan filled Vivian in on everything she had missed while she had been resting. The Reverend came by after the private counsels were finished, to see how Vivian was feeling. He assured Ryan and Vivian that he had spent the night praying for Vivian's speedy recovery, and was grateful that God had been listening.

Ryan told the Reverend that Marcus and Melina had gone out in search of more food. Although he wished them a safe return, he was dismayed that they had not spoken to him first. Then, the Reverend went into another speech about the community and how they should always come to him, so they could decide together what was best for everyone.

That said, the Reverend went to replace some of the candles that had burned out during the night. Before he left, he leaned down and gave Karma a pat on the head. Ryan noticed that Karma leaned her head away as if to avoid his touch. It was very subtle, but after the experience with Mikey, he had learned to watch Karma's reactions to people very carefully. Her reaction wasn't obvious enough for Ryan to become alarmed, just enough for him to take note.

Vivian spent most of the afternoon lying down. She made a few valiant attempts to walk around, but still felt dizzy and her head continued to ache. Ryan and Karma stayed close to her side for most of the day. Periodically, Ryan would open the big church doors and peer out into the rain. The street below was now a river of water. He doubted the pick-up truck carrying Marcus and Melina would be able to get through such deep water. He tried to stay optimistic, but it didn't look good. And the rain showed no signs of slowing.

And so it went for two more days.

The rain never faltered. Outside the church, the street had disappeared and now, even the parking lot was beginning to flood. Soon, the church itself would start to take in water.

Vivian continued to improve with each new day. Her dizziness was gone, and her head only ached at night when she was weary. Their rations were still small, and they were constantly hungry. Due to the never ending rain, at least thirst was never an issue. Every night they placed jugs outside and refilled their drinking water supply.

The Reverend continued his sermons and private counsels. He talked about how they must put their faith in him and trust that he would guide them through this. The Reverend continued to be strong and hopeful, but the people were suffering. As time went on Ryan noticed a change coming over many of their community. With the rain relentlessly pounding down and the food dwindling, the people seemed to be losing their grip on sanity. More than a few spent their entire day kneeling down, muttering prayers over and over again. The only thing they seemed to respond to was Reverend Holmes. They hung on every word of his sermons with desperate anticipation.

They all knew that if the rains didn't stop, they would probably die in the very church that they came to for salvation. The lack of food was wearing them down, and now the only thing left to cling to was the strength of the Reverend. Ryan was afraid to think what would happen if he eventually fell apart too. Although the people were weary and distraught, the Reverend seemed fit and energetic. He never complained of hunger and always kept his appearance neat and together. His spirits were always high, and he never seemed affected by their bleak situation.

Ryan and Vivian were hungry and tired as well, but escaped the overall feeling of despair that plagued the rest of the people. Even though they knew that Marcus and Melina could never make it back, they still had each other. Even Vivian, who had been in a deep depression less than a week ago, managed to keep her spirits up. Instead of clinging to the Reverend, they counted on each other for support. And through it all, Karma was always there. Tail wagging and tongue licking, she never seemed phased by the hysterical people around her.

The three of them were joined by Leo, who at Ryan's request, had brought his limited belongings and sat beside them. He was the only other person who seemed to still have all of his wits about him. They spent the days getting to know one another and talking of better times.

Ryan awoke on the morning of their fourth day in the church to the familiar sound of rain beating against the stained glass windows. He got up slowly, trying not to wake up Vivian, who was nestled amongst a tangle of blankets. Karma was already awake and waiting for their soggy morning walk.

As Ryan stood and stretched, Vivian rolled over and opened her eyes. "If you see the sun anywhere out there, come get me."

"Not likely," Leo said from his pile of blankets.

Ryan walked over him with Karma close behind. "Sit tight. I'll be right back with today's weather report."

The walk to the church doors every morning was always nerve-wracking. He could feel his heart beating faster as he approached the two wooden doors. As always, he held his breath as he swung the big door open and got his first view of the water level. Ryan always held out some small hope that even though it was still pouring, today he might actually see the street again. Even though he knew deep down that it was an impossible dream, he still hoped.

This morning, like the others, carried the familiar sting of disappointment. Upon opening the door he found that the outside water level was right at the door. If the water rose any higher, the church would begin to take in water. Unfazed, Karma stepped out into the rain and went about her morning business. Even though she sloshed through water up to her belly, she walked around as if she didn't notice it.

Watching Karma from the doorway, Ryan was struck by how quickly he had bonded with the dog. He and Karma had only been together for about a week, but they behaved like they had known each other for years. With the exception of that first night he found her at his doorstep, Karma had never been on a leash, yet no matter what was going on, she stayed close to Ryan.

Ryan had a few friends with dogs, who over the years had become very attached to them. He and Karma had developed that same connection in a fraction of the time. It was hard to believe that something like that was possible, but Karma was definitely not your average dog.

After she had finished her walk, Karma came back into the church foyer, and as was becoming her ritual, shook herself off and looked up at Ryan.

Ryan smiled down at her. "You don't know how lucky you are Karma. It must be nice to have no worries."

Karma tilted her head quizzically. He closed the door and led Karma back to Vivian and Leo, who were sitting on the floor talking as Ryan approached.

"You're never going to believe this, but it looks like rain for today, with a good chance of rain, followed by some rain," he said, sitting in the first pew.

"How much longer do you think we have before we get wet?" Vivian had to ask.

"Not long at all," Ryan replied.

"What are we going to do?" Vivian asked, not expecting an answer.

Leo frowned. "The old me would have told you that God will show us the way, but now I'm beginning to think that he must be a little angry with us."

"Careful," Ryan said. "Don't let this group hear you talk like that. You'll start a riot."

The Reverend and his two helpers passed out the morning's meal with their usual zeal. Today's banquet consisted of a piece of pound cake and water. The food was merely a tease to Ryan's stomach and just seemed to make him hungrier.

Ryan watched the two men helping the Reverend. Their names were Jerry and Carl. Jerry was about thirty years old, with a thick, stocky build that made it obvious he was no stranger to physical activity. Long brown hair slightly covered his white, freckled face and a bushy mustache sat on his top lip. His partner Carl was a tall black man, close to forty years old with a thin build, clean shaven face and bald head. He must have suffered some kind of injury because he walked with a slight limp.

Both men seemed to be holding up rather well, compared to everyone else. They didn't have the weak, desperate appearance of the other church-goers. Ryan started to wonder if they might be sneaking extra food for themselves. The Reverend seemed to trust them enough to let them have access and distribute the food, but could they really resist the screams of hunger while they divided up the days meals?

There was something else strange about these two men. Ryan rarely saw them. They didn't sleep out in the nave with everyone else and rarely spoke to the other people in the church. They also seemed to have a few changes of clothes available. Every day they were wearing something different. Today Jerry wore a black fleece pullover and jeans, while Carl was dressed in tan cargo pants and a Louisville Zoo t-shirt.

Ryan couldn't believe he hadn't noticed it earlier. The shirt was one that Melina had packed in their bag before they left the zoo. Were they just taking what they needed or greedily helping themselves to the community's shared belongings? Ryan wondered if the Reverend realized what was going on. Ryan decided he would have to have a little talk with the good Reverend about his two trusty helpers.

That thought would have to wait, because now it was time for the Reverend's morning sermon. Standing in the center of the sanctuary in his white robe, the Reverend waited as his disciples gathered in the first few pews. Many of the candles had burned out and they had apparently run out of new ones, because the Reverend had stopped replacing them. The dim lighting cast long shadows and made the Reverend appear ominous.

"My children," he began. "I hope the morning finds you in good spirits despite our situation. A new day brings new possibilities. Do not despair, for as the hour grows dark, our will must remain strong. We will still persevere.

"It once rained for forty days and forty nights. Noah, in his ark, could have given in to despair. He could have doubted the Lord. But he did not! He trusted in God, did as he was instructed and was given the grace of the Lord.

"You may ask yourself, why should I go on? And I am here to tell you that everyone here needs you. I need you, this community needs you, and God needs you. Our day of redemption is almost upon us. I can feel it. God has shown it to me. It will get dark, but the dawn will be glorious.

"So I ask you, my brothers and sisters, do you believe in God?"

"Yes!" the crowd replied loudly.

"Do you believe in me?"

"Yes!" they screamed.

"And I believe in you!" the Reverend yelled back at them. "Together we will survive the rain. Together we will make it to tomorrow. We may have to sacrifice to get there, but we will make it. And if the Lord asks you to sacrifice, you must be ready. Keep your faith strong and He will make it known what is expected of you. And if you love Him, and you believe in Him, your prayers will be answered. And through it all, I will be here to guide you. Because I am here for you, as God is for us all."

The Reverend paused to let his words sink into the desperate faces before him. Then he bowed his head and said, "Let us now commence the morning's private counseling. I feel that today's sessions are particularly important, so please be ready to speak your mind and bare your soul."

Then he walked into the counseling room and shut the door. A second later, a haggard looking woman walked quickly to the door and knocked. She was probably in the neighborhood of forty years old, but now appeared much older. She seemed to have aged ten years since Ryan had arrived at the church. Leo had told him that her name was Abby. She had gotten separated from her husband during the beginning of the rains, and has been praying for his return ever since. She was very distraught and her eyes appeared more vacant every day. Abby spoke to no one but Reverend Holmes and spent her days praying intently.

The Reverend must have told her to enter, because she went inside, closing the door behind her.

"Ryan," Vivian said from her spot on the floor.

Ryan immediately noticed the troubled look on her face. She came over and sat beside him in the first pew.

"What are we going to do?" she asked.

"I'm not sure," he told her. "We don't have a lot of choices."

Vivian dropped her head and took his hand. "I'm scared."

"I know. I am, too," Ryan said in a soft voice. "I'm working on thinking of some possibilities for us."

Vivian tilted her head toward him.

"Assuming that the rain doesn't stop, we are going to need to float or swim out of here," Ryan continued. "I've been looking around outside and this seems to be the highest place in the immediate area. So there may not be too many places that will be dryer than here. But soon we're going to have no choice, but to risk it. We'll have to find something around here that will float and hope for the best."

"What about Karma?" she asked.

Ryan looked down at the sleeping dog. She was curled up in a pile of blankets breathing deeply.

"I don't know," he said somberly. "She's only been in my life a short time, but I've really come to love her. I won't leave her. We'll find a way."

Ryan lifted his gaze from the dog and turned back to Vivian. She was staring at him intently, her face soft and calm. Slowly, she reached up and put her hand on the side of his face. Then, she gently leaned in and lightly pressed her lips against his.

Her lips were soft and warm, and Ryan's pulse quickened as she kissed him. Vivian slowly pulled back and gazed into his eyes. Ryan's mind was spinning as he tried to figure out what to say.

Before he got a chance, Vivian leaned in and kissed him again. This time, grabbing his shoulder and pulling him into her. It was a much more passionate kiss, and although Ryan was hesitant at first, he soon gave into the moment.

When they finally separated, Vivian found his hand again and held it firmly. Ryan's head felt clouded as he struggled to sort out his feelings.

"Thank you," he heard himself say.

Vivian smiled at him. "I'm sorry if I surprised you, but it's just something I had to do. Something I've wanted to do for the past couple of days, and I guess I just couldn't take it any longer."

Ryan thought for a moment, trying to organize his thoughts. "I'd be lying if I said I haven't thought about kissing you. But I'm not sure it's the right thing for us to do. You've been on an emotional rollercoaster these past few weeks, and are obviously trying to deal with some serious feelings." Ryan paused, taking a deep breath. "And I think you may just be getting caught up in the moment. I mean, we've been through so much these last few days, and I think it may be the trouble and turmoil of our situation that is drawing us together. Once things calm down, you may find you feel differently."

"Ryan, I've always been attracted to you," Vivian told him. "When you first moved in, I used to look across the courtyard to your apartment and wonder what you were doing. When you would tell me about a girl you were dating, I would think how lucky she was, but I never acted on my feelings. We had become such good friends, and I was afraid to jeopardize our relationship. Even when I was with Brad, my mind would still return to you. Looking back on it now I realize that I probably wasn't even in love with him. I just wanted to be loved by someone, even if he wasn't the right person for me. And when Brad left me, I was devastated. Not because I loved him, but because no one loved me."

Vivian wrapped both her hands around his. "You have been, and continue to be, here for me. And my feelings for you have always been strong. Besides, it seems like we'll have plenty of trouble and turmoil ahead to keep us going."

Ryan had to agree. He squeezed her hand and gave her a kiss on the cheek.

Not wanting to be left out, Karma ran over, put one front paw on each of their legs and delivered licks to both of them.

"I guess we're just one big happy family," Vivian said, rubbing Karma's head.

Ryan got up and gave both his girls a wink. "I'm going to run to the bathroom."

He walked past Leo, who flashed him a quick smile, and into the room that held the piles of clothing. He was just about to enter the bathroom when he heard muffled voices.

Ryan paused and looked back. The voices were coming from behind the opposite wall. He walked over and leaned his head in close to the wall. He could faintly hear two voices. One was a bit deeper than the other, so Ryan assumed it was a male and a female talking to each other.

Thinking for a moment, Ryan realized the Reverend's counseling chamber was on the other side of the wall. The voices must belong to the Reverend and Abby. Feeling like he was intruding on their privacy, he turned and headed back toward the bathroom. He was at the door again when a sound stopped him.

Going back to the wall, he leaned in and tried to make out the sound. Ryan couldn't be positive, but it sounded like the Reverend was moaning. The moans seemed to increase in intensity and frequency, before they suddenly stopped. There was silence for second or two and then some brief conversation then silence again.

Forgetting the bathroom, Ryan went back out into the church in time to see Abby quietly walking back to her usual spot in the fourth pew. Her shirt was hanging outside her black pants, and Ryan was pretty sure it had been tucked in when she had entered the counseling room.

Ryan didn't know what to do. He wanted to run right over and confront the Reverend, but he wasn't one hundred percent sure what had happened. There was only one other person who could tell him what the Reverend was up to.

Ryan walked to the fourth pew and sat down next to Abby. She looked at him, confused.

"Hi," Ryan said, not knowing how to proceed. "My name's Ryan."

Abby just stared at him blankly.

"I just thought I would introduce myself and see how you were doing," Ryan continued.

"Leave me alone," was all she said.

"How are you holding up?" Ryan proceeded anyway.

"Fine," she replied. "Now go away."

Abby wasn't exactly warming up to him, so Ryan decided to be blunt. "I know what you're doing with the Reverend."

Abby's expression changed to alarm, but there was also guilt in her eyes.

"It's okay," he said. "I'm not judging you. I just want to know how it happened."

"I don't know what you're talking about," Abby said, looked around to see if anyone was listening in.

"Abby, you can trust me. Tell me what happened."

"Get away from me," she slid down the pew a few feet, her eyes beginning to water.

"Did he force himself on you?" Ryan asked, after he scooted over to her.

"Stop asking me questions. You can't help me or him," she whispered angrily.

"I don't think the Reverend needs any help. He seems to be doing very well for himself."

Abby looked annoyed. "Not the Reverend, you idiot, my husband. I know he's out there somewhere and I need him to find me. I've prayed so hard for God to show him the way, but it hasn't worked. The Reverend is helping me to get God's attention. By sacrificing my body to the Reverend, God will see that I'm willing lay down myself for the safe return of my husband. He will see how much I love him and lead him back to me."

Abby's eyes were wide, but she seemed detached from her words.

"Now leave me alone and stop interfering with my prayers," she snapped.

Realizing that Abby's mental state had deteriorated some time ago, and that she was no longer thinking in a rational way, Ryan got up and walked back to the first pew where Vivian was talking to Leo.

"Are you all right?" Vivian asked him. "You look a little funny."

Ryan didn't know where to begin or how much to tell them. He decided to just tell them everything. Beginning with his suspicions about Jerry and Carl and finishing with his conversation with Abby.

Vivian was stunned. "I can't believe the Reverend would do something like that."

"I knew there was something not quite right about him," Leo declared.

"The big question is, what do we do about it?" Ryan said.

None of them seemed to have a good answer.

They sat in silence for a moment, then Leo calmly stated. "We do nothing."

Ryan and Vivian both stared at him, surprised.

"I know it sounds callous, but what does it matter now?" Leo continued. "Very soon we're all going to be swimming for our lives. You yourself said that we don't have much time. These people don't have much left. If we expose Reverend Holmes, we take away the only thing they have left: their faith. If they're going to die, let's let them die still believing in something."

Ryan didn't like letting the Reverend off the hook so easily, but Leo did have a good point. And so they said nothing and went about the day trying to pretend that this new information wasn't bothering them. They decided that it would be best if they skipped their morning counseling. None of them wanted to be that close to the Reverend again.

After the midday rations, the Reverend retired to his chambers. Ryan wondered exactly what he did in there all day by himself. Was he so ashamed of his deeds that he couldn't face his "community?" Somehow Ryan doubted that.

Somewhere around mid-afternoon the three friends were sitting with Karma under the Virgin Mary statue, trying to decide on a plan of action, when the time came to flee the church.

A shrill cry from the back of the church caused everyone to turn. Ryan saw Rebecca, the old woman Marcus and Melina had introduced him to, running down the center aisle toward the altar.

Ryan caught her as she reached the first pew. "What's wrong Rebecca?"

"The water seeks us," she wailed. "It's coming for us!"

Ryan looked over her shoulder to the foyer. Water seeped under the doors and was streaming into the church.

Next to Ryan, Karma barked.

This was not good.

"We've got to get organized," Ryan told Vivian and Leo. "I'm getting the Reverend, and we're going to get everyone together."

Ryan ran up the sanctuary steps and burst into the Reverend's chambers. Reverend Holmes was reclining in a big wooden chair with his feet up on the desk in front of him. His white robe was open down the middle exposing a gray shirt coving a small pot belly. The not-so-good reverend was spooning food in his mouth from an open soup can. On the desk in front of him were a number of snacks including a candy wrapper, an open bag of chips and a half eaten box of cookies.

Startled by Ryan's harsh entry, he sat up quickly, spilling a spoonful of soup on his lap.

"Ugh . . . Brother Ryan," he stammered. "What ever happened to knocking?"

Ryan walked into the room and noticed there were bags full of food behind the desk. He was speechless. But only for a second.

"You son of a bitch," he said.

Jerry came running into the room behind Ryan and grabbed him hard by the arm. "You're not supposed to be in here."

"It's okay, Jerry," the Reverend said, regaining his composure. "Please, leave us. Brother Ryan and I need to discuss a few things."

Jerry roughly let go of Ryan's arm. "I'll be right outside if you need me," he said, sneering at Ryan as he closed the door.

"Brother Ryan, I know how this must look -"

"Don't call me your brother ever again," Ryan told him. "Everyone out there is starving, and you're in here stuffing your face."

"Rationing the food is important. But I need my strength to

lead these people," the Reverend explained.

"Bullshit!" Ryan was enraged. "These people trusted you. They put their faith in you, and you lied to them. You selfish bastard."

"I have given hope to the hopeless!" the Reverend shouted, as he stood up and walked up to Ryan. "These pathetic fools were cowering in the corner when I got here. They were ready to give up and die. I stepped in and gave them a reason to go on living. Isn't that worth some food?"

Ryan was starting to put everything together. "You wanted them to be weak. You needed weak minds and weak bodies so that they would be easily swayed to your thinking."

"Ryan, let's just calm down," the Reverend said nervously.

Ryan ignored him. "That's it, isn't it? Weak minds are more likely to do what you tell them. That's how you persuaded Abby to have sex with you. You used her faith in God and love for her husband to have your way with her."

The Reverend seemed panicked. "I . . . gave them hope . . . kept them alive." The Reverend reached out and took hold of Ryan's shoulders. "I did what I had to in these troubled times."

Ryan pushed him away hard. The Reverend stumbled back and fell on the floor.

"God only knows what other sick acts you made these poor people commit. There's nothing holy about you."

On the floor the Reverend looked pathetic. With all of his poise and rhetoric gone, he was nothing but a slimy con artist.

"Listen," he said, climbing to his feet. "I've done wrong. I know it. But I'm tired of the lies as much as you are. What would you have me do? Confess? Fine, I'll tell them everything. They might as well know the truth before we all die."

That last sentence made Ryan remember why he had come to the Reverend in the first place.

The Reverend was still speaking. "I want to make things right. But please let me explain myself to them. Even though I haven't been fair with them, they do have faith in me. I'm not asking for leniency; I just want them to hear it from me."

Ryan didn't want to give the Reverend any breaks, but they had more important things to take care of.

"Reverend today is your lucky day," Ryan said. "I'm going to let you talk to them one last time. But only because, for some unknown reason, they respond to you. The church is taking in water and we don't have much time. I need you to get these people organized so we can build some kind of a makeshift raft."

The Reverend thought for a moment and then nodded. "Okay, I can do that. No matter what you think, I really do care about those people out there. Just give me a minute to collect my thoughts and then I'll be right out."

Ryan left the room, pushed past Jerry and joined his friends at the first pew.

The people in the church were getting hysterical. An inch of water covered the floor, and everyone was standing on the pews screaming prayers toward the altar. Most had carried their limited possessions with them, piling them up in the pews beside them. The ever-constant rain drumming on the stained glass windows combined with the cries of the church-goers created an almost musical rhythm.

Karma was barking up at Ryan as he looked around the church for anything that might float. Leo and Vivian, who had been unsuccessfully trying to calm some of the people down, soon returned to Ryan's side.

"They've lost it," Vivian said.

"The water coming into the church has cut the last thread of their sanity," Leo added. "The one place they counted on to be safe is now gone. They have nothing left."

Finally, the Reverend came out. He stopped and said something to Jerry and Carl, who were waiting for him outside his chambers, and then turned to his audience.

"Reverend!" a middle aged man yelled. "Help us!"

The Reverend held out his hands. "My children, hear me," he said loudly over the commotion. "It seems that the rains continue and have now entered our sanctuary. We have prayed and suffered all these days and still God has shown us no mercy. This does not mean He has not heard us! Everything has happened for a reason. We have just not realized its purpose. But, He has made it known to me!

"When Noah was told to make his ark, the Lord told him He would make rain fall on the Earth like never before. He said He was doing this to wash away the sins of man! He was cleansing the Earth of evil to save the good. Once the evil was vanquished, the rains ceased and the world was reborn!"

The water level in the church was rising inexplicably fast. Ryan, Vivian and Leo, standing in the front, glanced down to see the water climbing up their legs. Everyone else was standing on the pews, as if they were afraid to let the water touch them. Ryan hoped the Reverend would get to the point soon. Karma was barking her head off, as the water reached her belly.

The Reverend continued over the noise, "We now find ourselves in the same position. The rains are upon us and evil is being washed away. But we have no ark to keep us safe - only each other. So we must work together! Together we can survive this day! The world has become impure and evil must be destroyed before the world can be reborn! I ask you, do you believe in the Lord?"

"Yes!" the mob screamed.

"Will you do His bidding without question?" the Reverend yelled.

"Yes!" came the reply.

"What must we do?" shouted the middle aged man.

The Reverend paused for a moment, while Karma continued to bark at him. "God will not answer our prayers until the evil on this planet is gone forever. The rains will not stop until His will is done! We have the power to end this today! For evil is among us in this very church! There!" The Reverend thrust his arm toward Ryan and his companions. "There is the evil among us! Those who lie down with the beasts! They are impure and God will not stop the rains until they have been washed away from this Earth! They must be sacrificed! Kill them!"

Ryan didn't think it was possible, but things just got a whole lot worse.

CHAPTER 10

The Rise and Fall of The Reverend

Ryan, Vivian and Leo stared in disbelief, as the assembled people of the church charged toward them. With mindless abandon, they clawed and lunged over the pews. Although Ryan didn't regularly attend church, he was pretty sure this was not part of the normal service.

Meanwhile, the Reverend, Jerry and Carl ran down the far aisle. Ryan was about to say something to the charging crowd but saw the crazed insanity in their eyes and knew there would be no reasoning with them. They seemed to have gotten over their fear of the water, because most of them had thrown themselves off the pews without a second thought and were now vigorously splashing forward.

Ryan cautiously stepped back as the mob closed in. Vivian and Leo, behind Ryan, soon found themselves up against the wall. When he finally bumped into Vivian, Ryan turned and realized their location. They were backed into the front left corner of the church next to the Virgin Mary statue. The door leading to the bathroom was right behind them, but Ryan knew that was a dead end and the window in the bathroom was much too small to climb out of.

Trapped in a corner was not a good place to be. A bark from Karma turned Ryan toward the side aisle. She was halfway down the aisle looking back at him.

"Follow me," Ryan yelled over his shoulder, as a flailing hand reached for his head.

The hand belonged to Abby. With anger in her eyes she scratched at his face. "Give me my husband back!"

Ryan threw his weight forward and knocked Abby back into the next hysterical woman who was charging for them.

Luckily, the people were totally unorganized. They were all coming from the same direction, causing them to bump into one another and slow their progress.

Ryan ran through the rising water in the side aisle with Vivian and Leo close behind. The middle-aged man who had spoken up earlier jumped off a pew and threw himself at the fleeing friends. His outstretched hands managed to grab Leo's leg as he fell into the water. Leo let out a yell as he fell forward, but managed to get up quickly as his attacker fumbled to stand.

A loud sound stopped everyone in their tracks. It took Ryan a moment to figure out the sound was actually the wail of the church organ located on the balcony above the foyer. Someone was up there playing it very badly. Looking up, Ryan saw the Reverend standing in the middle of the balcony next to the organ pipes, sneering.

Pointing down at Ryan, he yelled over the organ, "The sinners must perish now! The Lord demands justice!"

His words sparked the people to action with renewed energy.

The water had now risen up to their knees and slowed their progress, but not their rage.

Karma was barking once again, as she hopped through the water to the back of the church. Ryan pushed Leo and Vivian forward, while he met the next crazed church patron.

A man in his fifties swung his fists wildly at Ryan screaming unintelligibly. Ryan's patience with these people had long since gone. He cocked his arm back and punched the old man in the face, sending him backward into the nearest pew.

Not waiting to see who was coming next, Ryan ran after his friends. He reached them as they turned into the foyer. Karma was at the front doors of the church with her front paws up on the door, while the organ music continued to play overhead.

The three friends pulled at the doors, but could only get them to open an inch or so.

"It's stuck," Vivian said, pulling.

Ryan realized that the rising water was providing too much resistance for the doors to fully open. And even if they did manage to get the doors open, where would they go?

The splashing bodies behind them were closing in once again. And as usual, Karma led the way. She hopped up the stairs to the right, her head just above the water. Ryan grabbed Vivian and sloshed after Karma, with Leo right behind him. The stairs leveled off at a landing where they made a one hundred and eighty degree turn and went up again to the balcony. Ryan made the turn and was almost to the top when he realized that Leo was no longer behind him.

"Leo!" Ryan shouted, as he turned and headed back down the stairs.

Ryan reached the landing and looked down the stairs. The mob was crowded at the base of the stairs where two men were holding Leo's struggling body underwater. Leo's arms were swinging wildly, as he desperately reached up.

Ryan knew he had to act fast. He came down two steps, grabbed a hold of the banister on each side of the stairway and threw himself forward, feet first. He hit one of the men solidly in the temple and the other the shoulder. Both of them were sent backward into the water, crashing into the mass of advancing church patrons. Ryan's momentum sent him over Leo's body where he landed on his feet in the water. Turning, he quickly pulled Leo up.

Leo coughed out some water then gulped a lungful of air. Ryan grabbed hold of him and they both scrambled up the stairs. They met Vivian and Karma on the stairs, and they all ran up to the balcony together.

The balcony ran the full length of the church, but was only as wide as the foyer. The stairs on either side of the church's main doors led up to the balcony. Against the railing overlooking the church was a small organ, where Carl sat playing an off key tune. The Reverend and Jerry stood on each side of the organ watching the scene below. Directly behind them on the front wall of the church was the big round stained glass window.

Before they could notice him, Ryan ran forward, put an arm around the Reverend's neck and backed him to the stained glass window where Vivian, Leo, and Karma were already waiting. Carl stopped his playing and turned with Jerry toward the group.

Just then, a few people made it up the stairs, stopping short at the sight of the Reverend in such a compromising position.

"The Reverend has been lying to you," Ryan said to the panting few who had made it up the stairs. "He's been giving you small morsels of food, while he eats like a king in the back room."

"Don't believe him. He's evil," the Reverend said, but then Ryan tightened his grip and silenced any further comments.

The people looked confused, but unconvinced. Carl and Jerry hesitated for a second, and then started advancing forward.

Carl smiled, "Let's usher these sinners to hell."

They only got a step or two before Karma ran in front of Ryan snarling. She bared her teeth and barked threateningly, stopping the two men in their tracks.

"Get rid of this dog, will you Jerry." Carl said, not taking his eyes off Karma.

When Jerry didn't move, Carl turned toward him and saw fear in his eyes. "What the hell's the matter with you, it's just a dog," he said.

"I'm afraid of dogs," Jerry quietly said.

"You've got to be kidding me!" Carl said, and started forward.

Karma growled and snapped at him causing both men to back up against the organ.

For a moment nobody moved or said a word. Then a voice from below broke the silence.

"Everybody!"

It was Rebecca yelling from the altar. She was holding one of the bags of food from the Reverend's chambers. "I found all of this food back here. He's been hiding it from us."

The people gathered on the stairs looked from Rebecca to the Reverend, unsure of what to make of all of this.

Ryan let out a deep breath, relieved that the people of the church finally knew the truth. Unfortunately, the feeling only lasted a few seconds.

"They're all in this together. They're all evil!" Rebecca screeched. "We must get rid of all of them! Only then will we be saved! Kill them all!"

"What?!" Vivian cried in horror, as the group at the top of the stairs surged toward them.

Ryan pushed the Reverend into the rushing people and ran to the other stairway, where Karma was already heading down. Apparently, the irrational mob hadn't thought about charging up both sets of stairs. Ryan started down the stairs, but Vivian was grabbed by Jerry before she could follow.

Jerry had her by the shoulders and pulled her in close to his face. "Where do you think you're going?"

Vivian got her footing and threw her knee upward with all her might. Jerry let out a pained groan as soon as the knee connected with his groin, and he dropped to the floor.

"Nice shot," Leo said, as they ran down the stairs.

Ryan and Karma made the turn on the landing and were coming down the last flight of water-covered stairs when the church doors exploded inward. The concussion sent Ryan diving back for cover.

When he raised his wet head he saw the bow of a boat sticking through the cracked doors. Ryan heard the roar of the boat's engine as it backed out of the doorway.

Karma jumped from the middle of the steps, plunged into the water, and swam out the doors. Ryan, Vivian and Leo followed. The water was now up to their waists as they waded through the splintered doors. Most of the church people must have filed up the opposite staircase, because they were able to get out without any further resistance.

Once outside, Ryan was almost knocked over by the boat as it idled in front of the church. The boat was about forty feet long with a blue underside and white topside.

Ryan led the others around the bow of the boat. As they made their way to the back, they saw Karma being lifted into the boat by a pair of big hands. When they finally reached the small platform at the back of the boat, they saw the welcome sight of Marcus standing above them. He reached out and helped each of them into the boat.

The boat appeared to be a small yacht, complete with seating for ten, a covered cockpit and a few rooms below. A metal railing wrapped around the bow of the boat and ended in the middle of each side.

"Welcome aboard," Melina said from the driver's seat.

"What'd we miss?" Marcus added.

A crash from above sent pieces of stained glass down on the boat, as the Reverend's body thrust through the big round window and landed on top of Ryan. The Reverend beat his fists down on Ryan screaming, "You've ruined everything! I'll kill you all!"

Marcus picked up the Reverend and threw him roughly on the other side of the deck, where he lay crumpled in a heap.

Ryan had the breath knocked out of him, but he was otherwise okay. Vivian was helping him to his feet when a chair fell from above and hit the bow of the boat.

Up above, they saw the crazed community of the church screaming down at them through the big broken window.

"Get us the hell out of here!" Ryan yelled to Melina in the cockpit.

She hit the throttle and they sped away through the half

submerged trees, as the church people threw things from above.

Ryan held on to the side of the boat, trying to catch his breath and regain his composure. He sat on a cushioned seat and raised his head to the sky.

It wasn't raining. He must have been so consumed with their hurried escape from the church he hadn't realized the rain had finally stopped. Clouds still covered the sky, but the lack of rain gave him hope. Even though his clothes were soaking wet, the dry air felt good.

Ryan looked down at the Reverend curled up on the floor. Bending down, Ryan lifted the man upright. The Reverend was still wearing his oversized white robe, but it was now wet and streaked with blood, pieces of stained glass and dirt. His hair that was always so neat was now a matted mess, and his face was covered with cuts from his jump through the window.

"You make me sick," Ryan said, disgusted.

"We should have left him with those weak minded lunatics," Vivian added.

The Reverend wiped blood from his eyes, "I did what I had to do to survive."

"You took advantage of those poor desperate people and then tried to kill us!" Vivian shot back.

"Are you even a real reverend?" Ryan yelled down at him.

The Reverend turned away.

"Are you!?" Ryan yelled again.

"All right! I'm not a reverend," the man on the floor said. "Are you happy? I came to the church to get out of the rain with Jerry and Carl. We saw the shape these people were in and could see that they were just waiting to die. Someone had to take charge. I just provided them with a leader. Trust me, those people would have been long gone if I hadn't come along. They needed something to believe in and I gave it to them. And they loved me for it. Hell, they worshipped me!"

"That's why your sermons sounded so cheesy," Leo said. "I always thought you were a little too TV evangelist."

"Is Holmes even your name?" Ryan demanded.

"No," he said. "My real name is Harold Feeney. I just thought Holmes was a nice warm name that people would trust."

Ryan felt outraged by the matter-of-fact way in which Harold spoke about what he had done. "You cowardly bastard. They *did* trust you. And you toyed with that trust." He paused, and then said, "And you used it to stuff your face with their food and have your way with grieving women like Abby!"

Ryan finished his statement with a kick to Harold's side, causing him to roll over and cover his head with his hands.

When no more kicks came he lowered his arms and looked up timidly. "I was scared and thought we were all going to die. So, I decided to have a little fun before I did. Is that so wrong? Come on, I'm only human."

That last statement stole Ryan's desire to argue. Only human. He never realized how much of an insult that statement could be. He thought about all of the horrible statistics that Melina had told them a few days ago. In his mind, Ryan pictured two animals talking to each other about all the horrible injustices man has done to the planet and saying, "Hey, what do you expect, they're only human." It seemed like such an insult. Only human.

Looking down at the ex-Reverend in his dirty, blood stained robe, Ryan couldn't be more ashamed to be human. He shook his head and turned around, unable to stand the sight of him anymore.

Melina, who had been navigating the boat around trees, houses, and other obstacles, finally killed the engine. The boat slowed and finally floated leisurely next to a large, partially submerged building.

She came out from behind the seats that separated the cockpit from back deck and stood next to Marcus, who was struggling to piece together what must have happened to his friends.

"So, what are we going to do with him?" Leo asked.

Harold squirmed around on the floor and muttered, "They worshipped me . . . and you ruined it . . . ."

Ryan turned back toward him and was about to say something when Harold sprung up at him and screamed, "You ruined it!"

Harold swung his arms wildly as he lunged at Ryan. Instinctively, Ryan ducked down, bending at the waist. Harold struck Ryan's body, his momentum leaning him over Ryan's back. Ryan stood up fast, and flung Harold over his back and into the water.

Harold's body hit the dark water with a dull splash, spraying water onto the deck. Ryan looked down at the drops of water that had landed on his arm. It was inky black.

In the water Harold broke the surface and gasped for breath. Thick black liquid dripped down his face leaving muddy streaks.

"Help me!" he cried as he thrashed about.

Ryan thought for a second and said, "Oh hell." Then leaned over the side of the boat and reached out for him.

The black water seemed to be weighing Harold down because his movements were very slow and he was having trouble keeping his head above water. Ryan's hand was a few inches from Harold's black coated fingers. He tried to stretch a little further, but his pants were stuck on something in the boat, stopping him from getting any closer.

Harold let out a final gargled cry as his head slipped beneath the surface. The last thing anyone ever saw of Harold Feeney was a robed hand slowly disappearing into the black water.

Ryan leaned back into the boat, reaching around to untangle his pants and found that his pants weren't actually caught on something. Something had caught him.

Karma had a mouthful of his pants at the left knee and had been pulling hard. The dog let go as Ryan straightened up.

"Wow, she really had a good hold on you," Leo said.

"Yeah, but was she making sure Ryan didn't fall in?" Vivian asked. "Or making sure he didn't reach that bastard?"

Ryan bent down and looked into the dogs eyes. They seemed so innocent.

"Some questions are better left unanswered," Melina said.

"What's wrong with the water?" Marcus asked, peering over the side of the boat.

"That," Melina said pointing at the half submerged building next to the boat.

In big black letters the words 'Essex Petroleum' could be seen just above the water line.

"That's pretty gross," Vivian said.

"Oil floats on water and spreads out quickly," Melina told them. "This is nothing. In 1989 when the Exxon Valdez ran aground in Alaska, it spilled about eleven million gallons of oil into the water. The impact on the environment was massive. Even now, over three decades later, the effects can still be seen."

Vivian shook her head. "That's horrible."

Ryan stared down at the black surface of the water. "Let's get out of here."

Melina returned to the cockpit and started the engine.

Once they were moving again, Ryan said, "Nice boat you got here."

"She's a beauty, isn't she?" Marcus said, smiling with pride. "You have the pleasure of riding in a Sea Ray 390 Sundancer Sports Yacht. I always wanted one of these beauties."

"Very nice," Vivian said. "Where did you get it?"

"The Gulf of Mexico," he calmly replied.

"Are you kidding?" Ryan said in disbelief. "The Gulf of Mexico has got to be five hundred miles from here!"

"Not anymore."

"What?" Vivian stammered. "Wait, what happened to you guys? We were afraid we'd never see you again."

"Well, I'll tell you," Marcus began. "Going out for food was not as easy as we had hoped. We didn't know where we were going and we didn't see any place that would have food. Finally, we came to a busted up supermarket and loaded up. The problem was that most of the roads were flooded. So, we just went whatever way was drivable and hoped that we'd be able to get back to you.

"It was not a fun ride. But that woman," he gestured to Melina, "can drive. I mean really drive. There were times I thought we were dead for sure, but she somehow steered us clear. We drove until the water finally overtook the truck. We were lucky enough to get out and climb into a high office building before it filled up. We even managed to save most of the food. Not knowing what to do next, we just waited.

"The next morning we saw all these boats floating by. Sail boats, catamarans, speed boats, big boats, little boats – you name it. There's not too many bodies of water around here that are large enough for some of those boats, and a bunch were definitely ocean vessels. They must have washed in from the Gulf."

"Anyway," Marcus continued. "When I saw this baby coming, I couldn't resist. So, we loaded up and made our way back to you. We had a bit of a hard time finding you though. The water was rising so fast that all of our visual landmarks were underwater. We've been looking for you for a day and a half."

"That's one hell of a tale," Leo said.

"Well, thank God you got to us when you did," Ryan said. "I thought we were done for."

Melina turned and asked, "Where to, gang?"

Nobody really had an answer. After a brief discussion, they agreed to head west and see what kind of condition the other half of the United States was in.

Ryan filled Marcus and Melina in on everything that happened at the church. Since they had separated, both groups had been through so much that it was exhausting just talking about it.

The day remained gray, but the lack of rain made everyone feel somewhat cheerful. Melina and Marcus stayed in the cockpit, using the boat's compass to keep them heading westward. Ryan sat in the back with Karma at his feet, while Leo and Vivian made small talk next to him. Watching the boat go around half submerged trees and houses was a surreal sight. He wondered how long it would take for all this water to drain away somewhere, be absorbed by the Earth or evaporate.

Soon they all remembered how hungry they were and went below to fill their bellies. The kitchen, or galley as Marcus corrected them, had everything you could ask for: coffee maker, refrigerator, freezer, stove and even utensils. Since the boat had its own power supply they were treated to electricity and fresh food that had been left in the refrigerator. The freezer contained hamburgers and chicken. Marcus quickly fried up some burgers and they had the best meal since their adventure began.

No one wanted to think about the reality of their situation. They were sailing across a seemingly endless sea of water with no real land in sight and no hope for the future. Instead, they tried to focus on the fact that the rain had stopped, they had plenty of food, a place to sleep (four of them even got beds) and even the luxury of electricity. If it were any other time, they would feel like they were on vacation.

They traveled like this for two days. Marcus and Melina had done a good job stocking the boat with extra gasoline, so stopping for fuel wasn't an issue yet. They would spend their days scanning the horizon in search of dry land, and at night they would anchor the boat to a tree or house. They got to know each other pretty well. With nothing to do but talk, they learned about each other's childhood, families, hopes and fears. The conversations on the boat brought them even closer together.

Clouds continued to blanket the sky, but no more rain fell. The water level was slowly dropping, exposing soggy trees, buildings, and houses. Although they were living better than they had at the church or the zoo, by their second night afloat they were all yearning for the sight of land.

The next morning Ryan was sleeping soundly next to Vivian in one of the beds, with Karma curled up between them. Just after sunrise, Karma jerked up, sniffing the air. Before Ryan could fully open his eyes, Karma jumped off the bed, barking all the way up to the deck.

Soon, everyone was awakened by Karma's barking, and one by one they made their way topside. Judging by the tree the boat was tied to, the water had dropped about two feet overnight, which meant that they were only floating in about four feet of water. Every night they made sure to tie the boat up very loosely in case the water level went down dramatically. They didn't want to wake up one night with the boat hanging from a tree.

Not too far in the distance, they all saw a beautiful sight: solid ground. Beyond that there was a plume of smoke rising into the gray sky. Karma was standing on the rear seat of the deck watching the smoke and barking.

The land was about a half a mile away, and Ryan judged the smoke to be a mile or so past that.

"Land ho!" Melina announced.

"I never thought I would be happy to get off this boat," Marcus said looking over everyone's head at the land.

"It served us well," Ryan said, patting the big man on the back.

"It sure did," Marcus said yawning. "Man, did I sleep good these last two days. When Mel and I were off searching for food it was terrible. I could never get comfortable."

Vivian smiled and said, "You probably just feel safer knowing I'm here to protect you."

"He's right," Melina said. "I had the same problem. But not the last couple of nights though."

"Well, even though it's going to feel good to put our feet on the ground again, in about a day we'll be missing this boat, big time," Ryan told them.

They had a quick breakfast, during which they talked about what they might find on dry land. Although they were all eager to leave the water, the prospect of the unknown left them more than a little apprehensive.

Once everyone ate their fill, Leo led them back onto the deck.

"I know we're all a bit scared," he told the group. "And even though there's no telling what's out there waiting for us, we can't stay here and just wait for things to happen." He paused and put a hand on the rope connecting the boat to the tree. "No, it's time we set out to meet our future head on."

With a confident nod, Leo reached up and untied the boat.

Leo's wise words made Ryan think of his father, who had always been prepared with the perfect advice whenever Ryan needed it. He never really had the time to think about the fate of his parents, but suddenly he was overcome with sadness. He missed them. Although his heart assured him that they were alive and well, his mind wasn't so sure.

As Ryan started to feel his emotions coming to the surface, Leo's smiling face was before him. It was his knowing smile that told Ryan he wasn't alone, and without a word he felt comforted. It was then that Ryan saw the similarities between Leo and his father. Not in appearance, but in attitude and spirit.

"What do you say?" Leo asked him.

Ryan felt new determination within himself begin to grow. "Let's do it."

Leo patted him on the shoulder as Melina got the boat moving.

Karma ran along the side of the boat and took up watch on the bow, keeping her eyes on the approaching shoreline, which consisted of a rising hill with what must have been, at one time, a main road. A few cars stood drying out at various angles, probably tossed around by the water.

Marcus was looking ahead through the cockpit windows behind Melina, who was steering them toward the uncovered roadway. Karma remained on the bow staring intently, the momentum making her floppy ears flutter.

Leo came up beside Marcus and said, "Karma seems ready to get off this boat."

"I hope that's all it is," Marcus replied, concern in his voice.

"What do you mean?"

"That dog knows stuff that we don't," Marcus told him.

Leo looked up at the big man, confused.

"You'll see," was all Marcus would offer.

Ryan and Vivian were standing in the back watching the half submerged houses go by.

"The air is so still," Vivian said.

Studying the trees, Ryan saw that the leaves were still and unmoving. And with the exception of the boat's wake, the surface of the water didn't have so much as a single ripple.

"It sure is calm, isn't it?" he asked.

"Or is it the calm before the storm?" Vivian added.

Melina increased their speed as they approached the shore. "Hold on, we're coming in!" she yelled over her shoulder.

Trying to stay clear of any hard asphalt, Melina aimed for a muddy spot alongside the road and ran the boat aground. It slid to a jerky stop and tilted slightly to the right.

Melina cut the engine and turned. "Looks like we're docked. Feel free to disembark at your leisure."

Karma was the first to jump off the boat. She leapt off the bow, into a foot of water, then trotted up the hill and shook off. Everyone else gathered some supplies and carefully hopped off the boat one at a time.

Once everyone was together, they started walking toward the road. Marcus adjusted the large backpack full of food on his back and glanced back at the boat one last time, then turned and caught up with the others.

Karma led the way, as usual. She would run about twenty feet ahead, then turn and wait for the slow moving bipeds to catch up.

They were walking through what was once a fairly populated area consisting of various sized houses and a few local businesses. The ground was soggy, but everything seemed fairly dry, which meant that the floods had dropped here at least a day before.

The plume of smoke hung in the sky ahead of them. After about a half mile, the road turned to the right, angling away from the smoke in the distance. Off to the side of the road was a single figure sitting on the hood of a beat up car.

As they got closer, they saw it was a man dressed in a bright green jumpsuit with big white polka-dots on it. He had on big oversized shoes, and his face was covered in full clown make-up.

CHAPTER 11

The Circus Comes to Town

Karma raced past the clown without so much as a sniff. She stopped on the road about twenty feet ahead, and looked back.

The clown stared straight ahead, seeming not to have noticed the white and brown dog running past. He was totally motionless with the exception of his feet, which he slowly raised up and down. The big, black, oversized shoes he wore made a metallic thud every time one of his heels came down on the dilapidated car he sat on.

As they got closer, Ryan saw that the clown's makeup was streaked in places and his green jumpsuit was dirty and torn. Although his makeup gave him a permanent grin, there was no smile on his face.

Ryan's small group stopped directly in front of the clown, watching him with curiosity. The clown continued his blank stare, even though there were five strangers standing right in front of him.

After a few seconds, Marcus waved a hand in front of the clown's face. "Hello? Anyone home?"

The clown jerked his head, finally noticing them. "Snuck me up, did ya'll? Come see Bi-Top-Bill. Not me fault, ya know."

Marcus stepped back, looking confused.

"I tode 'em da packies wuz mad, I did," the clown continued. "Step right up, they did. No mo' Bi-Top."

The clown's face was thin and his baggy jumpsuit hung limply from his skinny body. His head was bald on top, with a bushy semicircle of red curly hair going around the back of his head from ear to ear.

"I'm sorry," Ryan said. "What did you say?"

The clown shook his head. "Dem packies did it. I woked away. I done woked away, I did. No one left, so I woked away." His speech had a thick southern drawl that made his gibberish even harder to understand.

Ryan exchanged puzzled glances with the others, as the clown continued lifting his feet up and down on the car.

"Do you know where that smoke is coming from?" Leo tried.

The clown turned and stared at Leo for a while before answering. "Bone Bro dat way. Bad. Damn bad."

"What?" Leo said, puzzled.

"Da Bone Bro kee ya dead," the clown added.

Karma let out a sharp bark, getting everyone except the clown's attention. She was in the same spot at the bend in the road, but took a few more steps away once she had their attention.

"I think she wants to go," Vivian surmised.

"Let's keep moving," Ryan said. "This clown is giving me a headache."

Ryan led the group past the clown and over to where Karma waited. Once they were all together, Karma turned and hesitated. She looked down the bend of the road, then up at the smoke that rose over the trees in front of them.

"Not sure which way you want to go, huh, girl?" Melina asked, watching her.

Karma shifted her head back and forth one more time, let out a soft groan and jogged around the bend of the road, away from the smoke.

They followed Karma down the road, leaving the bizarre clown to continue his mindless kicking of his big-shoed feet. The road wound its way around a few houses, but soon left the residential area and opened up into a number of dusty fields. Simple brown wooden fences went along the road on both sides, enclosing various pastures.

"Do you guys always follow the dog?" Leo said to Marcus in a confused tone.

"Karma always knows best," he told him. "You'll see."

Up ahead they saw a huge red tent set up in a large field. There were a number of smaller tents set up around the big red one and several tractor trailer trucks and hitches parked on one side of the field. The right side of the field was empty, and judging by the many tire tracks, was used as a parking lot.

Karma ran down the dirt road and led the way to the tents. She was apparently in a hurry and had everyone moving quickly. Once they neared the vehicles they saw "Big Top Bills Traveling Circus" painted on the side of most of the trucks.

"I think we found Crazy Clown's home," Marcus said.

They walked up to the main tent, and were about to go inside when Karma rattled off a series of barks from in front of another tent off to the side.

"Okay Karma, we're following," Ryan said, as he turned toward her.

As soon as Karma saw her friends approaching, she darted into the tent.

They smelled the elephants before they actually saw them. That strong musky animal odor filled the air in and around the tent. Once inside, they stood before four of the huge creatures. The elephants were standing side by side against the back of the tent, each of them chained by the back legs to large metal stakes stuck into the ground behind them. They eyed the group, and slowly shifted their weight from one foot to the other.

Once he was able to take his eye off the elephants, Ryan noticed that there was a body lying on the ground next to the row of elephants. It was a man, face down, wearing red pants and a black-tailed tuxedo jacket. His left arm was pinned underneath his body, but the right one was outstretched over his head, still clutching a long black rod.

Vivian knelt down and inspected the body. "He's dead. Looks like he was trampled."

Melina circled the elephants, studying them carefully.

"Look at this," she said, pointing to a patch of discolored marks on the side of one of the elephants. "These poor guys have been abused. Probably for years."

Marcus stood over the crumpled body. "Then I'd say this guy got what he deserved."

"Big Top Bill, I presume." Ryan said, standing over the body.

"And the 'packies' that crazy clown was jabbering about, are probably these four pachyderms," Melina explained to them. "Which is kind of another word for elephants."

Ryan, along with everyone else, was so preoccupied with the body that they almost didn't notice Karma standing between two elephants right under their feet. She was staring up at them, while the elephants took turns moving their trunks along the length of her body. Ryan was amazed at how gently the big animals were moving. Considering their size and bulk the elephants controlled their bodies with a surprising graceful tenderness.

Marcus leaned down and grabbed the black rod from the corpse's hand. He turned it around in his hands trying to figure out exactly what it was.

"That's an electric prod," Melina said. "Circus handlers use it on animals as a training and disciplinary tool. It delivers a powerful shock that can injure or even kill the animal."

"I have a feeling that you're not a big fan of the circus," Leo said.

Melina shook her head. "The Circus is just a P.O.W. camp for animals. They live a miserable life of confinement and violent training, forced to perform ridiculous tricks that they can't comprehend."

"Don't get her started, Leo," Marcus said.

Melina ignored him and continued. "Here are four examples of circus life," she said pointing to the elephants. "They have whip and shock marks all over their bodies and their legs are bloody messes from being constantly chained up. Circuses are just another example of how humans have exploited animals with no regard for their welfare."

Leo looked up at the gentle giants. "We've got to help them."

As if she understood their conversation, Karma ran over to

one of the metal stakes the elephants were chained to and started digging furiously.

Ryan, Leo and Marcus ran over and joined Karma in her digging. The ground was surprisingly hard though, and made their progress slow and painful.

"I think these will work better, boys," Vivian said, holding a set of keys that she discovered hanging on one of the tent's support beams.

Ryan looked up and smiled, "They just might."

"Where would you silly boys be without us?" Melina asked, putting an arm around Vivian, as Ryan fitted a key into the first shackle.

It wasn't until all four elephants were free that the animals slowly moved forward. In single file, they walked out of the tent and into freedom.

"Let's check the rest of this place out and see if there are any more animals that need rescuing," Ryan said as they followed the elephants outside.

The elephants lumbered off into a nearby field. Ryan watched them and hoped that better days would find them. He didn't think that African elephants had much of a chance living in the American Southwest, but anything other than circus life would undoubtedly be an improvement.

Walking around the main tent, they let Karma take the lead once again. She quickly padded around to the back where the trucks were parked. Single and double tractor trailer hitches sat motionless with blocks behind the tires. Some of the trucks had swinging doors along the sides. Most hung open revealing individual animal cages built right into the trucks.

After a quick inspection, they counted two lions, three brown bears, five horses and seven small dogs, all held prisoner. The cages were small with little ventilation, and the floors were covered in feces. Ryan found it hard to believe that anyone would let an animal live in such conditions.

All the animals were very skittish and wary of the people peering in on them, but that changed when they saw Karma. She leaned up on each cage, and stuck her face between the bars. Each animal came immediately over and touched noses with her.

The cages were all padlocked, but Ryan found the appropriate keys on the ring they found in the elephant tent and opened all of the cages. Instead of charging out as the cage door opened, the animals slowly and calmly strolled out of their enclosures. Each gave a final look to Karma and ran off.

"It's like they knew we were here to help," Leo said as the last animal disappeared from view. "And they really seem to connect with Karma."

"Don't worry, Leo, my boy," Melina said. "You'll get used to this kind of thing soon enough."

They walked around the trucks and discovered a group of about fifteen small tents. They were cheap two and four person tents that were used for camping, and they were all charred and melted. The black marks of small fires marked the grass under and around the tents.

"What the hell happened here?" Marcus said as he stuck his head in a partially collapsed tent. Inside were the burnt figures of two people. "Yikes," he said withdrawing his head.

They walked around the camping area and found a similar sight in each tent.

"I bet this is where the circus staff lived," Vivian said.

Marcus checked out the surrounding area and returned back to the group. "This is the only spot that is burned like this."

"What could have done this?" Melina asked.

"Lightning," Ryan replied.

Everyone went silent as they considered the scene around them. With the exception of the clown and Big Top Bill, all of the circus workers and performers appeared to have been burnt to a crisp. Yet the animals were unharmed.

They decided to split up and check out the entire area. Ryan found himself in the main tent where the show must have taken place. There was a single large ring of painted wood in the center of the tent surrounded by rows of bleachers. Above, in the rafters, were two trapeze swings tied to the tent support beams.

Ryan walked into the center of the ring and looked down at the ground. There were footprints everywhere: some human, some animal. He knelt down and placed a hand in the round print that must have belonged to an elephant. He wondered what the elephant was thinking when he was forced to perform here. He wondered if the animal realized why he was continually whipped and prodded. Probably not. Ryan pitied the animals that were paraded out in the ring night after night, in town after town. He remembered coming to the circus when he was a kid with his parents. He loved watching the animals and thought they were having fun all dressed up in outfits and jumping through hoops of fire. Only now did he think back and realize that whenever an animal did a trick, it was prompted with a whip or stick. Ryan wished he had known then what he knew now.

Karma strolled up and licked Ryan in the face. He rubbed her ears and smiled.

"Good Karma."

After one last look at the elephant print, Ryan and Karma walked out of the tent to find the others.

A search through the remaining large tents revealed no more caged animals. One tent was filled with various supplies and equipment, another held costumes and make-up and one was set up to be someone's private quarters - most likely Big Top Bill's.

After their inspection of the circus was complete, they found themselves back at the burned tents. A nudge at Ryan's legs made him look down. He found Karma gazing up at him. Ryan reached down and gave her a pat on the head. When he straightened up, Karma jogged forward a few feet and turned.

"I guess our work is done here," Ryan said, moving toward her.

Once she saw everyone was coming, Karma darted across the grass field behind the campgrounds. After about two hundred feet, the field ended at a lightly wooded area. Ryan noticed they were again headed in the direction of the rising smoke cloud.

The day remained gloomy. Clouds continued to hide the sun, washing eerie gray light over the landscape.

Karma waited at the tree line, looking back impatiently.

"Into the trees it is," Ryan said, moving forward.

Karma led them through the woods. The trees weren't that thick and they could see houses off to the sides as the path sloped downward. After a short walk, the trees ended midway down a big hill. Karma stood just out of the cover of the trees watching the scene below.

The trees gave way to grass, as the hill continued for another thirty feet to a six foot tall iron fence which wrapped around a massive cemetery. Rows upon rows of grave stones lined the interior of the fence. The stones were set so close together that, in some spots, you lost site of the grass, making it appear like the land was completely paved over. Every so often the pattern was broken by the square box of a small mausoleum.

The cemetery went on for acres and was the biggest Ryan had ever laid eyes on. Ryan looked at the seemingly endless rows of grave markers and frowned. *Even in death*, he thought, *human beings litter the Earth.*

It appeared as if many of the graves had been dug up. Piles of dirt were scattered around the cemetery and many headstones were knocked over.

The plume of smoke was coming from a large bonfire about two hundred feet from the main gates off to the left. A group of men in cowboy hats were gathered around it yelling and jumping.

A movement off to the right caught Ryan's eye. At a mausoleum not far from the fire dancers, were two people. They were on their knees and bound by ropes to the columns in front of the mausoleum doors. One was an older man, the other a young woman. Their feet were tied together and their hands were secured behind their backs. Another length of rope then connected them to a column on each side.

"What the hell is going on down there?" Melina asked.

The men around the fire were dressed in western button-down shirts, jeans and pointy cowboy boots. A few of them wore brown chaps over their jeans and some had bandanas around their necks, while others wore cowboy hats. They only stopped jumping around when they paused to take a gulp out of one of the bottles that were being passed around.

At the mausoleum, a man came out of the small enclosure. He kicked the man in the side causing him to hit the ground hard. Then, he grabbed the girl by the back of the head, brought her face close to his and said something. The girl struggled as the man gave her a forced kiss and threw her down by the hair. The man said something else and then walked to the fire.

"We've got to do something," Vivian said, appalled by the site.

Ryan thought for a minute, trying to figure out what could be done. He counted eleven cowboys by the fire, but there could be more in the mausoleum or elsewhere. They would be greatly outnumbered in any kind of a physical confrontation.

"We need to get them away from that mausoleum," Leo said. "If they were distracted elsewhere, maybe we would be able to go down there and free those two."

Everyone thought for a moment, trying to think of a course of action that wouldn't leave them tied to the mausoleum like the two prisoners below.

"I bet two pretty girls could turn their heads," Melina said nudging Vivian.

Ryan turned and faced the women. "Are you crazy? Look at those guys. They're savages. You'd never make it back in one piece."

"Those bumpkins are half in the bag," Melina told him. "We'll just stay on the other side of the fence and lead them away."

"I don't like it," Ryan said. "It's too dangerous and too many things could go wrong."

"Oh, don't be such a worrier. We're tough chicks." Melina winked at Ryan and turned to Vivian. "What do you say kid?"

Vivian didn't look too confident about the plan.

Marcus was still staring at the scene below. "Forget it, Ryan's right. It's too much of a risk."

"Well, we've got to do something," Melina said. "We can't just sit here and watch this."

"No, we can't," Marcus agreed. "I'll take care of it. You guys just get them out of there."

"What makes you think you can do any better than us?" Melina asked.

Marcus calmly replied, "When I was in prison I had to handle myself with packs of assholes like that every day. Trust me, I know what I'm doing. I'll walk in and grab their attention. Wait until I get them to move away, get in there, free those two and run back into the cover of the woods. Don't wait for me. I'll get myself out of there and circle around to meet you. Give me about an hour. If I'm not back by then, move on without me."

"Goliath, we're not going to leave you," Melina said for all of them.

"Just do what I say, all right," he said.

Ryan regarded at the big man. "Are you sure about this?"

"Yes," Marcus replied. "Now let's move before they decide to take any more liberties with their captives."

Ryan didn't like this idea much better, but there weren't a whole lot of options. And he figured that Marcus would do better than any of them if things got physical.

Marcus gave them a nod and started down the hill, pausing to give Karma a pat on the side.

"Be careful," Vivian said.

They watched as Marcus walked down the hill and through the cemetery gates.

Once Marcus entered the cemetery, Ryan led everyone to the

edge of the trees on the hill directly above the main gates. They all held their breath, as they saw Marcus reach the fire and the drunken cowboys.

Marcus made sure he stood nice and tall as he walked down the center road of the cemetery. The fire was directly ahead of him, in the middle of an intersection of two roads that cut through the interior of the cemetery. The fire was big – about thirty feet in diameter. Instead of firewood, they were using caskets to create the blaze. Marcus kept his eyes fixed on the reveling men he was approaching. He was about twenty feet from them before he was finally noticed.

"Intruder alert!" yelled a young man wearing a big white cowboy hat.

The men abruptly stopped their hooting and dancing and looked over at the big man striding toward them.

"What have we here, boys?" said a bearded man wearing a brown hat with a metal band. He walked forward and met Marcus ten feet from the fire, with the rest of the men falling in behind him.

"What the hell do you think you're doing?" the man in the brown hat asked with a thick southern twang.

Marcus quickly sized up the men. They all seemed in pretty good shape and full of fire themselves. Five of them held half empty bottles of what looked like whiskey and most of the men had the swagger of a few too many drinks. Still, they would probably put up a good fight. Then he noticed something that alarmed him. All of the men had a thick, leather band draped around their shoulders. Hanging from these bands were what appeared to be human bones. The oversized necklaces held everything from small broken pieces to full skulls.

Marcus calmly said, "Just passing through."

The man in the brown hat stood directly in front of Marcus. Even though Marcus towered over him, the man showed no fear. "Not here yer not, partner" he said. "This here's the Bone Yard. Ain't no one allowed in the Bone Yard 'cept one o' the Bone Brothers."

The rest of the cowboys spread out in front of Marcus grinning.

"I don't want any trouble," Marcus said. "I saw your fire and wanted to see what was going on. I haven't seen too many people around here, and thought I might find some company."

A powerfully built guy in a black shirt and hat pushed forward. "You won't find no friends here, nigger."

Marcus stared down at the man and saw a haze of alcoholic hatred.

"I'll do the talkin', Billy Bob," the cowboy with the brown hat said with a wave of his hand. "Now listen here boy, you just stepped into our territory. And the' Bone Brothers don't need no company." He turned to the men behind him and then back to Marcus. "You see there are two kinds of people in this new world, those that are led by us, or those that are dead by us."

That brought a round of "yee-ha's" from the cowboys.

"Well then, maybe I could be of some service to you," Marcus told him.

"You ain't good for nothing, nigger, except adding to my collection," the mean looking guy in black said as he held up his long necklace of bones.

The man with the beard smiled and said, "I don't think Billy Bob likes you, boy."

Marcus was trying his best to control his rising anger. "I know where there's a whole stash of booze right here in this cemetery," he said. "I stashed it here myself. How about I take you to it?"

The bearded cowboy considered this information for a second and then said, "I don't think so. You see, boy, the Bone Brothers only trust one o' their own. And you ain't a brother of the Bone."

"Then let me join and we'll all have some fun," Marcus replied loudly.

The bearded cowboy shook his head. "It ain't that easy, partner. As you can see, we only take the strongest, toughest and craziest hombres into the Bone Brothers. You may be big, but yer gonna have to prove you're bad enough to hang with the likes of us."

Marcus thought for a moment, then in a sudden motion, slammed his fist into the black-hatted cowboy's face.

Surprised shock showed on the man's face right before Marcus's fist connected with his left temple, sending him to the ground, where he collapsed motionless. The rest of the cowboys watched in stunned silence. The bearded man in the brown hat took a step forward and looked down at his fallen associate, then back to Marcus.

"Well, I guess that's good enough fer me," he said, then leaning down once again. "How about you Billy Bob?"

The rest of the cowboys erupted in laughter, and a few even walked over to pat Marcus on the back.

"I'm Duke," the bearded man told Marcus. "Now if yer gonna be a Bone Brother, yer gonna need to get yerself some bones."

Marcus looked at Duke, afraid where this was going.

"Every Bone Brother has to dig his own. Then we can find yer booze and have some fun with our new lady friend over there."

Duke pointed over to the mausoleum where the man and girl were tied. Marcus saw that the girl was Asian, with a skinny frame and long, straight black hair. She wore a long, dull yellow sun dress with tan leggings and brown hiking boots. She must have been in her early twenties, and by the look in her eyes, was absolutely terrified. Her companion was a man of about forty, with bushy light blond hair that fell to his shoulders. He was beaten up pretty bad. His left eye was almost swollen shut and his tan shirt was dotted with wet blood stains.

"Do ya like the rodeo, partner?" Duke said.

"Uh, I've never been to one," Marcus said, taking his gaze off the two captives.

"Well, today's yer lucky day, boy. Most of us Bone Brothers are from the best dang rodeo in all of Texas."

"Really," Marcus said, but his mind was on Duke's last word. They had made it all the way to Texas. He couldn't believe they had come so far. He tried to remember what New York was like. It seemed like a lifetime ago that he sat in that tiny jail cell wondering how his life had gone so wrong. He felt like a totally different person now, but he wasn't sure if that was a good or bad thing.

"We're gonna let that guy go and whoever ropes 'em first, gets to kill 'em," Duke told Marcus. "But first you need to become a brother."

Duke led Marcus by the arm to the edge of the fire, where the others were drinking and laughing.

"Okay boys!" Duke announced to the crowd. "This fella here wants into the Brotherhood."

"Yee-ha!" was the response from the drunken cowboys.

"So let's get 'em ready for the walk 'o the dead!" Duke yelled.

Another "Yee-ha!" from the crowd signaled their approval.

Marcus looked down at Duke. "What do I have to do?"

Duke was smiling. "If you wanna be a Brother, you gotta take the walk and pick yer bones."

Marcus followed the cowboys as they walked through the cemetery. There were so many headstones that if Marcus didn't watch his steps carefully, he would trip over one. Duke led them to the middle of one of the center lots. Marcus glanced back to see how far they were from the mausoleum that held the two captives. Only about fifty feet. He needed to give his friends a little more distance.

"All right, partner," Duke said to him, holding up a bandana. "We're gonna blindfold ya nice and tight. Then you get a shot 'o whiskey and we spin ya. And then ya stumble yer ass around until you find a grave ya like. That's when we'll give ya the shovel so ya can claim yer bones."

The thought of digging up someone's grave made Marcus's stomach turn, but he had to play along so that Ryan and the others could get out with the prisoners.

He squatted down and let Duke blindfold him with a long length of soft leather, then stood up and accepted the bottle of whiskey. Marcus put the bottle to his lips, leaned his head back but only pretended to take a long gulp. He didn't want any cheap whiskey dulling his reflexes. He had a strong feeling he was going to need them very soon.

As soon as he brought the bottle down, someone snatched it away from him and then he was being roughly spun around. They turned Marcus around in a sloppy circle for about thirty seconds, then released him. As soon as he was on his own the cowboys started yelling and screaming. The spinning did its job, as Marcus staggered around trying to stay on his feet. He wanted to put some more distance between the cowboys and the captives, but he wasn't sure which way was which. He tried to get his bearings by listening for the fire, but with all the shouts and cheers of the cowboys he couldn't hear it.

Not having any other choice, Marcus walked forward and hoped he was moving in the right direction. He got about two feet before his feet hit a headstone and sent him to the ground. He got up slowly and started moving again, this time crouching down low as he walked with his hands out in front of him. By doing that he was able to navigate ahead by feeling the headstones with his hands before colliding into them.

Marcus kept moving forward for a minute or two, while the cowboys continued their hollering. But their patience soon ran out and he was stopped by Duke's voice.

"That's enough, partner," Marcus heard him say. "Make yer choice."

Marcus reached to his left and walked into a headstone, tapped it with his hand and stood up.

"Oh, that's too bad," he heard Duke say, as he removed the blindfold. "Ya picked a fresh one. That means y'all have a lot o' stuff to skin off."

Marcus panned around to see where his blind walk had taken them. He didn't do too badly. They were facing the back of the mausoleum with the prisoners, about seventy-five feet away. Marcus hoped it would be enough.

One of the cowboys handed Marcus a shovel and he looked down at the grave marker. It read "In Loving Memory of Carla Shannon, 1973 to 2015." She was buried only a year ago and already her grave was about to be desecrated. With great reluctance, Marcus thrust the shovel into the earth.

Ryan and the others watched from the cover of the trees as Marcus brought the shovel down into the ground. They had almost run down when Marcus punched out the cowboy in black, but Melina had assured them that Marcus knew what he was doing.

Although Ryan was hoping Marcus would lead the cowboys farther away from the captives, it seemed like this was going to be their best chance to make a rescue attempt.

They crept down to the front gates of the cemetery, trying to keep as low as possible. Ryan was worried about Karma running ahead, but she seemed to know they were going for a stealthy entrance, and kept behind Ryan.

Slowly, they continued their crouch-walking through the graves. Luckily, the mausoleum with the captives was directly between them and the cowboys, so it wasn't too difficult to stay out of their sight.

The young Asian girl was tied to the right column, and saw the group coming before her friend. At first, her eyes went wide with fear, but then she must have realized that the approaching group looked nothing like the brutes that had been terrorizing her, and her face brightened a little.

Once they reached the mausoleum, Melina and Vivian went to work on untying the girl, while Leo and Ryan walked around to free her friend. Ryan peered around the side of the mausoleum and saw Marcus throwing dirt over his shoulder while the cowboys continued to hoot and holler.

As Ryan and Leo frantically worked to free the man's knots, they became very concerned with his condition. His left eye was severely swollen, he had a number of cuts and bruises all over his body and he seemed to be on the verge of passing out.

Ryan looked into his one good eye and whispered, "Hang on, buddy. We're getting you out of here."

The man seemed to understand and did his best to stay upright on his knees.

The knots were tied very tightly and made their progress much slower then Ryan felt comfortable with. Melina and Vivian had the girl's hands free and were now working on her legs. Meanwhile, Ryan and Leo were still struggling to untie the man's hands.

That's when Karma's growl made Ryan stop and look up. Near the fire, the cowboy in black, that was knocked out by Marcus was slowly rising to his feet, holding his bruised head.

Billy Bob seemed to still be dazed, and stumbled in a circle before finally standing up straight. Slowly, he turned his head to where his buddies were gathered with Marcus.

Ryan kept his eye on Billy Bob as he and Leo finally got the ropes loose enough to slip the man's hands through and started on the ropes around his feet. Ryan pulled on the rope hard, causing the bound man to let out a groan.

The noise was a little too loud, and Ryan watched as Billy Bob turned toward them. It took a second or two for the image to register in Billy Bob's stunned brain. But when it did he let out a yell.

"Hey!" Billy Bob screamed toward the other cowboys. "Hey! They're stealing our livestock! Over here! Hurry, they're taking our fun!"

The cowboys that circled Marcus all turned their heads toward Billy Bob, who was jumping up and down, pointing at the mausoleum where the prisoners were held.

One of the cowboys stepped over a few feet to get a better view of the mausoleum and saw the rescuers working on the leg ropes of their prisoners.

"Coyotes in the barn!" he screamed, causing all the cowboys to run toward the mausoleum.

"Hurry up girls," Ryan said over his shoulder, as he watched the rushing gang of hillbillies close in.

Melina and Vivian finished untying the girl and started running to the cemetery gates with Karma in the lead.

It was another few long seconds before Ryan and Leo finally freed the guy's feet.

"Leo, get out of here," Ryan screamed, as he helped the man up.

Leo nodded and ran after the girls, while Ryan took the wounded man by the shoulders and helped him down the steps.

Ryan immediately saw he was in trouble. Even with Ryan's help, the injured man could only limp forward slowly. The screams of the approaching cowboys were getting alarmingly closer, and Ryan peeked back to see that they were almost on top of them.

"Keep going," Ryan told the man. "Don't' stop no matter what happens."

Then Ryan turned to meet the charging cowboys. He had no

idea what he was going to do. He only knew that he had to give his friends a little more time to escape.

A whiskey bottle shattered at Ryan's feet, right before the cowboys were upon him. Ryan swung a right hook at the first cowboy in front of him, connected solidly and sending him backward. The next two, however, were able to land punches in Ryan's midsection and shoulder. The punches stunned him, making him unprepared for a third punch to the face.

Ryan lost his balance and fell to the ground. He looked up as Duke and the rest of the cowboys loomed over him.

"The Bone Brothers are gonna make ya hurt bad, partner," Duke said, smiling.

The smile didn't last too long though, as the group of cowboys was hit hard from behind, by something with the force of a charging bull. Ryan turned his head into the dirt as cowboys went flying everywhere.

The charging bull turned out to be Marcus. He had followed behind the cowboys and waited until all their attention was on Ryan and then ran into them like a linebacker. The drunken cowboys had all gathered around Duke, so when Marcus's hurtling body and outstretched arms hit them, they fell to the ground like bowling pins.

Marcus landed on top of the stunned cowboys a few feet from Ryan. Raising their heads, the two friends looked at one another.

"You're pretty good at these diversions," Ryan said, as he stood up.

Marcus climbed off the cowboys under him and stood up as well. On his way to Ryan, Marcus noticed a cowboy in black trying to get to his feet. Marcus grabbed the back of his shirt and pulled

Billy Bob upright.

"I thought I made myself clear the first time," Marcus said, as he punched the startled Billy Bob in the nose, snapping his head back and sending back to the ground.

The rest of the cowboys were starting to get back on their feet, so Ryan and Marcus decided it was time to get out of there while they still could. They ran through the cemetery gates and to the base of the hill that led to the woods.

Ryan looked ahead and saw the beat-up blond man limping up the hill. Vivian, Melina, Leo, and the young Asian girl were shouting encouragement from the tree line on top of the hill, while Karma barked at their feet.

Yells from behind made Ryan and Marcus turn. The cowboys were in pursuit again, this time clutching small hatchets. They streamed out of the cemetery and headed toward the hill.

Ryan and Marcus started up the hill as a hatchet flew past Ryan's head, landing in the grass a few feet from him. The blond man was catching his breath near the top of hill when a hatchet embedded itself in his back, causing him to topple forward.

"No!" the young girl screamed, and ran to her fallen companion.

She knelt down and clutched his already lifeless body. Then she stood up, stunned, with tears streaming down her face while the cowboys charged up the hill.

Out of the corner of his eye, Ryan saw Duke take aim with his hatchet and say, "Adios muchacha."

Ryan yelled at the girl, "Get down!" But she was in a shocked daze and just stood frozen in front of the trees.

Ryan ran up the hill as Duke cocked his arm back. As soon as he got to the top, Ryan dove at the girl, tackling her to the ground as the hatchet zipped past their heads and sunk deeply into the tree the girl had been standing in front of.

Both Ryan and the girl looked up at the hatchet.

"You saved me," she said.

"Thank me later," Ryan said, as Marcus reached them.

Ryan was about to get to his feet when the cowboys finished climbing the hill. With hatchets and knives in their hands, they slowly walked up the last few feet. Eight cowboys circled in.

"Ya bastards got a lot o' nerve," Duke said to them. "I think we'll all be wearing some new bones tonight."

The other cowboy grinned menacingly as Ryan tried to think of some way out of this. Somewhere behind him, he heard Karma bark. Then, with a loud crack, a large tree over to their right came crashing down.

All the cowboys stared up in amazement as an elephant strode over the fallen tree, trumpeting. Then trees on the left side came down followed by three more elephants.

The cowboys couldn't seem to decide if this was an apparition of their drunken minds or the real thing. They stumbled back a few steps with their mouths hanging open, staring at the huge animals.

The first elephant rushed forward, swinging its large head and knocking two cowboys down the hill. Then the other three elephants came forward, trumpeting loudly. Soon all the cowboys were in full flight down the hill. The elephants chased them all the way back into the cemetery where the cowboys scattered and disappeared from view. Then, the large animals walked back up the hill, stopping in front of Ryan and the others.

Karma walked from Ryan's side and touched the extended trunk of one of the elephants with her paw.

Although he should have been intimidated by such an imposing animal, Ryan felt strangely calm. He took a few tentative steps forward and stood at the elephant's side and gazed into its dark eye. The elephant brought it's trunk up and rubbed it against Ryan's arm.

Such a magnificent creature, Ryan thought to himself.

Soon the others stepped forward and everyone exchanged gentle touches with the elephants. Staring into its eye, Ryan wished he could tell the elephant how thankful he was, and how badly he felt about their mistreatment at the circus. Even though he knew it was impossible, Ryan felt the elephant understood what was on his mind and in his heart.

The moment ended with the elephants slowly bowing their heads and returning back into the trees, leaving everyone with a feeling of wonder and kinship.

CHAPTER 12

The Savior is Here

Marcus pried the hatchet out of the man's back. Blood had soaked his shirt and stained the grass beneath him. The young girl informed them that the man's name was Zach and that they had been traveling together for the last week. In that time, they had encountered no other people. They came across a number of dead bodies, but no one living. So when they saw the smoke coming from the cemetery, they hurried over in hopes of finding other survivors. The cowboys who called themselves the Bone Brothers immediately made obscene advances toward her. She and Zach tried to run away, but the cowboys were all around them. Although Zach tried to protect her, he was outnumbered, and they beat him and tied them both to the mausoleum columns.

Her name was Nabi, and although she looked much younger, she was actually twenty-six years old. When Melina asked about her ethnic background, she explained that she was Korean, but her family had lived in the United States for two generations. She had a soft voice and spoke perfect English.

Underneath the dirt and dried tears, she had a sweet, innocent face and kind eyes. She was only about five-foot-two, but her hiking boots made her another inch taller. Her faded yellow sun dress hugged her thin body all the way to her knees, where she wore tight tan leggings. It seemed an odd outfit, and she explained that it wasn't her choice of attire. She had been driving to meet a few friends for dinner, when the lightning storms hit. She crashed her car and took cover in convenience store. The next day she went back to her car and ditched her nice leather shoes for the hiking boots that she always kept in her trunk. She knew it was going to get cold at night, so she grabbed the leggings from the convenience store, and started walking.

All of the populated areas seemed to be getting hit the hardest by the lightning, so she decided to get away from civilization. Her Dad was a wildlife photographer and had taken her on a number of long camping trips throughout her life, so she was well versed in outdoor survival. She was very adept at finding food, water and shelter when needed. It was while she was setting up a camp site one night that she met Zach. He was hopelessly lost and very dehydrated. She got him some food and water and shared her camp with him. Although they had spent the last week together, she didn't really know much about him. He never said much about his life or talked about anything personal. At first she thought it was odd and didn't really trust him. But as the days past, he proved to be a nice guy and she didn't give it much thought.

Nabi cried on Melina's shoulder, as Marcus inspected Zach's body. Looking at all of Zach's injuries, Ryan was amazed that the guy had made it as far as he did. They decided it wouldn't be right to just leave his body lying on the hillside. After a brief discussion they agreed to bring him to the other side of the woods and bury him in one of the fields next to the circus.

In spite of the protests from the others, Marcus went back into the cemetery and collected the shovel that he used during their rescue. He kept his eyes open, but didn't see any of the Bone Brothers. If they were still in the cemetery, they were in hiding somewhere out of sight, still shaken up after their encounter with the elephants.

Marcus carried Zach's body while they walked through the trees in silence. Even Karma seemed a bit solemn. As everyone was waiting for Marcus to return with the shovel, Karma had walked over to Nabi and sat down right next to her, with her body leaning on her leg. Nabi seemed to calm down as she pet the dog and even smiled.

Once they reached the field, they let Nabi decide where to bury Zach. She picked a nice grassy area near the edge of the trees. Marcus, Ryan and Leo took turns digging the grave, while Melina and Vivian sat down with Nabi and talked, as Karma stretched out beside them.

"You have such a beautiful name," Vivian said. "Does it have any special meaning?"

"It means butterfly," Nabi told her. "In Korea, it is believed that yellow butterflies are bringers of good fortune."

"Well, then I guess it's lucky for us that we found you," Melina said holding up the end of her yellow dress.

"It seems like I was the lucky one," Nabi said, then lifted the corner of her dress. "Yellow has always been my favorite color."

A dull rumbling under the ground made everyone stop and look at one another. It only lasted for a moment and then stopped just as suddenly as it started.

"What was that?" Leo asked.

"Just a tremor," Nabi said. "We've been getting a lot of those the last couple of days. Nothing major so far though."

Ryan exchanged a nervous look with Marcus, and then continued digging.

Nabi watched the men as they dug Zach's grave and her eyes started to well up. "Zach seemed like such a good guy, and now he's gone and I have nobody."

Nabi lowered her head and covered her eyes with her hands.

"Don't you worry, honey," Melina said, putting a hand on her shoulder. "You've got us now."

"That's right," Vivian added. "We've traveled all across the country and we're still alive."

Nabi looked up, wiping her eyes. "You came from the East?"

Vivian nodded.

"Is it any better over there?" Nabi asked.

Vivian took a deep breath. "Not really. I think the entire world is going through some kind of a change."

Melina and Vivian talked with Nabi, trying to keep her mind off the grave being dug just a few feet away. Although it seemed like crazy talk, they explained about Karma and how special she had proved to be.

When they finished, Nabi considered the sleeping dog. "She sounds like a unique dog."

"I know it's hard to believe," Vivian said. "If I didn't live it, I would be skeptical too. You'll see for yourself soon enough."

It took the men about an hour to dig a hole big enough to fit

Zach's body. Everyone gathered around as Marcus placed the body in.

Nabi looked down with tears in her eyes. "Goodbye my friend," she said softly.

Ryan covered the body with dirt. When he had finished smoothing the surface of the grave, everyone stood around it in silence. They had no headstone, but Melina and Marcus gathered some small stones and framed the grave.

Then they lowered their heads as Leo led them in a brief prayer. "Zach was a good man and deserves more than we can offer. As we lay his body to rest, may his soul be at peace and his spirit free. The world will miss him, but he will live forever in our hearts."

Quietly, they all paid their last respects and stepped away from the grave. Nabi remained for a minute longer, and then she too stepped away. Melina and Vivian put their arms around her as the group followed Karma across the field and onto a paved road.

After about an hour of steady walking, Karma left the road and jogged down a long driveway leading to a small ranch. A long rust colored house with screened windows spread out at the end of the driveway. The property around the house was mostly grassy fields dotted with trees and thorny bushes.

On the lawn in front of the house was a large tree. The trunk was about four feet in diameter at its base and divided into two large separate branches that rose up about twenty-five feet and then branched off in several directions. Two rope swings were attached to one of the big branches, hanging a few feet from the ground. The tree had lost most of its leaves and a lot of its bark was flaking off.

Karma walked onto the grass and sat down next to the tree. Ryan walked up to the door and knocked, while Marcus went around to the back of the house. When no one answered, he put his hand to a nearby window and peered in. Looking into the living room, Ryan saw old colonial wooden furniture in front of a fireplace, but no people. He knocked again, but when there was no response he walked over to the tree where Melina, Vivian, Leo and Nabi were gathered, gazing at the tree's trunk.

Ryan leaned over Vivian's shoulder to see. It was covered with carved writing. A quick walk around the tree showed that the entire trunk was etched with letters. The carvings even went up into the tree for about six or seven feet where it finally met a line of live bark. There were initials, words, even whole sentences engraved into the trunk. Some of the letters ran into one another making it difficult to read or distinguish one thought from another.

Marcus finished his lap around the house and walked back to the group.

"That's a whole lot of graffiti," Marcus said, considering the tree.

Melina ran her hands over the tree's scars. "I'll never understand why someone would desecrate a nice tree."

"I guess people don't think about trees as living creatures," Leo said.

Melina shook her head. "That's exactly the problem, they don't think."

"Did you find anything around the back of the house?" Ryan asked Marcus.

"Nope, all's quiet. No sign of anyone."

"We need to rest," Ryan said to the group. "Maybe we'll let ourselves in and have something to eat."

"That sounds good to me," Vivian said. "I'm starving."

The doors were all locked, so they were forced to break a window to get inside. Besides the living room, the house had a dining room, kitchen, a screened in sun porch, bathroom and three bedrooms. Marcus went into the kitchen and opened up the large backpack of supplies he carried. The house had some non-perishable food items that they added to their current rations, so it didn't appear that food would be a problem.

Marcus, Vivian and Nabi prepared the food while Ryan, Melina and Leo gathered some wood and got a fire going. Marcus put a few cans of soup in a large pot and held it over the fire to warm it up. Everyone met on the porch with a hot bowl of soup and a few pieces of stale bread.

The room was completely enclosed and carpeted, with floor to ceiling screened windows. A wicker sofa and matching loveseat sat against the wall in one corner, and a big cushioned chair was placed opposite the loveseat in front of a wooden coffee table. There was nothing on the back wall, allowing for a good view of the rear property.

Ryan and Vivian sat on the loveseat with Karma at their feet, while Nabi and Melina got comfortable on the couch. Leo took a seat in the chair, leaving Marcus to recline on the floor with Karma. They ate their food in relative silence, enjoying the hot meal.

Everyone was just about finished with their meal when the Earth began to shake again. Windows rattled and the glasses of juice they were drinking shifted on the coffee table. Vivian put a hand on Ryan's leg for support, but the vibrations shuttered to a stop before anyone got a chance to take action. They looked at one another, waiting for another tremor.

When none came, Vivian said, "What's happening to this

planet?"

"I don't know," Marcus said from the floor. "But it certainly keeps things interesting."

Melina sat up in her seat. "I have a theory."

Everyone looked to Melina, eager to find some kind of explanation for the fantastic events of the past few days.

"Mankind has lived on this Earth for many years. We have evolved very quickly and made huge advances in technology and industrialization. And in our haste for development and discovery, we continually ignore the impact our greed has on this planet. Even though we know that our progress pollutes the water, land and air, we continue. Although we know that many animal species have become extinct, and many more are threatened as a direct result of our actions, we continue. Despite our knowledge of the repercussions that our actions have on this world, we still continue to destroy it.

"Take tigers, for example. If nothing changes, tigers will be extinct in the wild within the next five years. We know this, yet nothing changes and the animals continue to die.

"When we think that an animal population is too high, we systematically kill a number of them in order to control their numbers. That's the most hypocritical action I've ever heard of. Do you know what the most overpopulated animal on the planet is? It's humans. Soon this planet will be filled to its capacity of us. We will use up all of the remaining resources and have nowhere else to throw our waste products."

Melina glanced around at the room. "Human beings have abused this planet for far too long, and now the planet is taking matters into it's own hands. Every so often the Earth gets so messed up that it is beyond repair. No one knows why the dinosaurs died, but there are many speculations. Maybe they became so successful that they outnumbered their resources. Maybe they caused so much harm to the environment that the ecosystem equalized things by wiping them out.

"I think that good old Mother Nature has watched us destroy her planet for way too long, and now it's time to restore balance and start over."

"Then I guess you think that we're all doomed and it's just a matter of time before Mother Nature eliminates us too," Marcus said.

"It's unfortunate, but the actions of the majority may condemn all of us," she replied.

They sat in silence for a moment digesting the possibilities.

"I've been thinking about a slightly different scenario," Leo said softly.

"I hope it's got a brighter future than the last one," Nabi said.

Leo sat up. "It's kind of spiritual, so I ask that you keep an open mind and hear me out." He paused to see if anyone objected, then continued. "Believe it or not, I think that crazy reverend may have been right about something."

"I find that very hard to believe," Ryan said.

"In one of his last sermons he was talking about Noah's Ark," Leo went on. "I didn't think much about it at the church, but as time has gone by it's making more and more sense to me.

"According to the scripture, God was saddened by the violence and evil of man. So much so, that He decided to fill the Earth with water in order to wash away man's sins. Melina is right; mankind has done the world many great injustices. And perhaps God has now decided to wipe the slate clean and start anew.

"Look around at our little group. We are a very culturally and physically diverse bunch. I, personally, believe in God. And I think that He has a plan for us and that everything happens for a reason. So maybe we've been brought together for a specific purpose. Maybe we have survived, while others have died, to be the new beginning of the human race."

"I'm sorry, Leo," Ryan said, shaking his head. "Maybe it's because I'm not that religious, but I find the whole thing a bit farfetched."

"I think God chose to start this with you, Ryan," Leo told him. "And it continues to grow as you move across the country and possibly even the world."

"Are you kidding me?" Ryan said, standing up. "That would mean that I'm Noah in this little scenario, right?"

"Maybe something like that," Leo replied.

"But if I remember correctly, didn't God speak to Noah?" Ryan asked. "Didn't he help and guide Noah through the whole thing? So when is he going to find me?"

"I think he already has," Leo said, and looked down at Karma.

All eyes went to Karma, who was lying on the floor with her eyes closed.

"You're trying to tell me that God is a Pit Bull?" Ryan asked, giggling.

"God doesn't necessarily have to be an old man with a beard," Leo said. "He could be black, or a woman or even a dog. Or maybe Karma is God's messenger, sent here to make sure we go where we are meant to go and see what needs to be seen."

"I don't know," Ryan said, bending down to pet Karma.

"Hold on a second," Marcus interrupted. "Leo, what do you do for a living?"

Leo looked at Marcus, confused. "I'm a therapist, specializing in grief and stress counseling."

"Don't you see?" Marcus said. "Take a look at all of us. Not only are we a culturally mixed group, but between all of us, we have the experience and background to survive. Before prison I was a carpenter. I don't like to brag, but I can build just about anything, Vivian's a nurse, and can take care of us when we're sick and patch us up when we get hurt. Melina knows everything about animals and the environment. She knows what humans have done wrong and knows the ways to make it right. Leo, the therapist, can help us deal with all of the psychological issues that lay ahead. And Nabi, you said you were good at building shelters and finding food and water in the open country, right?"

"Yeah," she said. "My dad taught me everything there is to know about survival in the wild."

Marcus looked up at Ryan from the floor with excited satisfaction.

"That's great," Ryan said, standing. "But how do I fit in? I'm just an average guy with no real skills to help our little group do anything."

Marcus slowly shook his head. "Ryan, you're the most important person here. First of all, there's Karma. Whatever you believe in, I think we can all agree that she's much more than a simple dog. And although she may like all of us, you're the one she's leading."

Ryan was about to object, when Marcus put a hand up silencing him.

"More importantly, you are our protector."

"What?" Ryan said in disbelief.

"Think about it," Marcus said to him. "You've saved every one of our lives."

Ryan thought for a moment. He went back in his mind over all the events that had happened since he left New Jersey.

"That's quite a wild idea, and you almost had me starting to believe it," Ryan said. "But what about Vivian? I've been with her the longest and I haven't saved her life."

Marcus was quiet as he tried to reassess his thinking.

Then, Vivian softly said, "Yes, you did."

Ryan, along with everyone else, turned to Vivian. She was sitting on the edge of the loveseat with her knees close together and her hands clasped on her lap, staring blankly at the coffee table. As she felt everyone's gaze upon her, she looked up at Ryan.

"That night you came to my door and brought me over to your place to see Karma and make me dinner." Vivian paused, and then continued with some difficulty. "I was about to commit suicide."

Ryan sat down beside her. "What? What are you talking about?"

"I was going to slit my wrists in the bathtub," she continued. "If you didn't drag me out of that apartment, I would be dead right now. You saved me."

Ryan couldn't believe what he was hearing. Everything was swirling around his head making him feel dizzy.

"Face it, my man," Marcus said. "You're our guardian."

The black of night took hold and they decided to stay in the house until morning. Everyone split up and found a bed to sleep in. Ryan and Vivian got the master bedroom, Marcus and Melina shared a queen bed in one room, and Leo and Nabi settled for bunk beds in what was obviously a kid's room. True to form, Karma curled up next to Ryan and Vivian on the bed.

Ryan's head was still spinning from their early conversation. He knew he should try to relax and get some sleep, but he didn't see how that was going to be possible. He had so much to think about. He couldn't believe that Vivian had been so close to taking her own life. Maybe he should have tried harder to talk to her. Maybe he should have made her come over for dinner a week earlier. It seemed like there were so many things he could have done that might have made a difference. And even though the others congratulated him for saving Vivian when he did, Ryan felt that he should never have let her get to that point.

And then there was this nonsense about Karma being God or God's messenger. Ryan didn't buy into a lot of religion, but he did believe that something might be out there somewhere. He just couldn't convince himself that it was a dog.

Although Ryan was fully prepared to toss and turn all night trying to sort out what was happening to them, as soon as his head hit the pillow, he was asleep.

The next thing Ryan felt was a warm lick to the face. He opened his eyes and was greeted by Karma's big brown eyes and wet nose. Sitting up, he saw that Vivian was already awake and out of bed. Ryan got out of bed and stood at the bedroom window. The day was another gray one: wall to wall clouds without so much as a crack of blue sky. Ryan was starting to forget what a nice clear day really looked like.

Sounds from the kitchen turned Ryan away from the window. He walked down the hall and into the living room where Marcus sat on the floor, sorting through the supplies from his big backpack.

"Good morning," Marcus said, cheerfully.

Ryan gave him a smile, "Good morning."

In the kitchen, Melina and Vivian were putting together some food for breakfast.

Ryan walked over to them. "Good morning ladies," he said, taking a glass of cranberry juice from Vivian. "What time is it?"

"Day time," Melina said. "And how is *the chosen one* doing today?"

"Fine, if you stop calling me that," Ryan replied.

Melina nodded, "Whatever you say, my savior."

Ryan shook his head, but couldn't help cracking a smile. Vivian gave him a kiss on the cheek and they both sat down.

During breakfast, they agreed to relax in the house for another hour or two and then gather whatever supplies they thought they might need and head out.

With a full belly, Ryan found himself on the front lawn, watching Karma sniff around the bushes. Nabi found a tennis ball lying on the ground and brought it over to Karma.

"Hey, Karma," Nabi leaned down, holding the ball out. "How

do you feel about a little game of fetch?" Then she threw the ball across the lawn.

Without any hesitation, Karma raced after it. The ball took one high bounce off the ground before Karma caught up to it and snatched it out of the air. Then she charged back to Nabi and deposited the ball at her feet.

"Good girl," Nabi told her, and she picked up the ball and threw it again.

Vivian walked out the front door and toward the swings that hung from the tree. Ryan followed, and they both sat down in a swing and gently rocked back and forth.

Ryan watched Karma sprint across the lawn after the tennis ball. She looked like such an average dog now. But he couldn't forget all of the unusual events that had happened over the past two weeks.

"Do you really think Karma could be . . . God or something?" Ryan asked Vivian.

Vivian thought for a few seconds as she swung. "I don't think it matters if you believe Karma is God, or you believe she's Mother Nature, or you believe she's a guardian angel. The important thing is that you believe in *something*."

Vivian paused and looked into Ryan's eyes. "You can believe in Karma, in me, or, more importantly, you can believe in yourself. Personally, I believe that we're all in this mess together for a reason. And that gives me hope. I also know that whatever happens, I'm happy to be facing it with you."

Ryan smiled. "You know how beautiful you are?"

"Of course I do, but I like to be reminded as much as possible."

Together, they continued to swing and watch Karma race back and forth after the ball. Ryan lost himself in the simple happiness of the moment, gently swinging next to Vivian as Karma played close by. It made him forget the hectic race for survival that life had become in the last two weeks. Ryan felt happy. He hoped that someday in the future, they could share moments like this all the time.

Ryan's smile was short lived though, as another tremor shook the ground beneath them. This one was more than just a little quiver. Anyone who was standing had to hold onto something fast or fall to the ground. Inside the house, pictures fell, glass shattered and furniture moved across the floor.

Ryan heard a crack as the branch holding the swings broke off the tree and sent him and Vivian to the ground on their backs. They watched in horror as the big branch fell from above and came crashing down on the grass, landing an inch or two from their heads.

Then, all was quiet again. Although Ryan had never been in an earthquake before, he knew that everything they had felt so far had been minor. This tremor was the biggest they had experienced, and was nothing compared to a major quake.

Karma ran over to Ryan as he was helping Vivian to her feet.

"Is everyone all right?" he asked, looking around.

Nabi had been thrown to the ground on the front lawn, but she picked herself up as soon as the Earth stopped moving. The front door opened, and out came Melina, Marcus and Leo, who were visibly shaken, but unharmed.

"They seem to be intensifying," Leo said.

"Maybe we should get moving," Ryan told them.

Melina nodded in agreement. "We might as well – everything in the house is now a mess."

It took them about a half hour to gather their stuff and pack up some supplies. Marcus threw the big backpack over his shoulder, while Melina carried a smaller backpack. Leo and Ryan both carried small duffle bags that they found in the house. Most of the bags held food and drinks of some kind, with the exception of Leo's, which contained some extra clothing.

Walking side by side, the six travelers left the ranch with the scarred tree behind them and headed out into the dreary day. Karma jogged ahead, pausing every so often to wait for everyone to catch up.

For two hours they walked without a break, stopping only when they came across an abandoned car or truck. Unfortunately, all of the vehicles they encountered either didn't have keys or didn't have gas. They saw no other living things, although they found a few dead bodies along the way.

They were walking through the main street of a small Texan town when they finally found a vehicle with keys and gas. Although it wasn't the most effective form of transportation, they all piled into the ice cream truck.

The truck was old and the tires were a bit bald, but it definitely beat walking. It was about the size of a large van, with a big opening on the right side to allow the driver to hand out ice cream to eager kids. Colorful stickers showing the different ice cream choices covered the sides and back of the truck, and a red stop sign was attached on the left, ready to be flipped out in case traffic needed to be stopped. There was one door on either side, leading to the only seat in the truck. The passenger side door had a round hole in the middle with a cartoon dragon painted around it. Inside the truck, just under the passenger side door, a cardboard box sat on the floor to collect garbage after it was thrown into the dragon's mouth.

The back of the truck held the freezers. It was a single unit made out of steel and ran along the left side of the truck. It was divided into three compartments, each having a separate door that swung up and back. The freezers must have stopped working a long time ago, because the remaining ice cream was a soupy, smelly mess.

They quickly got rid of the mushy boxes of leftover ice cream and filed in the truck. Melina climbed into the driver's seat. After hearing Marcus talk about her driving in the rain, she was the unanimous choice to steer the truck. Ryan tossed the box of garbage in the back and used a turned over milk crate to sit next to Melina. Vivian, Leo and Nabi made themselves as comfortable as possible on top of the freezers, while Marcus chose to sit on the ledge of the opening on the right side of the truck. Karma sat on floor by Marcus, occasionally leaning her head out of the opening.

The ride was bumpy and uncomfortable, but no one complained. They traveled through the bleak morning and into the afternoon. Although they kept their eyes open for any sign of other survivors, they saw none. Debris was scattered among the buildings and cars littered the road like unwanted toys.

Ryan looked out of the streaked window of the ice cream truck. The world seemed so big and empty. He imagined that this is what it would be like if the world powers ever waged war on one another. But then again, maybe this was a kind of world war. Only in this war, the world itself was taking action.

Another quake rocked the Earth and almost knocked the truck on its side, but Melina's ace driving kept them upright. The trembling lasted a solid thirty seconds this time, and was the longest one they had been through so far. That fact was on everyone's mind, although none of them verbalized their fears.

As they continued east, they noticed smoke rising in the air up ahead. Marcus leaned out the side of the truck and counted as many as twelve separate plumes. The last time they followed a cloud like that, they had been forced to run for their lives, so everyone felt more than a little nervous as they got closer.

Melina stopped the truck in the middle of the road once they were in full view of the cause of the smoke. Everyone stepped out of the truck and stared out at the city in front of them.

"I knew we were missing something these past few days," Marcus said. "What would the end of the world be without some good old fashioned rioting?"

CHAPTER 13

Picking Up Strays

The scene before them looked like something out of a movie. The road they were traveling on led into what was once a populated southwestern city. It lacked the gray tall buildings and wall to wall concrete that Ryan was used to from New York City. Instead, the buildings were only about three stories high and almost all of them were colored some shade of brown. Immobile cars and trucks lay in the streets at all angles, most of which were dented with broken windows. Fires burned in a number of garbage cans that lined the streets and sidewalks, causing a haze to drift through the air. Some buildings in the interior of the city must have been burning as well, because smoke clouds rose overhead not too far away.

Standing next to the ice cream truck, Ryan tried to picture what the place must have been like before all the disasters struck. The city probably had a relaxing charm that you didn't get from a metropolis with giant metal buildings towering above you. He imagined people exchanging smiles as they walked down the street on their way home from work, while others sat at outdoor restaurants sipping a cold drink.

It would have been a nice town to visit. But not anymore. Storefront windows were shattered, garbage littered the streets and the fires transformed the air into a smoky haze. Figures occasionally ran from one building to another, some stopping just long enough to throw a rock or brick at a nearby window.

"Do we really have to go in there?" Melina asked.

Ryan reached down and gave Karma a pat on the side. "What do you think girl?"

The dog looked up at him, stepped forward a few paces, and turned back to them.

"Damn," Marcus said. "How did I know she was gonna do that?"

Ryan convinced Karma to join them back in the truck and they drove into the town.

Melina drove slowly as she steered the truck around cars and burning garbage cans. They could see shadows of people watching them from windows and every so often someone would dart across the street and into the cover of a building.

They had only driven a couple hundred feet into town when Karma started barking. Melina stopped the truck. "What's going on?"

As soon as the truck stopped Karma leapt out of the big opening of the truck and ran to the sidewalk.

"Karma!" Ryan called, opening the door.

Everyone followed Ryan out of the truck and over to the sidewalk where Karma stood waiting. When they got to her, she turned and ran into the open door of a nearby building. Some movement in the street ahead of them caught Ryan's attention. Through the wafting smoke they saw a few people running out of the broken window of a small shop with their hands full. Ryan stepped forward into the street to get a better look and saw that they were coming out of a jewelry store.

"Looters," Leo said, coming up next to him.

"Why the hell would they bother stealing jewelry?" Ryan asked. "I don't see how it could have any value anymore."

"Greed is rarely rational," Leo replied.

A loud bang startled the group, as a rock hit the side of the truck and bounced into the street.

"I think it's safe to say that we're in a hostile environment," Melina said.

Ryan looked at the buildings around them, but couldn't see anyone. A bark from Karma brought his attention back to the building in front of them. She was standing in the doorway, squinting in the smoke.

"Let's see what she wants to show us," Ryan said, walking toward the doorway.

Marcus put a hand on his shoulder. "Maybe I should stay out here and watch the truck."

Ryan considered it for a moment and then told him, "I think its best that we stay together. You never know what's going to happen and I don't want to take a chance of getting separated."

Melina grabbed the keys out of the ignition while everyone grabbed their packs and bags, then everyone followed Karma inside the building. The front of the building didn't give any indication as to what was inside. Above the door there was only the number sixty-three, painted in white lettering.

Karma led them down a dark hallway. There were doors on either side, but she jogged passed them without even a casual glance.

Ryan peeked in each one as he walked by. Judging by what he saw, they must be inside of a small office building. Each door they passed contained a messy arrangement of desks and chairs. Forgotten paperwork covered the desks and most of the floors.

Karma continued down the hallway, which eventually turned to the left. Still following, Ryan and the others made the turn and then continued down the hall until Karma finally stopped in front of a glass door on the right. Gray light filtered through the glass and illuminated the dark hallway. Karma stared at the closed door as Ryan reached her. He looked through the glass door and realized that they had made it to the back of the building.

Ryan pulled the door open and Karma ran out and started jogging across a small parking lot toward a dark brown building on the other side. Following, Ryan saw that the parking lot was enclosed by the backs of a few buildings, with a narrow alleyway leading out to a street.

They were halfway across the parking lot when the ground started to shake. Ryan held his arms out and tried to keep his balance, but was soon sent to the ground, along with everyone else. Ryan landed on his stomach and lifted his head to see the nearby buildings cracking, their windows shattering as the frames of the structures shifted. The three cars in the parking lot shuddered as the rumbling shifted them over a few feet. Pieces of cement and stucco fell from the cracks in the buildings and the big glass door they had just walked through fell forward and smashed onto the asphalt of the parking lot.

The earthquake continued for a few more seconds and then came to an abrupt stop. Ryan pushed himself back to his feet and helped the others up.

"That was not fun," Marcus said, brushing himself off.

"They definitely seem to be building in strength," Vivian said.

Nabi agreed. "Yeah. I think we should get out of here and find a nice unpopulated area, where there are no buildings to crash down on our heads."

"Let's see where Karma is taking us first," Ryan told them. "Then we'll get out of here as fast as we can. I promise."

They found Karma waiting for them in front of the dark brown building. There was a square white sign next to a door that read "Sunrise Animal Shelter."

Ryan opened the door and Karma darted inside. The room was dark, with only a few small windows letting light in. As their eyes adjusted, Ryan guessed they were standing in some kind of reception room. There was a desk on the left and rows of chairs lined up against the three walls opposite it. There was a door behind the desk and another one opposite the door they had just come through.

Nabi let out a startled cry and turned her head into Vivian's shoulder.

"What?" Ryan asked.

Nabi motioned behind the desk, where he saw a woman's body crumpled in the corner. As Ryan walked past the desk toward it, a weak voice said, "Get out of here you scoundrels. There's nothing left for you."

Vivian let go of Nabi and knelt down with Ryan, lifting up the woman's head. She was an older woman, probably in her mid-sixties, with tan skin and shoulder length dark black hair that was now a knotted mess. She was clothed in tan pants and a loose fitting white blouse that was marked with dirt, blood and even a few boot prints. Her face was covered in cuts and bruises, and the woman seemed on the verge of unconsciousness. Her eyelids were almost closed and she was apparently in a lot of pain.

Vivian did a quick inventory of her visual injuries. The woman appeared to have been beaten and left for dead. She was badly bruised and her right arm hung limply from her shoulder, obviously broken.

"What happened to you?" Vivian asked, moving the hair away from her face.

The woman gazed up at Vivian as if trying to recognize her. "There's nothing left. You've taken it all already. Get out."

Leo leaned down. "Don't worry; we're not here to hurt you. Tell us what happened, so we can help."

The words took a moment to sink into the woman's aching head, but she seemed to understand. "Oh, thank God." She coughed and winced in pain.

"Who did this to you?" Vivian asked.

"I don't know who they were," she said, between labored breaths. "They were breaking into all the buildings. I guess they were just locals who figured that the law no longer mattered . . . They've been looting stores, ransacking houses and starting fires. I never thought they would come in here."

The woman cringed with every word, as if speech was a painful process.

"And they just beat you up?" Marcus asked, appalled by the thought.

"They were taking all the food . . . I'm a volunteer here, and the animals need that food. I couldn't just let them take it . . . I tried to stop them, but it was no use. They kept hitting and kicking me . . . I begged them to stop. I told them that the animals would die without the food, but they didn't care . . . They took it all."

The woman wheezed the last few words out and drifted off into unconsciousness.

Ryan put a hand on Vivian's shoulder. "Do what you can for her. I'm going to check out the rest of this place."

"This is a little over my head," Vivian said. "But I'll try."

Ryan turned and saw Karma sitting in front of the door to the side of the desk. Marcus and Melina joined Ryan as he opened the door and followed Karma inside.

The door led them into a large room with a row of individual animal cages holding dogs. They ran along the entire wall, with hand printed pages clipped to the front listing the names and specific information of each animal. On the far right side there were two big rooms made out of chain link fencing. One room held five small to medium sized dogs, while the other held four bigger dogs. All the way on the left side, was a small room with a large glass wall that held smaller cages containing cats.

Ryan walked across the room and looked at the various dogs. Normally, the dogs would be running around their cages in excitement. But not on this day. There was no jumping or wagging of tails in greeting, as you might expect from shelter animals who were begging for a home. These dogs just watched Ryan as he passed them. Most were very thin and in poor condition. They seemed to perk up a little when Karma came near, some pushing their noses against the bars of the cage.

Karma looked back and forth down the row of cages and then up at Ryan.

"These poor pooches," Marcus said.

Ryan reached down and opened a cage belonging to a yellow lab named Bailey.

After the door swung completely open, Bailey slowly walked out and touched noses with Karma. Karma licked the skinny dog on the face a few times, and then walked to the next cage.

"Let them all out," Ryan told him.

Ryan, Marcus and Melina opened all of the cages, allowing the rest of the dogs to get their welcome from Karma.

Once all the dogs were free, they went into the cat room and opened all the cages. The cats were in similar condition, and calmly walked out of the room to join the dogs. Surprisingly, the dogs didn't react to the cats coming into the room.

There were sixteen dogs and twenty-one cats in total gathered around Karma. Each animal took a turn touching noses with Karma or rubbing against her side. It was a weird sight, seeing all of these dogs and cats standing together so quietly.

"They probably haven't been fed for days," Melina said. "They need food in a bad way."

The door opened and Leo, Nabi and a teary eyed Vivian walked into the room.

Vivian wiped her eyes and said, "She's dead."

Ryan put an arm around her, "She was too far gone. There was nothing you could do."

"What are we going to do with all of these guys?" Nabi asked.

Ryan looked around at all of the animals at their feet. There were all different breeds of cats and dogs, in all shapes and sizes. The only thing they had in common was that they were all homeless and hungry.

Ryan thought for a moment.

"Let's get these animals a meal," he told everyone as he opened one of the duffle bags.

"Are you crazy?" Marcus said. "Look at all these guys. We'd have to use the rest of our supplies to feed them."

"I'm very aware of that," Ryan said. "But we can't just let them out into that cruel world without some food. They would never make it."

Marcus just shook his head.

"Who knows how long they've been orphaned here," Nabi said. "And now, without food. I think it's the least we can do for these poor animals."

"They will need some nourishment if they're going to have any chance of survival," Melina added.

Ryan, Melina and a reluctant Marcus gathered all of the food from their bags and backpacks, while Vivian, Leo and Nabi lined up food bowls on the floor. They put some food in each bowl, trying to make sure every animal got a decent portion. Although some of the bowls were filled before others, none of the dogs or cats started eating until all of the bowls were filled. But once they started, they chowed down hard and fast. They finished every last morsel of food in their bowls and then licked it clean. They didn't try to steal any other animal's food. Once finished with their meal they just patiently waited by their bowl.

Karma stood next to Ryan watching. She didn't seem to mind that every animal was eating except for her.

Marcus on the other hand, couldn't let it go. "That's it. We have no more food."

Ryan looked over at the big guy. "These animals needed this."

"I know," Marcus said. "But what the hell are we going to do now?"

"It was the right thing to do," Leo said.

"Yeah, Goliath," Melina said, walking up to Marcus. "Our good deed here will be rewarded in the future. Or don't you believe in karma?"

Marcus looked from Melina, down to the dog at Ryan's feet and smiled. "Yeah, I guess I do. Just make sure you remind me of how good this was when my stomach is grumbling later."

They held the doors open and watched, as all the animals followed Karma out into the parking lot. Outside, the stray dogs and cats trotted past Karma, across the parking lot and down the alleyway. Karma watched the last dog disappear around the corner and then turned back to her human friends.

Silently, they walked back through the office building. Although Ryan felt a little uncomfortable leaving the body of the woman in the shelter, they had no choice. There was nowhere to bury her and that last earthquake had made him feel the need to move out quickly. Vivian covered the woman's body with a blanket and they had a brief moment of silence before they left the small building.

When they made it back to the ice cream truck, they found two teenage boys inside, rummaging around. The boys were dressed in dirty jeans and long sleeve shirts, and didn't notice the group coming back to the truck.

Marcus made it to the truck first and slammed his hand down on the hood. "Hey!" he yelled at them through the windshield.

The two teens took one look at the big guy and made a hasty exit through the big opening in the side of the truck. Marcus watched them disappear around the corner of a building across the street and then stuck his head in the trucks opening to see what they were up to.

"They didn't do anything," he told the others. "They were probably searching for stuff to loot, but luckily for us, we have nothing."

Ryan glanced around the smoky streets, then down at Karma, who was also surveying the area.

"Well," Ryan said. "I guess we should continue down this road and see where it takes us."

Everyone assumed their positions in the ice cream truck and Melina got them moving again. She steered around the many obstructions, as Marcus kept watch out of the big opening for any signs of trouble. They could hear raised voices coming from a couple of windows, as well as sounds of breaking glass. Occasionally, they would see a few figures run out of a local store with an armload of merchandise.

The street curved around to the left and headed into a small traffic circle. In the center of the circle was a grassy island with a flag pole in the middle. A big American flag hung loosely on the pole. There was a light breeze blowing through the smoky air, which made the flag gently flap overhead. Directly on the other side of the circle was a large white building with long columns on either side of a series of steps. There were two army transport vehicles parked on the right side.

As Melina drove the ice cream truck around the circle, a soldier stepped out from behind one of the columns, aiming his rifle at the truck.

"Stop right there!" the camouflaged man shouted in a stern

voice.

"Looks like we've got some more excitement," Melina said, as she hit the brakes.

The soldier came down a few steps, keeping his rifle aimed at the truck. Karma jumped out of the truck and ran toward him.

"Now what?" Ryan said, watching Karma gallop up the steps.

The soldier seemed a bit startled by the approaching dog, but kept his gun pointed at the truck. When Karma reached him, she pranced at his feet, wagging her tail and looking up at him. The soldier glanced down and his face seemed to soften a bit.

Ryan opened the door of the truck and stepped out, while Marcus jumped out of the service opening.

The soldier jerked his attention back to the truck. "Where the hell do you think you're going?"

Ryan raised his arms unthreateningly. "Hey, take it easy. We're on your side," he said, although he wasn't sure there were any sides.

"I'll be the judge of that," the soldier snapped back. "Everybody out of the truck and keep your hands up."

The soldier couldn't be more than twenty-one years old. Behind the rifle was a baby face with a brown crew cut. His military pants and long sleeved shirt were camouflaged, and his black boots were shiny.

"Where are you going?" the soldier asked, clutching his rifle.

"Uh, we're not really sure," Ryan said. "We've been traveling around, just trying to stay alive."

"In an ice cream truck?"

"Yeah, the Ferrari's in the shop," Melina replied.

"It's all we could find," Ryan said, ignoring Melina. "We've used a number of vehicles the last couple of weeks. Are you with the army?"

"That's right," the soldier said.

Marcus turned to Melina, "I feel safer already."

"Better be careful, Big Foot," Melina muttered. "This guy's liable to drag your ass all the way back to your New York cage."

The soldier glared quickly at Melina. "What did you just say?"

"Uh, sir, I'm sorry, sir," she replied condescendingly. "Just a little friendly banter with the big guy."

"No, did you say you were from New York?"

"Some of us are," Ryan said, trying to keep the soldiers attention on himself and not Melina's mouth.

The soldier lowered his rifle. "The Colonel is gonna want to talk to you. Would you mind stepping inside?"

"I guess not," Ryan told him, not seeing any other alternative.

They followed the soldier up the stairs and inside the building, which they discovered was the town's public library. It appeared that the army had converted it into a makeshift command station.

They went through a small foyer, before glass doors led into the library. The main desk had been cleared off to make room for various electronic devices. To the right, two long tables held military equipment and supplies, and beyond that were the book stacks and library computer terminals. Off to the left of the main desk was the reference area, where about ten uniformed men were talking.

The soldier who brought them inside looked over at the men and said, "Where's the Colonel?"

They pointed to a door behind the desk. The soldier went around the desk and knocked solidly on the door.

Almost immediately, a voice from the room said, "Enter."

The young soldier opened the door and stepped into the

doorway. "I've got a group of people who traveled here from New York. I thought you might like to speak with them."

"New York?" the man's voice said. "Yes, send them in."

The soldier stepped aside and allowed the group to enter the room. The room contained a big wooden desk opposite three metal chairs, with filing cabinets lining the back wall. A few pictures of desert landscapes adorned the walls and a big potted cactus sat on a table on the right side.

A serious looking middle-aged man was standing behind the desk, dressed in camouflage. He was fairly tall with short black hair, and his face was a maze of lines and creases giving him a weathered appearance.

Once everyone was inside, the young soldier stepped out of the room and shut the door. The man behind the desk studied the people before him intently. His eyes went from person to person slowly, ending with Ryan. Finally, he glanced down at Karma standing at Ryan's feet.

"Good looking dog," the man said.

"Thanks," Ryan replied, feeling a little nervous.

The man walked around the desk and took a seat on top of it. "I'm Colonel Cartwright of the 7th Infantry Division. I understand you came in from the east coast?"

"Yes, we did," Ryan replied.

"Good," the Colonel said. "I wonder if you wouldn't mind telling me what's going on over there? We lost contact with all of our bases in the East about a week ago and I would love to know what the hell's happening."

"It's not a pretty sight," Marcus said. Thinking back on all of the destruction and death they had witnessed, Marcus's face reflected everyone's pain and loss.

"Please, tell me what you know," Colonel Cartwright said.

Ryan told him their tale, leaving out the unusual events with Karma. Every so often one of the others would jump in and add something, but for the most part they let Ryan do the talking.

After Ryan finished, the Colonel shook his head. "So I guess I shouldn't count on hearing from any of our men in the East?"

"I wouldn't hold my breath," Marcus said.

"Excuse me, sir, but why are you stationed in a library?" Vivian asked.

The Colonel got up off the desk and started to slowly pace.

"We were sent down from Fort Carson in Colorado Springs to assess the situation and assist the locals. We needed a temporary HQ, and there was something about that big flag outside that made me feel welcome. The people were pretty freaked out by the time we arrived, but we tried to keep them calm and help in any way we could.

"Then, a few days ago, things got a little out of control. Food and water were becoming scarce, and the people were turning to us for help. Unfortunately, there wasn't a hell of a lot I could do for them. They started rioting and were aggressive toward my men. We tried to keep order, but after one of my men was jumped and beaten to death, I ordered everyone back here to hold up until we get word from General Cox."

"Who's General Cox?" Melina asked.

"General Cox is the commanding officer here. He went west to check in on two other military bases. He assured us that he would be back in four days. That was a week ago."

"So what happens now?" Ryan had to ask.

"My orders are very specific," the Colonel told them. "We are to stay here until the General returns."

"But what if he never returns?" Melina said. "Haven't you felt the earthquakes? It's not safe here."

"I have to give him some more time. General Cox is a demanding man and he doesn't like it when his orders are disobeyed. Are you heading out or staying in town?"

Ryan looked around at his friends. "I think we're going to get moving."

Everyone nodded in agreement.

"Well, thank you for your time. I wish you a safe journey," the Colonel said, as he showed them to the door.

They went outside and found the young soldier back at his post next to the column.

"Good day," he said, as they walked down the stairs.

Ryan opened the ice cream truck door, let everyone go inside, and then stepped in himself.

"Aren't we forgetting someone?" Melina said behind the wheel, pointing up at the library doors.

Karma was standing next to the young soldier, looking down at them.

"Karma, let's go!" Ryan called out the door.

Karma held her ground and let out a bark.

"Maybe we're not done with this place yet," Vivian said from her perch on the freezer. "Maybe that soldier is supposed to come with us."

"Great," Ryan said, throwing his hands up. "How the hell are we going to convince soldier boy there to ignore his orders to come for a ride in an ice cream truck?"

Vivian jumped off the freezer and put a hand on Ryan's shoulder.

"She's never steered us wrong. Let's just go up there and talk to him for a minute. I'm sure we'll figure out what needs to be done."

"Oh, all right," Ryan conceded.

Everyone filed back out of the truck and walked up the stairs. Karma's tail started wagging as they climbed the steps.

Ryan knelt down and rubbed Karma's head and whispered, "What are you up to?"

The young soldier smiled. "She's a nice dog."

"And don't think she doesn't know it," Melina said, stepping forward. "What's your name soldier?"

"Private Shawn Mathers, ma'am," he replied.

"Don't ever ma'am me, Private Shawn," Melina told him sternly.

"Uh, sorry. I didn't mean any disrespect," he stammered.

"Don't worry about her," Marcus said. "She's like this with everyone."

Melina smiled at the soldier, "Just be glad I like you. It's this monster," she pointed at Marcus, "that needs to be careful. Let me ask you something, Shawn: do you like it here?"

"Here in New Mexico?" he asked.

"No, here in the army," Melina corrected.

"Yes, ma-," Shawn's face reddened, as he realized his mistake. "Yes, I guess so."

"No regrets about leaving your family and friends?" Melina asked him.

The soldier thought for a second. "Sure, I miss them. But this is the life I chose and I'm proud to serve my country."

Melina nodded. "I see."

Karma started barking.

Ryan and Vivian traded nervous looks, as Melina continued. "Now as I understand it, you're here waiting around for some general – who you may never see again - to get back and tell you what to do."

"Something like that," Shawn said.

"Does anyone ever question your orders?" Leo asked.

"No, a good soldier never questions his orders. Besides, General Cox is not someone you want to make angry."

Karma ran down the steps and started barking up at them from in front of the ice cream truck. Everyone looked down at her as the world started shaking again. Luckily, it was just a little tremor, lasting only a few seconds.

Ryan felt a growing feeling of dread in his stomach.

He turned and faced the young soldier. "Shawn, listen to me. Your General is never coming back. He's most likely dead by now. Things are getting very unstable here and we have to get out of here, before it's too late."

"Then by all means, go," Shawn said.

Karma continued to bark.

"Look at the world around you," Ryan continued. "It's falling apart. This is a different place than it was a few weeks ago. Everything is different now. There's no more society, no more organization and no more authority. It's now just a fight for survival. And if you cling to the orders of a past world, you won't survive in this new one.

"I know you just met us a few minutes ago, but believe me when I tell you, things are about to get a whole lot worse. You need to come with us now, if you want to live."

Shawn shook his head. "What are you talking about? I can't leave."

Vivian grabbed his hand. "Please. I know it sounds crazy, but you need to trust us."

"I'm sorry, but I suggest you get on your way," he said. "I'm not about to abandon my post."

Ryan was about to say something more, when the ground began shaking with renewed force. Within a few seconds, they all realized that this was much more than the little quakes they had experienced earlier.

Everyone struggled to keep their balance as the ground below them trembled. Cracks formed on the library's walls and chunks of cement broke off and fell to the ground. Karma's rapid barking was almost drowned out by the sound of the earth moving and the buildings around them breaking apart.

Ryan grabbed hold of Marcus. "Get everyone in the truck."

Marcus nodded, took hold of Nabi and started to help her down the stairs, with Leo, Vivian and Melina close behind. Their eyes got wide as the stairs began to crack apart underneath their feet. Large fissures streaked across the streets, opening holes and crevasses everywhere. Nearby buildings began to collapse, and the screams of people inside were lost in the roar of crumbling cement and bricks.

Marcus just about carried Nabi down the deteriorating stairs and placed her into the truck. Melina and Vivian stumbled down after them, as Ryan grabbed Shawn by the arm and pulled him toward the stairs. Somewhere underneath the library the earth split apart. The back of the building tilted down, as the library walls crumbled inward. With a shudder that sent everyone to the ground, the building broke free of the stairs and collapsed into a huge hole.

A falling column just missed slamming down onto Ryan and Shawn as they tried to get back to their feet. The shifting earth pushed the ground under the stairs upward as the crevice that engulfed the library continued to grow. Shawn had managed to get up on one knee, as a large chunk of the stairs next to him crumbled apart making him lose his balance and tumble toward the chasm. Shawn reached out for something to hold on to, but found only loose pieces of cement.

Ryan got himself upright in time to see Shawn skidding into the ever-widening hole. Quickly, he leapt for Shawn, sliding across loose rocks and pieces of broken cement. His hand found Shawn's, but their momentum carried them both over the lip of the rift. Ryan was somehow able to hook his free arm around a piece overhanging cement, stopping them both from plummeting into the gap.

Ryan glanced down and saw the frightened face of Shawn staring up at him desperately. He had no idea how deep the crevice was, because everything under them was obscured by rising clouds of dust. The pain throbbing in his arm from the strain of their combined weight was unbearable. He knew he couldn't hold them much longer.

Over the noise of the crumbling buildings he heard Karma's barks. Lifting his head, he saw her standing above him. Then, he began to feel Shawn's hand slipping out of his grip. He looked back down, as his hand separated from Shawn's. The soldier didn't make a sound as his body disappeared into the haze of dirt and debris.

Ryan stared down into the abyss, not willing to believe that Shawn was gone. A bark from Karma snapped him out of his trance. Ryan put his other hand on the ledge and started pulling himself up slowly. He got his right leg over the lip and dragged the rest of his body onto solid ground. Lying on his stomach panting, he realized that the ground had stopped shaking and the Earth was once again still.

CHAPTER 14

A Pleasant Gamble

Ryan stood up slowly and gazed down into the chasm that had swallowed the library and Shawn. Although the earth had stopped shaking, he could still hear pieces of the building crumbling down.

As the dust started to clear, Ryan began to make out some images below. The crack in the earth had created a hole as big as a football field. The portion of the remaining stairway that Ryan now stood on had been pushed about fifteen feet upward. About thirty feet below his feet, Ryan saw that the library was nothing more than a large pile of rubble. If he didn't know what the building once was, he never would have recognized it. And lying on a crumpled column was the broken body of Shawn. His back was bent at an unnatural angle and there was blood dripping from his open mouth.

Ryan gazed down. He was filled with a combination of sadness and anger. He was sad that Shawn was gone and mad at himself for being unable to save the young soldier. He noticed Karma standing next to him, looking down. She was speckled with dirt, but seemed unharmed.

"Ryan!" Vivian's concerned voice called from behind Ryan. "Are you okay?"

Ryan slowly turned away from the crevice and started down the angled slope of the fissure, with Karma following. At the bottom of the newly formed hill, Vivian embraced him.

"Thank God you're all right," she said, giving him a final squeeze.

"Shawn's dead," Ryan told them.

Ryan looked at the faces of his friends gathered around him. Everyone seemed to be trying to determine what the implications of Shawn's death might be.

After a moment of silence, Marcus was the first to speak. "It's gonna be okay," he said. "We did all we could for the guy."

Ryan shook his head. "But I was supposed to save him, right? He was supposed to come with us, wasn't he?"

"We don't know that for sure," Melina said.

"Well, if I'm the savior, shouldn't I have saved him?" Ryan said, raising his voice in frustration.

"Not necessarily," Leo said, in a calming voice. "There's only so much one man can do, and not everything goes according to plan. Not even God's plan."

"We're just glad you're safe," Nabi added.

Ryan looked down at Karma trying to find some answers in her eyes. He stared into her big brown eyes, wishing that she could tell him exactly what she was thinking. Karma just looked up at him calmly, not offering much in the way of information.

The collapse of a building down the street made everyone take notice of the destruction around them. The entire town had been reduced to a dusty pile of debris. The big rift in the earth had consumed many of the buildings on the main street and most of the others had been shaken apart by the tremors. There was no sign of people anywhere, and with the exception of the occasional sound of shifting rubble, there was nothing but silence.

A sudden breeze started to blow, causing everyone to squint as dirt was lifted into the air. The place reminded Ryan of the cemetery; large stones covering the ground signifying death. He felt a feeling of despair wash over him, and he decided it was time to go.

Karma seemed to agree. She had moved over to the ice cream truck doorway, waiting for them.

"Let's get moving," Ryan told the others.

The rising ground had caused the ice cream truck to lean to the left slightly. Melina got in the truck and moved it to level ground before everyone filed in.

No one spoke as they drove through the remainder of the town, weaving around big pieces of cement and cracks in the ground. They left the battered town behind, and tried to avoid the more populated areas by traveling on minor roads with less development.

Ryan sat on the milk crate next to Melina, staring out at the desert landscape. There were so many doubts going through his mind. Although he would never have admitted it, Ryan had been starting to believe that Karma was some kind of a higher being, perhaps Mother Nature or even God. He even began to consider the outside possibility that he was put here to be the traveling group's protector and keep everyone safe from harm.

Deep down, Ryan wanted to believe that he wasn't just an

average guy, leading an average life. He wanted his life to be more meaningful, and have some real purpose. And after thinking about everything that was said back at the ranch, he had begun to really believe. But now, with Shawn's death, he doubted everything.

They had been driving for about an hour when the ice cream truck finally ran out of gas.

"That's all she wrote," Melina announced, as they coasted to a stop.

"Good," Nabi said. "My ass couldn't take another bump."

They exited the truck and took stock of their surroundings. They were on a small paved road with a faded dotted yellow line running down the center. There was nothing but trees, shrubs and dirt in all directions.

"What now?" Vivian asked.

Ryan gazed up into the gray sky. Clouds still covered the horizon and the light seemed to be fading a bit. He guessed it would be dark in an hour or two.

Karma jogged down the center of the road in front of the immobile ice cream truck.

"Looks like we're walking," he said.

Marcus and Melina gathered their near empty backpacks. Without food, they only held a couple of extra shirts and a few other miscellaneous supplies.

"Nabi, keep your eyes open for any suitable spots to set up a camp for the night," Ryan said, as they walked down the road after Karma.

"Will do," she replied.

They followed the road as the wind picked up. Karma stayed in front, stopping occasionally to wait for her companions to catch up. Melina and Nabi walked side by side, swapping camping stories and outdoor adventures. Ryan and Vivian followed a couple of paces behind them. Vivian had tried a few attempts at conversation with Ryan, but he remained distant and preoccupied. Not far behind them, Marcus and Leo pulled up the rear of their little caravan.

"Man, my stomach is growling," Marcus said.

"We did what was needed back there," Leo told him. "Those animals needed that food badly."

"I know," Marcus said quickly. "I don't mean to sound uncaring. I just get a little grouchy when I'm hungry."

Leo looked up ahead at Ryan. He noticed that Ryan's head was lowered slightly and his shoulders were slumped. Years of experience told Leo that Ryan was carrying a heavy burden.

"I'll be right back," he told Marcus, quickening his pace.

When he was next to Ryan, Leo said, "How're you doing?"

Ryan glanced over at him, and then brought his eyes forward. "All right, I guess."

"What are you thinking about?" Leo asked.

"Nothing. Everything. I don't know," Ryan replied.

Leo stayed quiet, hoping Ryan would say more.

After a few seconds, he did. "I should have been able to save him. . . I think I was supposed to save him. But I didn't – I couldn't. What does that mean?"

Ryan paused and shrugged his shoulders. "Either I'm not who you guys think I am or I just messed up in a major way. I think you just might be wrong about everything."

"Don't be so quick to dismiss everything just because things aren't perfect," Leo told him. "Faith is easy to have when the path is certain, but that's not when it's most useful. True faith is only achieved when our beliefs are tested. That's when it's time to look to your devotion for support and guidance. You must have trust in your faith, wherever it may lie, and have confidence in your beliefs and yourself."

Ryan looked over at the man walking next to him. There was something about his kind eyes and the calm sound of his voice that made Ryan feel at ease.

"Maybe everything happened as it was supposed to," Leo continued. "Maybe you were not meant to save Shawn. It's possible that you were just being shown that you can't save everyone, even though you know them to be worthy and good.

"Or, maybe God slipped up," Leo smiled. "Even the man upstairs can have an off day."

Ryan smiled back.

"Don't beat yourself up over things that are out of your control," Leo said. "I have a feeling you'll have plenty more chances to prove yourself."

"Thanks," Ryan told him, feeling better.

Leo smiled and drifted back next to Marcus.

Whatever was responsible, Ryan was glad to be with these five people. He couldn't think of a better group to face the unknown with.

Up ahead, Karma was waiting for them to catch up again.

There was no better guide, either, Ryan thought.

Darkness was starting to descend and the wind continued to build. Nabi pointed out a few places that they could camp, but the spots provided very little shelter. And with the increasing wind, they all agreed they should keep moving forward.

Soon the last bit of gray light faded into night. They kept walking on the road, staying close together in the dark. Even Karma pulled in close to the group as they continued forward.

Ryan was just about to tell Nabi to stop them at the next possible camp site when Karma started barking.

"Is that a good news bark or a bad news bark?" Melina asked.

"I can never tell the difference," Ryan answered in the growing darkness.

"Hey!" Nabi called. "Check that out."

Ryan looked up and saw the faint glow of lights off to the left.

Curiosity got everyone moving a little faster. As they got closer they realized that the lights were coming from two large buildings.

"Are those electric lights?" Marcus asked.

"It sure looks like it," Vivian said.

"How is that possible?" Marcus asked, confused.

They followed the road toward the buildings. When they finally reached them, they realized that the lights were a series of small white and yellow spot lights pointed at a large sign. The sign read *Nightfall Hotel and Casino.*

Ryan stood in front of the sign, dumbfounded.

Behind the sign were two buildings. The one on the left was a three story hotel, with tall glass revolving doors in front. The oval building on the right was the casino, which appeared to be attached to the hotel. It was just as large, but only two stories high. And like all good casinos, had almost no windows.

"Don't tell me this place is open" Melina said

"There's only one way to find out," Marcus said excitedly.

As they pondered which door to enter, Karma made the decision and ran up to the casino doors.

"Looks like Karma feels lady luck calling," Marcus said, walking toward the casino.

The rest of the group followed as Marcus opened one of the two big glass doors leading into the casino. Inside, they found themselves in a large marble foyer. There were overhead lights on, illuminating a large circular fountain with leafy green artificial plants. Even though the water wasn't running, it was a pretty sight.

"I don't suppose you guys are up for a little craps," Marcus said.

"Not so fast, Too-Tall," Melina scolded. "First we need to find out what the hell is going on here."

A hallway branched off to the left and right from the lobby. Karma jogged toward the right hallway, her nails making little clicking sounds on the marble. They were about to follow her when they heard footsteps coming from the opposite hallway.

A large, beefy man in a tight black t-shirt shirt and dress pants strode confidently into the lobby.

"Good evening folks," he said in a husky voice, stopping next to the fountain. "Can I help you?"

The man had short, dirty blond hair and a body that looked like it was sculpted out of rock. His clothing was clean, his pants neatly ironed, and his black boots were shined. He regarded them calmly as if this were an average day at the casino. Ryan had to remind himself that this was not an average day.

"I don't know where to start," Ryan said.

Melina took a step forward. "We just swung by for a few games of blackjack and a Wayne Newton show."

Ryan put a hand up to Melina. "Uh, we've kind of been through a lot, and we saw the lights outside. . . How exactly do you have electricity?"

"I'm afraid I can't answer that," the man told them. "I can tell you that this is a private club now and all visitors have to be cleared to enter."

Marcus walked next to Melina. "Are you kidding me? Do you have any idea of the shit that's going on out there?" he said, pointing at the casino doors.

The man crossed his muscular arms. "The only thing that concerns me is the shit going on in here."

More footsteps echoed down the hallway, and a gray haired man in a blue suit walked in behind the big bruiser, as he exchanged stares with Marcus.

"Well, what have we here, James?" the newcomer asked.

"More roughnecks," he told him. "They came in off the street. I was just about to show them out."

"Now why would you do that?" the gray haired man asked.

James tilted his head. "I was told to keep all undesirables out of here."

"I think I can guess who gave you that order," he said adjusting his suit jacket. "Listen, James, I need to be informed of things around here."

"Hey, I was just doing what I was told," James said.

"I know. It's not your fault. That son of a bitch likes to give orders a little too much."

The gray haired man gave the big guy a pat on the back and walked past him and up to Melina and Marcus. "How do you do?

I'm Senator Walter Gibbons. Welcome."

Marcus shook the hand outstretched before him. "Nice to meet you. I'm Marcus."

"And you are?" he asked, moving over to Melina.

"Melina," she told him. "Roughneck supreme."

"I hope James didn't offend you," he said, looking at the rest of the group. "A few bad experiences with some hoodlums have caused us to lean on the side of caution."

The Senator shook hands with everyone else, and then took a step back. "So, where are you from?"

"Everywhere," Ryan replied. "How do you have electricity?"

"Why don't you come on in, have a seat and I'll answer all your questions," the Senator said. Then he turned to James. "Would you go and tell Yuma to switch on the lights in Desert Moon?"

James nodded, "Will do," and then strode back down the hall.

Senator Gibbons smiled at his guests. "Okay now. If you would please follow me."

Ryan was totally confused by what was going on, but curiosity won over caution, and he followed the Senator down the hallway to the right, and into a buffet style restaurant called *Desert Moon Café*.

"As I mentioned, my name is Walter Gibbons," he told them as they filed into the restaurant. "I am a United States Senator from Arizona. I was visiting when the disasters struck, and have been holding up here until the scope of the damage is known."

The place was dark, but the lights from the hallway were enough to see the general layout of the restaurant. There were circular tables of various sizes throughout the big room, with floral patterned chairs pushed in neatly around each one. Four empty, rectangular food service stations were set up in the middle of the room, with a few more along the back wall.

Senator Gibbons motioned to a table in front, big enough for everyone to take a seat. After their long walk, no one hesitated to sit down. The Senator remained standing,

"I don't mean to sound disrespectful," Ryan said, "but, are you really just hanging out in a casino hoping everything is going to go back to normal?"

The Senator leaned forward. "I have assembled a small group of powerful and influential people here to help in the rebuilding process when that time comes."

The lights in the restaurant came on, making everyone squint for a second. Ryan still couldn't believe they had electricity. He noticed the Senator's suit. It looked like it just came from the dry cleaners. Ryan gazed down at the filthy rags that clung to his body, and then back to smiling Senator. He wondered if the man before them had seen any of the hardships and tragedy that they had. Or if he knew what it was like have no idea when you might eat again. Or to run for your life time and time again. Ryan doubted it.

"Why are you in a Casino?" Vivian asked. "Shouldn't you be in a command center or bunker somewhere?"

"Unfortunately, things happened very quickly and I had to use the resources that were presented to me," he replied. Then he addressed the group, smiling. "I can tell that you are very curious about our little establishment here. Well, it is true we have electrical power. An associate of mine was able to supply us with a number of high powered mobile generators. They won't last forever, so we have a very strict policy of their usage. We only use the power at night, and only in the parts of the casino and hotel that are necessary. It helps us to feel civilized during this uncivilized time."

Ryan was trying to decide what question to ask first, when Melina beat him to it.

"You said you're going to start the rebuilding process when the time is right?" she asked him.

"Yes, that's correct," Walter replied.

"Rebuild what?" Melina said. "There's not a hell of a lot left out there."

"I know it looks tough out there now," he told all of them. "But I'm confident that we can come together and make this a great country once again. And I'll be ready when the time comes. The people are going to need a leader. Someone strong, who knows how to get everyone back together. I believe that I have the experience and fortitude to steer us where we need to go.

"So you see, we are waiting out the storm. Gathering our strength for that new beginning we know is just around the corner."

Ryan couldn't decide what to make of Senator Walter Gibbons. It almost sounded like he was campaigning. After listening to his speech, it seemed to Ryan that there was very little difference between the Senator and the fake reverend. Whether it's a presidential candidate or a fanatical preacher, the goal is always the same: to get as many people as possible to believe. And it didn't really matter if you believed in what they were saying, as long as you believe in them, and gave them your vote, money, and blind devotion.

The Senator's voice pulled Ryan from his thoughts.

"Well, I can tell that you've been through quite an ordeal. How would you like to get washed up, put on some fresh clothes and sit down for a hot meal?"

"I sincerely hope you're not toying with us," Melina said.

The Senator smiled. "Not at all. First, we'll get you a couple of rooms next door where you can rinse off. Then, I'll have someone bring you some new clothes and you can join us for dinner."

Ryan couldn't believe his ears. It sounded too good to be true.

Marcus didn't hear anything after the words "hot meal."

"Let's go," he said, standing up quickly.

They followed Senator Gibbons down the hallway, back through the lobby and down the opposite hallway. They passed the entrance to the casino, which was dark and unlit. Then they passed a restaurant on the left, where they saw some tables already being set. They continued down the hall, which eventually led over to the hotel.

The lobby was decorated in reds and oranges and had a strong southwestern flare, as did everything over on the casino side. They walked past the front desk and across to another hallway. They passed about five or six rooms until the Senator finally stopped in front of room number 104.

"I can spare two rooms right now, 104 and 106. Since we don't want to waste our electricity on the computers, we can't program the key cards," He told them as he slid a card into the slot on the door. A small light flashed green and he opened the door.

"Luckily, we have a couple of these master key cards, so we can open any door. The only problem is that you don't get your own key. Just keep the lock out when the door is open."

The Senator turned the lock on the door, exposing the bolt and stopping the door from fully closing.

"The electricity is only on in the rooms from seven to ten o'clock each night," he said, as he walked to the next door and did the same. "Make yourselves comfortable and I'll send some clothes over. Why don't you meet us for dinner in about an hour and a half? We'll be in the Regency, which is that nice restaurant we passed on our way over here."

Vivian was in the doorway of the first room already. "Thank you. You have no idea how much this means to us."

"It's my pleasure," Senator Gibbons said, and left them to their rooms.

The women took room 104 and the men went over to room 106, with the exception of Karma, who stuck to Ryan's side.

Inside their room, the boys made themselves comfortable. Marcus immediately collapsed on one of the two double beds.

"I can't wait to sink my teeth in some hot food," he declared, as he stared up at the ceiling.

"Hey! We have running water!" Leo yelled from the bathroom. "It's kind of weak, but it's water."

Ryan stood in the middle of the hotel room, thinking.

Marcus sat up and said, "Uh oh. What's the matter, Ryan?"

"Doesn't all this seem a bit strange to you?" he asked them. "The whole world is in turmoil and the Senator and his posse are hanging out in a casino. Don't you think there's something wrong with that?"

"Maybe they're just in denial," Leo said, as he walked out of the bathroom. "Everyone handles stressful situations differently. It's possible that they've created this little world here as a defense mechanism for facing reality."

"Hey, I don't care who they are or why they're here. I'm just glad we found this place," Marcus said.

"But we didn't find this place," Ryan reminded them. "Karma did."

"Yeah, so what?" Marcus said, standing. "She probably just

wanted to reward us for helping out all those poor starving dogs and cats."

Marcus bent down, put his big hands on Karma's ears and gave her a kiss on the snout. "I definitely believe in Karma," he said.

Ryan wasn't convinced. "I don't know. It doesn't really fit with everything that's happened so far. And I thought you guys believed that she's God or some kind of angel? Why would God bring us to a casino?"

Marcus stood back up. "Hey, even the man upstairs needs to have a little fun once in a while."

Ryan looked at Leo.

"The Lord works in mysterious ways," was all he could add.

"Don't worry about it, my man," Marcus told Ryan. "You'll feel better after you get cleaned up and have a belly full of food."

Although Ryan still felt a little uneasy, the thought of some clean clothes and a meal sounded great.

They took turns washing off. The flow of water in the shower wasn't much more than a fast trickle, but it did the job. There was soap and shampoo, which helped to wash away the dirt and grime they had accumulated since the rains. Ryan used a wet towel to clean the dirt off Karma. She stood in the bathtub without any complaints while Ryan cleaned her off as thoroughly as he could.

A man dropped off a clean set of clothes for each of them. Unfortunately for Marcus, they didn't have a big and tall selection. So while Ryan and Marcus got dress pants and white button-down shirts, Marcus got a tan t-shirt and pants about two inches too short. Nice dress shoes were also delivered. The Senator did a pretty good job of estimating their sizes, although the size thirteen shoes left for Marcus were two sizes too small.

Nothing could spoil Marcus's mood though. He just shrugged off the ill-fitting shoes and continued talking about what he wanted for dinner. Ultimately, he wore the skimpy pants and tight t-shirt, with his own boots. He was able to get most of the dirt off of them, making them look black once again.

It took them about two hours to clean up and get dressed. Ryan had to admit it did feel nice to be clean and wear some nice clothes again. He debated leaving Karma in the hotel room but he felt better with her at his side, and she also needed a meal. Once they were ready, they went next door and knocked on the girls' door.

"Just a minute," came Melina's voice from inside.

Ryan felt a little strange and awkward, like an eighteen year old waiting for his prom date. He had to keep reminding himself that this was still an unstable and dangerous time. Another earthquake could hit them at any time, and he had to stay alert and be ready for anything. Although he wasn't sure what he really believed, he definitely felt an overwhelming obligation to keep their entire group safe from harm.

The door opened and out walked the three girls.

Ryan was speechless. Having gotten used to seeing them covered in filth and sweat, he was totally unprepared for the sight before him. Not only were the girls clean, wearing beautiful dresses, but their hair was done nicely and they were wearing makeup.

They all wore the same style of dress, but each had a different color. Vivian wore red, Melina wore black and Nabi had royal blue. The dresses were long and elegant with a shiny satiny appearance and thin spaghetti straps. The women had been supplied with some hair care products along with the make-up, and they all wore their hair down.

"You are truly a sight for these sore eyes," Leo said, as the girls strutted into the hallway.

Ryan didn't know what to say. He had lived across from Vivian for three years and had spent the last few intense weeks by her side, but now he felt like he was seeing her for the first time.

"You look amazing," he said to her.

Vivian smiled, "Thanks, you clean up nicely too."

Marcus shook his head "A hot meal and these three lovely ladies. I must be dreaming."

"I would hope that you would dream yourself some clothes that fit," Melina said, eyeballing his outfit.

"It's all good," he said, smiling. "Now let's go eat."

They walked down the hall and across the hotel lobby. Ryan still felt that this was kind of inappropriate, considering what was going on the in world, but he had to admit it was a pleasant distraction.

They crossed over into the other building and turned into the restaurant. The room was an assortment of rectangular tables and cushioned dining chairs. Most of the tables were bare, with nothing but a white tablecloth on them. In the back, there were three tables filled with people eating and talking. An empty table to the right had six place settings neatly arranged and waiting.

As the group stepped into the restaurant, Senator Gibbons stood up from his seat at one of the tables.

"Ah, there you are. Please come in and make yourselves comfortable," he said, motioning to the empty table.

Marcus led the way, and everyone took a seat.

"I'm sure you're quite hungry, so why don't we skip all of the introductions until after dinner," the Senator told them. "You'll have to forgive us, but we had to start without you."

The Senator made a hand motion to a short man standing by what must be the kitchen doors. The man disappeared for a moment and emerged carrying two plates of food. The man had the distinct skin tone and features of a Native American. He was probably around Leo's age, with tan skin and short cropped jet black hair. He stood about five and a half feet tall, with an average build. As he crossed the room, Karma ran up and hopped around by his feet.

The man lifted the plates to get a good look at the dog and make sure he didn't trip.

"Karma!" Ryan called after her. "Get over here."

"I've also had them prepare some food for your dog," the Senator said. "Yuma will bring it out after you guys are taken care of."

"Thank you, that's very kind," Ryan said.

The man named Yuma set the plates down in front of Vivian and Nabi, then turned and headed back toward the kitchen. Ryan saw the man give Karma a smile and quick pat on the head before leaving.

After he was served, Ryan stared at the table. They each got a plateful of pasta covered with a thin tomato sauce. Two baskets of slightly stale sliced bread were placed in the center of the table, and they each had a glass of red wine to drink.

Ryan tried to begin eating with class, but it was hard to show restraint when he was starving. He grabbed his fork and scooped spaghetti into his mouth, gulping it down before he could even taste it. He forced himself to take the time to savor the second mouthful, thoroughly enjoying the taste.

After a sip of wine, he paused to watch his friends. Melina leaned over her plate totally focused on her meal, while Vivian and Nabi sat upright, slowly chewing, both wearing big smiles. Leo ate rather calmly, pausing with each bite to fully appreciate its taste. And then there was Marcus. He dug into his food with a vengeance that bordered on fury. Within a minute he was halfway through his dinner, with no signs of slowing.

As promised, Karma was brought a bowl of food. Ryan didn't get a chance to see what it was, because the dog gulped it down as soon as it was placed in front of her.

Ryan glanced at the people seated at the other tables while he ate. He couldn't shake the feeling that this was some bizarre dream instead of reality. How could there be people living like this, while the rest of the planet fought tooth and nail just to survive another day?

They casually talked and joked while they ate their meals. Each table held seven or eight men all wearing suits or nice dress clothes. All except for one man seated across from the Senator, who wore a green military dress uniform.

Their tables all had half-filled ashtrays in the center and many of them lit up a cigarette as soon as they finished their food.

Ryan noticed that the seat next to the Senator was vacant. Judging by the half eaten plate of pasta, someone must have just stepped away from the table.

Ryan was about to swallow another mouthful of food, when a familiar voice from behind him made his stomach drop.

"Tree-hugger-mother-fucker."

CHAPTER 15

When Luck Runs Out

Ryan sat, frozen at the table, with a mouthful of pasta. He knew the voice and who it belonged to. *How could it be possible?* Ryan thought. He swallowed the food down and slowly turned around in his chair.

The smug face of his old nemesis Reese looked down at him. He wore an expensive dark gray sports jacket and black pants. The white button-down shirt under the jacket had the first button undone revealing a gold necklace. In one hand held a box of cigars, in the other, a key chain holding about a dozen keys and green rabbit's foot.

"What an unexpected surprise," Reese said with a grin.

Ryan was unable to respond, as his mind desperately tried to figure out how this could be feasible.

Reese walked halfway around the table, looking over the newcomers.

"I knew we had visitors, but I had no idea it was an old friend," he said. "And accompanied by such beautiful ladies."

"How the hell did you get here, Reese?" Ryan finally said.

"What? No, 'glad to see you buddy?' No, 'thank heavens you're alive old friend?'" Reese asked. "Aren't you happy to see me?"

It seemed like a lifetime ago that Ryan had been stuck in that crappy sales job, being forced to put up with people like Reese. He hadn't thought about the job or Reese since he walked out of the office the day the disasters hit New Jersey: and that had been a good thing. Now, with Reese's arrogant face in front of him once again, it did indeed feel like old times.

Somehow, Ryan contained his disgust. "Of course, I'm happy you're alive," he said. "It's just a bit surprising to see you so far from home."

Reese continued his circle of the table. "Ah yes, that's it. Well, believe it or not, I am home. I was born not far from here. Although I moved when I was quite young, I still feel that my roots are right here. And by right here, I mean this casino. I've been coming here for years. This is always the place I come to when I need a few days to myself. And when the first disaster struck, I decided to do what everyone else was doing: go home. Luckily, I knew a guy with a private plane who owed me a favor. I landed safely here just as New York City burned to the ground.

"Well, I can see you have a lot to digest," Reese continued. "Eat up and we'll talk some more later."

Reese smiled at everyone seated at the table and then walked over and sat down next to the Senator.

Vivian saw the look on Ryan's face. "Is everything all right?" she leaned in and asked him.

"Yeah," he replied. "For now."

They continued eating their dinners, but Ryan found that he had lost most of his appetite. He forced down the rest of his meal, occasionally glancing over to watch Reese laughing as he smoked a cigar with the other men at his table. Ryan tried to concentrate on the conversations his friends were having, but found it hard to take his mind off the appearance of Reese.

Marcus was the center of attention at their table. With a full belly, he was in high spirits. He told stories, recapped their past adventures and even threw in a few jokes. Everyone laughed and enjoyed themselves. Doing something as normal as having dinner together, at a nice table with warm food, was a welcome distraction from reality.

After they finished every last crumb on their plates, Senator Gibbons walked over and invited everyone next door to the casino. Not wanting the fun to end, Marcus quickly answered for the table and everyone followed the Senator across the hall.

Leo walked next to Ryan. "You haven't been the same since the arrival of your old acquaintance. What's up?"

"He's not one of my favorite people and I'm sure he feels the same about me," Ryan said. "He's not to be trusted."

Leo nodded as they entered the casino's gaming room. Game tables filled the center of the room, while slot machines covered the back wall. Although most of the tables were empty, three were manned by a dealer or an attendant. The men ahead of them split up and gathered around their favorite tables.

Senator Gibbons approached the group as they watched the games begin.

"Tonight is a night of celebration," he said. "You have traveled far and endured many hardships to get here. You deserve a night of relaxation and fun. I'm extending each of you a line of credit in the amount of five hundred dollars. Have a few drinks and try your luck."

"I used to love blackjack," Marcus said, smiling.

"Right over there," the Senator motioned to a nearby table where three men, including Reese were being dealt cards.

"Something tells me you're going to need me," Melina said, walking next to Marcus, as he headed to the table.

The Senator turned back to the remaining friends.

"I think I'll just watch for now," Ryan told him.

"I've always wanted to try craps," Nabi said.

"Well then, craps it is," Senator Gibbons said, taking Nabi by the arm and escorting her toward the craps table.

Ryan, Vivian and Leo followed with Karma close by. As they reached the table, Reese called out.

"Who let that fucking dog in here?" he said loudly. "Is that yours, tree-hugger?"

Ryan turned to the blackjack table, feeling his blood pressure begin to rise.

Melina, who was standing next to Marcus at the table, leaned over to Reese and said. "Don't worry, she won't bother anybody."

Reese glanced at Melina, and then back to Ryan. "You're lucky you keep such good company, or else I would have thrown that mutt out where it belongs."

There was a lot Ryan wanted to say, but he realized it wouldn't be in their best interest, so he kept silent and turned to the craps table.

There were four men standing around the table putting chips

down on various spots on the table. Ryan had been to the casinos in Atlantic City back in New Jersey a few times, but was never much of a gambler.

The Senator brought Nabi up to the table, next to the uniformed military man.

"This is General Cox," the Senator said. "General, would you kindly tutor this young lady on the game of craps?"

"Of course," the General said. "It would be my pleasure. What's your name, my dear?"

"Nabi," she told him.

The General was a tall man in his mid-forties with a crew cut of brown hair. Although the others didn't seem to recognize the name, Ryan did.

"You're General Cox from Fort Carson?" Ryan asked.

"Yes, I am."

"What are you doing here?" Ryan continued. "I thought you were supposed to check out a few military bases and rejoin your men stationed in the library?"

The General turned away from the table and faced Ryan. "How would you know what I'm supposed to do, civilian?"

"Because we just left your men," Ryan told him. "They were waiting for you. Why didn't you go back to them?"

"First of all, I don't appreciate your line of questioning," the General said, his expression stern. "But if you must know, I finished my sweep and was heading back when I found this place. I realized that I might be needed here, so I stayed. They didn't need me there anyway. Colonel Cartwright is a perfectly adept leader."

Ryan met the General's stare. "Yes, he was. But because they were waiting for you, they stayed in that library while the ground opened up underneath them and the building was ripped apart. Every last one of your men died, while you were here playing craps."

"That is most regrettable," General Cox said. "But I fail to see how that is my fault. Colonel Cartwright had the authority to evacuate the area if he felt threatened in any way. Their loss is unfortunate, but these are unfortunate times. And we must all do what is necessary to survive."

The General's eyes remained locked on Ryan's for another second, and then he turned back to the table.

Ryan stood behind Nabi with Vivian and Leo, while the General began instructing Nabi on the game of craps. The friends were left a little unsettled by his callous attitude and Ryan was about to say more when a roar from the blackjack table caused them to turn around. Marcus had apparently just won a big hand and was pumping his arm up and down in celebration. Reese was patting the big guy on the back as he puffed on his cigar.

The uneasy feeling that Ryan had earlier was back again. None of this seemed right. He looked down at Karma, sitting at his feet, but she didn't offer any assistance.

After about a half hour, Marcus and Melina left the blackjack table and joined them behind Nabi.

"Well, how'd you do?" Vivian asked.

Marcus frowned and shook his head. "I lost it all."

"Big fool doesn't know when to walk away," Melina said.

"I was on too good a roll to quit," Marcus pleaded.

Melina laughed. "Well, your roll sure came to an abrupt stop."

"I thought you were supposed to be my lucky charm?"

"I was lucky," she replied. "Just not for you."

With that, Reese walked over and put his arms around Marcus

and Melina. "You've got some cool friends here, Ryan. Now, how about you and I take a walk and catch up?"

Without waiting for an answer, Reese took Ryan by the shoulder and led him away from the craps table. They walked off to the left side, into the high stakes room.

No one noticed that Karma had backed away and let out a soft growl when Reese came close. As Ryan went into the room with Reese, Karma walked behind them, stopping just shy of the room's opening.

Inside the high stakes area, there were four tables set up in the middle of the room, with big cushioned chairs and sofas arranged by the walls. Reese directed Ryan to a chair and then settled into the seat opposite him and leaned back.

Reese took a long drag off the cigar and blew the smoke upwards. "What are the odds the two of us would find each other again?"

"I was thinking the same thing," Ryan replied.

"It's funny how things work out," Reese said, blowing out more smoke. He reached into his inside jacket pocket and held out a cigar, offering it to Ryan.

Ryan put a hand up and shook his head.

"I mean, here we are, you and me. Together again," Reese returned the cigar to his pocket. "Listen, Ryan. I know we've had our problems in the past, and I can tell by your face that you're not too excited to see me, but a lot has changed. Like it or not, this world has turned to shit and now we have to live in it. To do that, we're going to have to count on the people around us. I say we forget the past and start over. Whaddya say?"

Ryan looked at Reese, trying to figure out what he was up to. Reese's motives were always selfish, so Ryan knew that he must have something up his sleeve. He would never trust him, no matter what the situation. However, at the moment, he didn't have enough information to figure out Reese just yet.

"I guess I can do that," Ryan lied.

"Super," Reese said, and then he turned toward the craps table, where Ryan's friends were gathered. "Who are your traveling buddies?"

"They're all good people," Ryan told him, watching them. "We met along the way and have been helping each other get through this mess."

Ryan watched as Marcus and General Cox helped Nabi with her craps game, while a few men talked and flirted with Melina and Vivian. Leo stood behind Vivian, occasionally glancing over Ryan's way. Seeing Vivian conversing with the strange men, Ryan was hit with a feeling of jealousy. Although he didn't like to admit it, he was becoming very attached to her.

"Is that redhead your girl?" Reese asked, as if reading his mind.

"Uh . . . yeah," he replied without taking his eyes off her.

Reese laughed. "That didn't sound too convincing."

Ryan brought his gaze back to Reese, noticing Karma staring at them from the main casino floor. "We're friends, but have recently become a lot closer," Ryan said, immediately hating himself for telling Reese anything.

"Well good for you, old friend. She's a beautiful girl," Reese said, standing up. "Now, what's your drink of choice?"

Ryan stood up as well. "I'm mostly a beer drinker."

"Beer?" Reese repeated with distaste. "I think we can do a lot better than that."

Ryan followed Reese out of the room and back to the others.

"Hey, Yuma," Reese called to the man who had served them their dinner. Yuma was passing out glasses of champagne to the ladies when Reese and Ryan walked up.

"Go back and fetch us a couple glasses of Glenfiddich," Reese ordered.

Yuma bowed his head and left without a word. A minute later he returned with two filled glasses on a serving tray, along with more champagne.

"Now, what do you say we drink and be merry," Reese declared. Marcus, Leo and the girls smiled and raised their glasses. Shrugging, Ryan raised his. They touched glasses and Ryan swallowed a gulp of the harsh scotch.

The rest of the night was spent in the casino drinking and gambling. Ryan never really felt the rush that real gamblers live for. The whole thing seemed a bit pointless to Ryan, since he was pretty sure that money didn't have any real value anymore. Nevertheless, everyone seemed to be enjoying themselves.

They were introduced to most of the other men in the room, and found themselves surrounded by lawyers and politicians. None of them were shy about talking – especially about themselves – and spent most of the time trying to top one another's stories. Just about every guy spent some time flirting with one or all of the girls. Vivian and Melina handled themselves perfectly, rebuffing any advances without insulting any of their hosts. Nabi was the only one who didn't seem to know what to do. She put up with more than a few insensitive comments and touches. That was until Marcus noticed what was going on and planted his large body next to her. The men gathered in that casino were all rich and powerful men, but every one of them hesitated when they were within Marcus's shadow.

Through it all, Karma just followed and watched.

It was well after three in the morning when they excused themselves and headed back to their rooms. Senator Gibbons provided them with a small flashlight, so they could navigate their way back to their rooms, and wished them a good night.

The walk back to the rooms was an entertaining one. With the unsettling appearance of Reese, Ryan made a conscious effort to avoid having too many drinks. Vivian and Leo seemed to have paced themselves well enough not to feel any major effects of the alcohol. Melina had a good amount of champagne, but seemed to have an amazingly high tolerance. Nabi and Marcus, on the other hand, were wasted.

It probably only took a few drinks for thin Nabi to feel a little tipsy, but Marcus needed a lot more. And he definitely drank a lot more than any of them, quite possibly more than all of them put together.

Marcus and Nabi sang off-key songs, as they swaggered down the hall. When they finally reached their rooms, they split up, three to a room. Ryan, Vivian and Leo took one, leaving Melina to put up with the drunks. She didn't seem to mind, telling them that she would make sure they were put to bed safely. Karma, of course, stuck with Ryan.

Inside their room, Ryan, Vivian and Leo got ready for bed. Ryan and Vivian shared one bed, while Leo got the other one to himself.

As they were lying in bed, Ryan said, "I know that everyone likes it here, and I agree it beats living out in the elements. But I don't trust these guys – especially Reese."

"I know you have a history with this guy, but they don't seem to mean us any harm," Vivian told him.

"He's not a nice person and nothing good can come from his appearance," Ryan said. "I think we should get out of here."

"And go where?" Vivian asked.

"Anywhere," Ryan replied. "As long as it's away from him."

"I think Karma brought us this way for a reason," Leo said. "Let's see if she'll give us a hint tomorrow."

"I guess," Ryan said. "But after what happened with Shawn, don't look to me to be the savior."

Karma jumped up on the bed and snuggled in between Ryan and Vivian. Soon, they were all asleep.

The next morning, Ryan awoke as Karma hopped off the bed and shook herself. He sat up and rolled his neck around to work out the kinks.

"That felt good," Leo said, turning over in his bed.

"Sleep well?" Ryan asked him.

"Oh yeah,' he replied.

"Me too," Vivian added, putting a hand on Ryan's back.

Ryan turned his head, smiled and winked at her. He stood up, stretched his arms out and walked to the window, yawning. Ryan pulled the heavy curtains aside, letting gray light into the room. The day was bleak and cloudy. The wind was still blowing hard, causing the glass of the window to rattle against its frame.

"Another beautiful day in paradise," Ryan declared.

After a brief stop in the bathroom, Ryan changed his clothes, as

Vivian and Leo rose out of bed.

"I'm taking Karma out for a walk," Ryan told them. "We'll be back in a few minutes."

Vivian smiled as she grabbed Ryan's hand, giving it a squeeze on her way to the bathroom.

"Let's go, Karma," Ryan said, opening the door.

With no windows, the hallway was dark. Ryan waited a moment for his eyes to adjust, and then started down the hall after Karma, who was already halfway to the hotel lobby.

The hotel was quiet. After the long night of drinking, Ryan figured that he and Karma were the only ones who were able to make it out of bed so far.

Ryan pushed open one of the two glass doors next to the revolving doors, and held it open as Karma jogged out. When Ryan got outside he was hit by a gust of wind that nearly pushed him over. Dirt and loose twigs blew across the ground, as the clouds above churned and swirled.

Karma barked off to the left, and Ryan squinted in the wind to find her. He looked up in time to see her running past the casino doors and around the side of the oval building. Ryan ran after her, as dirt and small pebbles, carried in the breeze, pelted against him.

Around the bend, in the back of the casino, were two fenced in tennis courts and a covered outdoor bar. The bar was open on three sides with a red tiled roof covering the top. It had a number of tall tables with bar stools around them. Hanging plants rocked back and forth around the edges of the roof. The back wall had a small bar set into it, with a doorway on the other side.

Beyond the bar, on the hotel side, was an Olympic-sized swimming pool, surrounded by rows of lounge chairs. In the back were five private cabanas that, in the casino's prime, could be rented out by the day for a hefty price.

Ryan spotted Karma running into the outdoor bar. She ran behind the bar and through the doorway. Ryan ran past the tennis courts and into the bar area, ducking away from a swinging plant. He went around the bar and into the doorway Karma had gone though, which led into a back storage room.

There was a man lying on the floor giggling, among piles of boxes and supplies. Karma was standing directly over him wagging her tail, preventing Ryan from seeing who it was.

"Karma, get off him," Ryan said, pulling the dog back to expose a grinning Yuma. "I'm sorry. Once she likes someone, there's no stopping her."

"Don't apologize," Yuma told Ryan, as he stood up. "She's just acting on her feelings. That's always a good thing."

"Yes, you're absolutely right. I don't think we got a chance to formally meet, I'm Ryan."

Yuma shook Ryan's extended hand. "I'm Yuma. Nice to meet you."

"I meant to thank you for taking such good care of us last night," Ryan said. "I hope you got some time to eat and have a little fun."

"I'm afraid my duties kept me pretty occupied," Yuma said. He then seemed to realize he should be working, and began removing various bottles of alcohol from the boxes around him and placing them in a separate box.

"I'm assuming you work here?" Ryan asked.

"Yes," he replied. "I've been working here for about a year now."

Ryan face showed his concern. "Yuma, why are you still working? Don't you realize what's going on around you? You should worry less about those ungrateful suits and more about yourself."

Yuma stopped packing his box and looked up at Ryan. "I am thinking about myself. My family lives in Arizona and I want to get back to them very badly, but I have no way of reaching them. Mr. Reese has promised to get me a ride back to them."

"Really?" Ryan asked. "How long has he been promising that?"

"Since the Earth became angry," Yuma replied.

Ryan could feel his hatred for Reese rising up once again. "You must know that he'll never keep that promise."

"I am beginning to doubt his sincerity, but I don't have many other options."

Ryan thought for a moment. "You can come with us. We're leaving today. We may not have a vehicle now, but we'll find one. I made it here all the way from New Jersey without knowing what my next ride would be."

"That's very kind, but I don't think Mr. Reese would allow it."

"The hell he won't," Ryan said, as his anger grew. "Don't you worry, I'll take care of Reese. You just get yourself packed and ready to go."

Yuma thought for a couple of seconds. "I don't know . . . ."

"Hey, my parents live in Arizona," Ryan told him. "We can find our families together."

Yuma looked hesitant, but eventually nodded and said, "Okay, if you're sure it will be all right."

Ryan instructed Yuma to meet them in the hotel lobby at noon and then left him to his chores. Karma was reluctant to leave, but eventually followed Ryan back outside. The wind was still blowing hard, and Ryan had to cover his eyes for the remainder of their walk around the hotel.

They made it back to the room to find the others waiting to go to breakfast. Marcus and Nabi both had headaches, but weren't as hung over as Ryan thought they would be. Marcus's mind was back on food, and he talked nonstop on the walk to the restaurant about what he wanted to eat.

When they got to the *Regency* they found only two men sitting at a table eating. Marcus was very dismayed to learn that breakfast wasn't a big meal here. There were only some assorted Danishes and pastries set out on a table. All of which had gone stale a few days ago. Large pitchers of orange juice and water were also set out.

They sat down at one of the tables in a corner with their hard baked goods and warm drinks.

Ryan told everyone that he wanted to leave by noon, which was about two hours away. Marcus suggested staying another night, but Ryan told him that he didn't trust Reese and he felt Karma was getting a little restless. Although they would all miss the comforts of the casino, they knew that they couldn't stay here forever.

Ryan also informed them that they would be taking Yuma with them. He told them how Karma reacted to him and how he wanted to get to his family.

"I had a feeling he would be joining us," Melina said. "While you drunks were partying it up last night, I had a nice long conversation with him. You know he's part Navaho Indian? Anyway, he has some pretty strong beliefs about what's happening on this planet."

"What did he say?" Vivian asked.

Melina continued, "His ancestors saw the Earth as a living, breathing entity. Every creature on the planet, including humans, are merely a branch on the great tree of life. While most people think of this planet as a resource to be used for their benefit, Native

Americans see themselves as stewards of Mother Earth, taking only what is necessary to survive. And Yuma believes that we've abused the Earth and now it's mad."

"That must have been some fun conversation," Marcus said. "I'm glad I was too busy talking to lady luck."

"Too bad Ms. Luck wanted nothing to do with you," Melina shot back.

"Anyway," Ryan said, "he's coming with us."

After the unsatisfying breakfast they went back to their rooms and began packing up their things. As was typical of the end of any hotel stay, they swiped all the soap, shampoo and anything else they thought they might be able to use.

Ryan was stuffing his clothing into a bag when he heard a knock at the door. Ryan opened the door and saw James's beefy body.

"Reese needs to see you," he told Ryan.

"I'm a little busy right now. What does he want?"

James's face showed no expression. "Don't know. I just know he needs to see you."

There was something in James's voice that told Ryan he wasn't going to take no for an answer. Since Ryan didn't want to stir things up when they were so close to leaving, he conceded.

"All right," Ryan said. "Just give me a second."

Ryan closed the door and turned back to Vivian and Leo.

"I'll be right back," he told them. "Finish packing and be ready to get out of here when I return. I'm leaving Karma with you."

"Okay," Vivian said. "But be careful with Reese."

"I will," he promised.

Ryan had a tough time getting out the door without letting Karma out too. She kept jumping at the door and trying to push her way out. It took a little maneuvering, but Ryan finally got into the hallway, closing the door.

"Follow me," James said.

As Ryan walked down the hall behind James, he could hear Karma barking inside the room and jumping at the closed door. He followed James past the *Regency*, through the casino and down the opposite hallway. At the end of the hall, they went through a door that led to a stairway. They walked up three flights and came to a small landing with a steel door. James opened the door and led Ryan outside onto the roof.

Reese was standing at the edge of the roof holding a rifle. He seemed to be searching for something in the distance, and simply nodded his head as James and Ryan approached.

"What do you need, Reese?" Ryan asked, as the wind gusted fiercely around them.

"Hold on a second," Reese told him, as he studied the ground below.

Something caught his eye and he leveled the rifle and fired a shot. Ryan saw a blur of motion as some kind of animal ran from bush to bush about one hundred yards away.

"Damn," Reese said, lowering the gun.

"What are you trying to shoot?" Ryan had to ask.

Reese took a step away from the edge and turned, swinging the gun around toward Ryan. "A rabbit. I'm usually a pretty good shot, but this damn wind is making it quite challenging. For some unknown reason there's been a stream of critters running through here. It's like a fucking animal parade. It has made for some good sport, though."

Ryan chose to stay silent.

"Why don't we head inside," Reese continued. "This wind is liable to knock us off the roof."

Ryan followed James and Reese back inside the doorway. Reese leaned the rifle against the wall and took the lead down the stairs. Instead of going all the way down to the main floor, Reese led them to the second floor. They walked down a hallway and through a door.

The door opened into a large, well-furnished lounge area. Black leather couches and chairs were arranged in front of small round coffee tables, there were flat screen TV's fixed into the walls and a fully stocked bar to the left.

"I'm willing to bet that you've never set foot in a VIP Room," Reese said, walking to the bar.

Ryan followed, saying nothing, while James walked across the room, and left through a door on the other side.

"What would you like to drink?" Reese asked, already pouring himself a glass of scotch.

"Isn't it a little early for that?" Ryan replied.

Reese put the bottle on the bar and then took a sip. "Maybe for you, but I've been up for about five hours already."

"Don't you ever sleep?"

Reese shook his head and set himself down in a big cushioned, leather chair. "So much time is wasted on sleep. Did you know that all great achievers sleep less? It's true. There's so much to be accomplished in those few extra hours that most people spend lying in bed, letting time pass them by. Not me. I'll sleep when I'm dead."

Reese motioned for Ryan to take a seat in the chair opposite him, as he took another drink from his glass. Ryan walked to the chair and sat down. It was a nice chair, but Ryan didn't feel the least bit comfortable.

"So, I hear you want to leave our lovely establishment," Reese said, leaning back in his chair.

Ryan wasn't sure what Reese knew, so he decided to play dumb. "What gives you that idea?"

"Oh, come now, Ryan. Let's not play these games with each other."

Ryan thought for a moment, and then said, "We had a great time here and appreciate all of your hospitality, but it's time for us to move on. We're going to head out in about an hour or so."

Reese stared at Ryan. "Is there anything else?"

"No," Ryan replied. "That's it. Like I said, you guys have been great to us. We're just ready to continue on our way."

"I see," Reese said, sitting up and putting his glass on the table.

The far door opened suddenly, and James pushed Yuma into the room.

Reese got up and walked around his chair. "Would you believe that I found little Yuma packing his things? Although he was reluctant at first, he eventually told me that he had intentions of leaving with you."

James had Yuma by the back of the neck and walked him over to a chair and flung him down. Ryan noticed a large bruise on the side of his head and there was blood in the corner of his mouth.

"What the hell is wrong with you, Reese?" Ryan asked, standing up. "All he wants to do is find his family."

"We both know that his family is probably dead by now," Reese said. "There is nothing out there for him. He's much better off here with us."

"It's his life. And if he wants to use it looking for his loved ones, that's his choice. What difference is it to you?"

"I need him here," Reese said, smiling. "He makes my drinks just how I like them."

Ryan didn't like the way things were going. "I don't think the Senator would approve of this kind of thing."

"Are you kidding me?" Reese sneered. "The Senator does what I tell him to do. Just like all good politicians, he's just a stupid puppet. I run the show here. Take a look around you. It's survival of the fittest. And I have to tell you, I'm feeling pretty damn fit."

Ryan was trying to get a handle on the situation and figure out what his next move should be.

"But if you want to leave? Fine, go ahead. But my favorite bartender is staying put," Reese said, motioning to Yuma.

Ryan wished he had grabbed Yuma and gotten everyone out before breakfast this morning. Now it wasn't going to be an easy task.

"Listen, Reese –"

"I'm not finished!" Reese yelled. "The three dames aren't leaving either. You see, I've always had a thing for redheads, and thanks to Mother Nature, my dating pool has been drastically reduced. General Cox has taking a liking to that slanty-eyed chink, and that big mouthed spic goes to my man, James here."

James smiled at Ryan, nodding his big head in agreement.

"You and the two other bozos will be escorted out immediately," Reese added, and then turned to James. "Take my little tree-hugger-mother-fucker here downstairs. Collect the other two jackasses and give 'em the old heave ho."

James took a step forward.

"There's no way I'm leaving without them," Ryan said, not sure how he was going to back up his words.

"Somehow, I knew you would feel that way," Reese said. "So to make sure you don't try anything heroic, James is going to shoot each of you in the leg. That should keep you sufficiently hobbled and out of trouble."

James pulled out a black pistol from the back of his waistband, and walked toward Ryan.

Reese smiled while James grabbed Ryan by the shoulder. As James was trying to steer Ryan toward the door, Ryan lunged up with both hands grabbing the big guy's wrist holding the gun. The motion took the cocky man off guard, but James adjusted quickly.

As Ryan struggled to keep James from angling the gun at him, he yelled to Yuma, "Get out of here!"

Yuma stumbled out of his chair and ran toward the far door. Reese saw the move and ran after him. Yuma, who was still feeling the effects of the beating he had gotten earlier, couldn't reach the door in time. Reese tackled him hard, then got to his feet and kicked Yuma in the side twice.

Ryan was no match for James's strength and soon felt his arms weakening. James brought his free arm back and punched Ryan in the side of the head. A second punch sent Ryan to the ground.

Dazed, Ryan looked up to into the barrel of the gun. Reese dragged Yuma back into the middle of the room and threw him down. Then he pushed past James and grabbed Ryan by the shirt.

"It seems like I'm on top again!" Reese yelled. "That was the most pathetic attempt I've ever seen. What did you think was going to happen? Yuma would run and get your friends to help you? Not gonna happen!"

Reese gave Ryan a punch to the face, and Ryan tasted blood.

Then, Reese straightened up. "Now you've pissed me off, and I'm going to make sure you know what pain feels like. And nobody's coming for you, tree-hugger-mother-fucker. Nobody! Only God can save you now."

Reese brought his leg back to kick Ryan, but was stopped by a voice.

"Be careful," Marcus's voice said. "God may be closer than you think."

Everyone's attention went to the door, where they saw Marcus standing just inside the doorway with Karma at his side.

Reese smiled and calmly said, "Shoot them all."

James raised his gun at Marcus.

Lying on his back on the floor, Ryan kicked out his legs, hitting James just below the right knee. James was built very solidly and barely moved. But it did shift his attention down to Ryan for a moment. In that moment, Karma and Marcus went into motion.

Karma galloped forward, with Marcus in close pursuit. James saw the charging dog and brought the gun up and fired twice, but both bullets missed their mark. Before he could pull the trigger again Karma was upon him. She sprang off the floor, jumping on the backpedaling man with her mouth open and teeth bared. Her strong jaw closed down on the wrist holding the gun, sending it skidding across the floor. Terror quickly replaced the cocky look on James's face, as he tripped on a chair and went flying backward with Karma on top of him.

Reese was so mesmerized by James's struggle with the dog that he forgot about Ryan. As soon as James and Karma fell backward, Ryan got his feet underneath him and swung his fist at Reese as hard as he could. The punch hit the distracted man square in the face. Reese staggered backward and looked over just as Ryan was on him again. Ryan grabbed him by the shoulders, pulling Reese's upper body down as Ryan drove his left knee up hard, hitting Reese in the stomach, knocking the wind from him. Reese collapsed to the floor, clutching his stomach.

Meanwhile, Marcus had reached James and Karma. The dog had torn a mean gash in James' wrist and was now growling savagely an inch from his face. James was frozen with fear, and merely stared at the dogs curling lips, trembling. Marcus noticed the wet patch on James's pants, and couldn't help but smirk.

Ryan was on top of Reese in a rage. The thought of this bastard hurting Vivian and the rest of his friends made Ryan loose himself to anger. He brought his fist down on Reese's head, again and again, as Reese struggled feebly.

Marcus finally grabbed hold of Ryan, who tried to deliver a last punch and then began to settle down. Ryan was breathing hard as Marcus turned him around.

"Ryan," he said. "I think we need to go."

Ryan had been so consumed with punishing Reese that he hadn't noticed Karma's barking. She had left James, who was curled on the floor holding his injured wrist, and was standing by the door, barking at them.

Ryan looked down at Reese as he groaned and shifted on the floor. "You're lucky, Reese, I was just about to help you catch up on your sleep."

Ryan turned, helped Yuma up and followed Marcus toward Karma. On his way to the door, Ryan noticed the gun on the floor and grabbed it.

Karma led the way down the hall to the stairway.

As they ran down the stairs Ryan said, "Thanks for saving me. How did you know where to find me?"

"I'd love to take the credit," Marcus said, as he jumped down the last few stairs. "But it was Karma. She was jumping and scratching at the door ever since you left. Finally, I let her out, and she took off. I was barely able to keep up with her, but she led the way right to you."

Karma was waiting for them when they got to the bottom of the stairs.

Ryan gave her a pat on the head and said, "Thanks, girl," then opened the stairway door and peeked out.

There was no one in sight, so Ryan opened the door and they ran down the hall. They entered the empty casino and ran around the tables, keeping a close eye ahead for trouble. They left the blackjack table behind and sprinted down the hallway toward the hotel.

As they ran past the *Regency* restaurant, they saw General Cox and a few other men sitting at a table eating. Ryan locked eyes with the General for a brief second as he whipped by.

Finally, they made it to the hotel lobby, where the rest of the group was gathered and waiting. Ryan and Marcus were tired and out of breath, and poor Yuma was exhausted, but, they had no time to rest. A few barks from Karma got everyone's attention. She was at the hotel doors, waiting for them.

"Let's move, quickly," Ryan told them, as Vivian released him.

Outside, the world was a dust bowl of blowing sand and dirt. The winds appeared to be gusting in every direction at once, forcing everyone to squint as they looked ahead for Karma.

They ran toward the road. Karma was about fifty feet away from the hotel and casino, with Marcus, Melina and Nabi in close pursuit. About ten feet behind them, Vivian and Leo ran, with Ryan helping the injured Yuma behind them.

Ryan glanced over his shoulder and saw General Cox come out of the hotel doors, followed by three other men.

"Stop right there!" The General yelled.

Ryan looked down at the gun he still held in his hand and considered firing at them, but couldn't bring himself to do it.

"Keep going!" Ryan screamed ahead as he ran forward.

The loud crack of a gunshot made Ryan pause and turn back. He saw the General and his men running after them, but they didn't have any visible weapons. As Ryan was turning back around, he noticed a figure on the roof with a rifle.

Through the wind, Ryan saw that it was Reese.

Reese aimed the weapon down and fired again. Ryan saw immediately that the shot was not aimed for him, but for someone up ahead. Although, Reese's first shot had missed, his second found its mark. Ryan watched in horror as the bullet hit Karma, causing her to let out a yelp and fall to the ground.

"No!" Ryan screamed.

On the roof, Reese was raising his gun over his head in triumph. Ryan's heart felt so incredibly heavy that he had trouble staying on his feet. In the short time he had been with the dog, Ryan had grown incredibly attached to her. Still, he wasn't prepared for the overwhelming wave of grief that came over him. Karma had come to symbolize their chance for survival in this harsh world, and had become a trusted and loving friend. Watching her get shot made everything Ryan was clinging to crash down.

Ryan almost lost the will to keep going. He felt tears in his eyes, and was about to give up and simply fall to the ground, when his sorrow shifted into anger. Anger for these men that thought themselves above everyone else. Anger at their greed. Anger at their apathy for the world. And most of all, anger at Reese.

Ryan straightened himself up tall and looked up at the roof. Reese was smiling down at him as he aimed the gun at Ryan.

The wind was blowing forcefully around them as they stared at each other. Ryan kept his gaze on Reese as he raised his arm with the pistol and squeezed the trigger, without aiming. Ryan had never fired a gun in his life, but his shot hit Reese in his chest, penetrating his cold heart.

Reese wobbled back a step, looked down at the growing red stain in his expensive shirt, then toppled over the edge of the roof and fell to the ground.

"Goodnight, you bastard," Ryan said softly.

The wind was now whipping around with renewed force. Ryan turned to see that the General and his men had stopped their pursuit and were staring over Ryan's left shoulder.

Ryan turned, and saw the wind was blowing dirt and debris in a steady spiral motion about thirty feet in the air. They all watched as the spiral continued to form and the tornado touched the ground.

General Cox and his men turned quickly and fled back toward the hotel. Ryan ran to where the others were gathered, and together they huddled down on the ground.

The twister grew quickly in size and strength as it moved toward the hotel and casino, picking up sticks, rocks and anything else in its path. The force of the wind pulled at Ryan and the others as the tornado skirted past them and rushed for the buildings. By the time it reached the hotel, the tornado was massive.

The General and the other men had made it to the hotel doors, when the wind grabbed hold of them. Two of the men helplessly reached out as a spinning current of air lifted them off their feet. Both men were spun head over heels into the thick of the tornado and swiftly disappeared. The General and the other remaining man, who Ryan remembered to be a corporate lawyer, both had their hands on one of the semicircle handles on the glass hotel doors. Their feet were stretched out behind them as the tornado pulled at their bodies.

The swirling wind made it hard for Ryan to see exactly what was happening. He turned his gaze from the hotel toward Karma. Ryan was surprised to see the dog standing up, eyes fixed on the tornado. There was blood and dirt covering the side of her white and brown body. The wind blew her floppy ears around her head as dirt and sand churned around her. Still, she kept her gaze concentrated on the scene in front of her.

Ryan looked up at the hotel in time to see the lawyer lose his grip on the door handle and be sucked into the spinning cloud. General Cox held on for another few seconds before he, too, was pulled and spun into the air, vanishing from view.

The tornado then moved right on top of the hotel and casino, ripping it apart, as it mowed over it. It seemed to stop there for a moment as the winds tore the very foundation of the hotel out of the ground. Then, it swirled to the casino sending pieces of wood, glass and furniture spinning into the air. Because of the magnitude of the tornado, Ryan couldn't see the buildings themselves, only the shredded fragments that were carried into the tornado's spinning mass.

After a few minutes, the twister started to dissipate. As quickly as it started, the tornado ended in a gentle corkscrew of wind. Then the air was still.

There was nothing left of the hotel and casino except blown apart wreckage. Most of the structures were spread out on the ground in every direction. Debris was everywhere, yet not a single piece had hit any of the small group of people crouched together on the ground.

Slowly, they all stood up and took in the view around them. Ryan glanced back to where Karma was standing and saw her try to take a step forward, and then collapse.

Ryan ran over to her and knelt down. She was lying on her side, and had a large stain of blood on her coat. Her eyes were closed and her body motionless. Ryan leaned down and gently put his arms around her, and was overcome with sorrow. The pain and loss he felt in his heart was overwhelming. He hadn't cried hard since he was a child, but now, clutching Karma, Ryan wept.

A strange warm sensation on his head and back made him lift his head. Looking up, with tears streaming down the dirt on his face, Ryan saw that the clouds had parted to reveal a blue sky and bright sunshine.

EPILOGUE

Seven figures walked along on an empty paved road, casting long shadows on the ground. The sun hung low overhead, causing the clear blue sky to begin to darken. The day had been a hot one, but now that the sun was starting to arc its way toward the horizon, the temperature was dropping. A flock of birds flew by on their way to some unknown destination, their squawking cries breaking the silence of the day, as they slowly faded away into the distance.

The coolness of night would be a welcome change from the hot sun of the long day. Although the sun had beaten down on him all day, making his body sweat and his breathing labored, Ryan enjoyed its brightness and reveled in its warmth. In the two weeks since the tornado ripped apart the hotel and casino, there had been only sunny days. Big, fluffy, white clouds would roll by on occasion, but the sun never disappeared for more than a brief time.

The first few mornings after the sun's reappearance, Ryan would tentatively look up at the sky for fear that the wall of clouds had returned in the night to blanket their world in grayness once again.

Now he had gained confidence that the sun would not leave them for such a long time ever again.

They had experienced no more disasters, either. No fires, no earthquakes, no tornados. The days had been calm and normal. A pleasant, uneventful day was something that Ryan would never again take for granted.

Even after two weeks, Ryan still found himself looking ahead, expecting to see Karma's spotted white body bouncing ahead of him. He glanced to his left and watched Vivian walking next to him. She was so beautiful. He had finally admitted, at least to himself, that he loved this girl with all his heart. Over the last two weeks, their bond had gotten stronger and their devotion to one another became clearer.

Ryan turned his head to the right and watched as Yuma explained the Native American belief of the circle of life to Nabi. Yuma had found his place in their group almost immediately. His shy, soft demeanor didn't hide the proud, strong person he really was. He still believed and practiced many of his people's traditions and beliefs, and found an eager student in Nabi. They had reached the small town where Yuma's family had been living and found broken houses and scarred land, but no bodies. Yuma believed that they had felt the unrest of the Earth and moved to safer ground. He seemed very confident that they were still alive and that their path would be made known to him soon enough. Ryan admired his optimism and courage.

Nabi had taken an instant liking to Yuma and spent most of her day learning about the customs and history of his people. Behind them, Melina walked between Marcus and Leo. Melina's witty teasing and care-free attitude had helped to lighten the mood whenever someone felt the weight of day to day survival getting too heavy. Her good cheer was always contagious.

Leo had also proven his worth to the group. After the day of the tornado, Leo and Ryan had spent more than a few hours alone together talking over the events. Leo always found a way to show Ryan the purpose in even the most trivial of incidents. He was a very spiritual man, but wasn't closed minded to new ideas or viewpoints, and Ryan always felt better after speaking with him.

Walking next to Melina, Marcus had removed his shirt in the midday heat, but he still carried the big backpack strapped to his back. He was a true friend, in every sense of the word. When Ryan was lying on the floor in the VIP room of the casino, he was not surprised to see the big man standing there in his hour of need.

Ryan had thought about that day often. It had all happened so fast, it seemed almost like a dream. But it had been all too real. Ryan could still feel the pain of seeing the bullet hit Karma. He could still recall the image of Reese standing on the roof, aiming the rifle down at him. He remembered thinking that he had to act fast, so he just raised his hand up and fired the gun. He had no explanation as to how his aim had been so accurate. In the strong wind, with no prior experience with firearms, there should have been no way that he could have made that shot.

Sometimes an unexplained situation should be left that way, Leo had told him. Ryan knew that Leo believed it was God's will that had guided the bullet, while Marcus said that their protector had done it again. Ryan, as usual, wasn't sure what to believe. One thing was certain to him though: there was something special about this group, and he had begun to realize that maybe the responsibility he felt for them went beyond simple camaraderie.

"Hey, Ryan," Marcus said, bringing Ryan away from his thoughts. "Do you think it's been enough time? I'm getting tired."

Ryan looked at Vivian questioningly.

"There's only one way to find out," Vivian said.

Ryan and Vivian walked up to Marcus. Sweat glistened on his muscular chest and the pressure of the straps of the backpack made his veins bulge.

"Turn around," Ryan told him.

Marcus spun his body around and Ryan came face to face with Karma. Only her head and neck could be seen sticking out of the big backpack. As Ryan and Vivian grabbed hold of the pack, Karma leaned her head out and started licking Ryan's face.

"Yes," Ryan told her. "I'm glad to see you too."

Ryan and Vivian got the pack to the ground and unzipped the large pouch. Karma stood up and stretched her back legs out. There was a makeshift bandage made out of a torn t-shirt tied to her side.

Vivian untied the bandage and exposed the wound.

"She's healing nicely," she said, inspecting the area. "I think she should be safe to try walking on her own."

"Hallelujah," Marcus said. "She's a lot heavier than she looks, you know."

Ryan moved his hand over the spot of dried blood where the bullet had entered. It was amazing that she wasn't more seriously injured. The bullet had hit her left flank, passed through her body, and exited by her right leg without damaging any internal organs. Vivian had dressed her wounds, and they made sure Karma stayed off her feet.

"All right, let's see how she moves," Vivian said.

Karma took a few steps, paused for a second to sniff the ground, and then trotted forward.

"I think she's feeling like her old self again," Melina said. "I call the next ride on Marcus's back."

Marcus groaned.

They continued walking forward, keeping an eye on Karma, making sure she wasn't in any pain.

Yuma and Nabi resumed their conversation about the circle of life, as the others walked in silence. Ryan began to think about all that had happened since that Friday when he had left his office for the last time. The world had decided to show the human race just how small it really was. In a relatively short period of time, everything had changed. Maybe it was all part of the circle of life, as Yuma said. The world they knew was gone, and this was a new beginning. Maybe Mother Nature had finally decided that the planet was messed up so badly that it was time for a do over.

The new beginning had already started to take shape. As they traveled west, they had seen a small group of lions hunting a herd of elk. The lions, obviously zoo refugees, had apparently decided to make Arizona their new territory. Other animals were also spotted living and adapting to their new homes. It made Ryan happy to see these wild animals running free without the confinement of cages or the fear of gunshots.

They had also noticed trees, grass and vegetation growing over crumbled buildings and through cement streets. Nature was quickly reclaiming the land.

Karma was up ahead of them where she belonged, leading the way once again. They walked around a bend and past a sign that read *Grand Canyon Lookout.*

The road led to a metal railing on the edge of a cliff. Together, the group walked to the edge, leaned on the railing, and gazed out.

"Welcome to the new world," Melina said.

Beyond the ledge where the Grand Canyon had been was the Pacific Ocean. The seas had risen so much that Arizona was now the coastline.

Ryan reached over and grasped Vivian's hand. She gave his hand a squeeze and smiled up at him. Ryan looked back and saw Karma sniffing around in the bushes. Then he turned back and faced Leo, who was standing on the other side of him, watching the sun glisten on the water.

"I still don't understand why God would come to Earth as a dog, or why Mother Nature would send a dog to guide us?" he asked.

"It makes perfect sense to me," Leo said, as he turned toward him. "Who better to save mankind, than man's best friend?"

Ryan smiled. He couldn't argue with that.

ACKNOWLEDGEMENTS

My name may be the only one on the cover of this book, however, there were many people who helped me get this story out of my head, on these pages and into your hands. I am very lucky, and tremendously grateful, to have some amazing people (and yes, one dog too) in my life who enabled me to finish this book.

It all starts with my supportive and nurturing parents who never try to talk me out of any of my crazy ideas (and I have a lot of them). Both my mom and my dad have been, and always will be, my foundation that everything I do is built upon. There are no amount of words here that could ever express my appreciation for their love.

Although I love to write, I'm not really trained or educated in the craft of writing and it usually shows. When I first wrote this book I didn't have any money to pay for a real editor and was lucky to have Chris Stratner come to my rescue and help me clean up my writing. Since that first edition came out I have written a few other books, and now have an expert editor on my team to make my written works presentable. Thank you, Meagan DeJong, for always finding the time to edit my projects and make me look good.

The saying goes, "behind every great man is a pack of girls." Well, maybe that's not the exact saying but that's how it goes for me. I have four women in my life that have given me superpowers to do things I never thought imaginable. First is the girl who started it all, my furry best buddy, Hayley. She was the inspiration for this book and was sitting at my feet the day I typed out the first word, and now 11 years later (she just turned 15!) she's still here at my feet inspiring me.

To pick up the slack for Hayley as she ages, my personal team has two new recruits, my twin daughters, Sabrina and Jada. Together, they are my head cheerleaders and I spend every single day trying to make them proud. Although I won't let them read this book yet (I don't feel like explaining what "tree-hugger-mother-fucker" means to two seven-year-olds) they are still very excited and supportive.

Leading us all is my amazing wife Michele. She is the main reason this book was ever completed and she continually pushes me to be a better person in every way imaginable. Her love and unwavering belief in me is why I'm able to accomplish anything. (Fun Fact: I actually proposed to her using this very book. When it was first published I took one book and put in a new acknowledgements page with an additional last line, which asked her to marry me. Then I had her Aunt read it in front of her family at a party to celebrate the book.)

Lastly, I need to thank my extended online family. All of my clients, rescue volunteers, podcast listeners and the growing online community (especially Janet Peterson for the proofreading help); thank you for being a part of my life and giving me the encouragement to keep putting myself out there. You guys rock! And that includes you. Thanks so much for taking the time to read this book. I truly hope you enjoyed the story and wish you nothing but good karma in the future.

ABOUT THE AUTHOR

Fernando spends most of his days as a Dog Behavior Consultant, helping people and their dogs enjoy a better life together. He has also created an abundance of online content to help owners around the globe with their dogs (www. FernDogTraining.com)

Fern loves to write and is the author of two books, *A Better Life with Your Dog* and *The Dog Rescue Handbook*. In addition to training dogs, Fern is passionate about training people to become dog trainers. He is the Founder/Director of The FernDog Rescue Foundation which is a foster-based rescue to help homeless dogs find homes.

Fernando lives in Northern New jersey with his wife, twin daughters, and his trusty Pit Bull Haley whom the character of Karma was based.